Life
Unexpected

Life Unexpected

A NOVEL

J.A. Stone

LAKE UNION
PUBLISHING

Published by Lake Union Publishing, Seattle

www.apub.com

Amazon, the Amazon logo, and Lake Union Publishing are trademarks of Amazon.com, Inc., or its affiliates.

ISBN-13: 9781503939998
ISBN-10: 1503939995

Cover design by Danielle Christopher

Printed in the United States of America

PROLOGUE

"You coming, squirt?"

Corey fought to open her eyes. When she did, she saw her dad's weathered face only inches from hers. For just a moment, she considered saying no, rolling over, and going back to sleep.

"Yeah," she mumbled. As pleasurable as sleeping in might seem at that moment, even in her half-awake state, Corey knew that she'd kick herself later if she didn't get up and go with him.

"Good," her dad whispered before straightening up and heading for the bedroom door. "Be ready in fifteen minutes."

"Okay." She threw back her covers. *Why do fishermen always have to leave so early?* Corey knew that she and her dad caught just as many fish midmorning as they did during the first couple of hours after dawn. So why couldn't they sleep just a little bit later?

Corey put on her swimsuit and then pulled on a ratty pair of shorts and an old T-shirt. She tiptoed down the stairs to keep from waking her sister, Diane, and her friend Fran, who were sleeping in the room next to hers. Her mother, in her faded-blue housedress, was standing behind the breakfast bar spreading mayonnaise on pieces of white bread. She looked up and welcomed Corey with a warm smile. "You want ham or turkey?"

"I don't care. Do I have to eat breakfast?"

"Of course."

"Why can't I eat a honey bun on the boat like dad?"

"You're wasting your time arguing. Hurry up or your dad will leave you."

Corey poured milk over a bowl of Cap'n Crunch cereal and began to shovel the food into her mouth. She watched as her mother wrapped the sandwiches in plastic and then put them into another plastic sack. She added a bag of potato chips and some cheese crackers. "Take off your shirt."

Corey paused long enough between bites to pull off her shirt. If she'd learned anything in her ten years of life, it was that her mother was serious about sunscreen. "Oh . . . that's cold." She arched her shoulders as her mother squirted Coppertone suntan lotion down her back. Her mother didn't reply but just kept rubbing vigorously.

"I'm done," Corey said as her mother wiped the remaining lotion onto the sides of her arms. Corey started to pull her shirt back over her head.

"Wait," her mother ordered. "Do you want to rub off what I just put on you? And here, take these sandwiches." With all her tasks done, she deposited a kiss on Corey's cheek and handed her the bag of food.

"Okay, Mom." Corey sighed as she headed out the door carrying both her shirt and the bag. Her father was already waiting for her in his old, red Dodge truck parked at the bottom of the stairs. He looked at his watch as she climbed in. "You're five minutes late."

"Mom's fault. Had to have breakfast and, you know, sunscreen. Besides, does it really matter what time we leave?"

"According to last night's fishing report, the best time to fish for Spanish mackerel is between now and nine a.m."

Corey let out another sigh. Her parents were as predictable and constant as the ocean's tides that her father followed so closely.

At the marina, her dad climbed into the flatbed of his truck and handed the fishing poles down to Corey. Then he jumped down, opened the ice chest, and put the sandwiches in. The air already seemed heavy as they started toward their boat slip. Corey struggled to balance the heavy fishing poles and keep the lines from tangling at the top. Ahead, she could see that their beach neighbors, Bob MacKinnon and his son, Tripp, were already on their boat. A curly-headed boy whom Corey didn't know was peering over the back of the boat, pointing excitedly at something floating in the dark water.

"Morning, Bob, Tripp." Corey's dad put the ice chest down in front of the MacKinnon boat. "Y'all heading out to the buoy line today?"

"Morning, Frank. Yeah, we're hoping to catch some Kings today. How about y'all?"

"We're going trolling for Spanish. I've heard they're striking close into shore."

During the adults' exchange, Tripp and the other boy pointedly ignored Corey. Feeling awkwardly uncomfortable, Corey wouldn't put the fishing poles down, figuring that if she did so, it would only encourage her dad to talk longer. Finally, her dad noticed her discomfort, finished with the chitchat, picked up the ice chest, and began walking again. As Corey followed him, she looked back over her shoulder to where Tripp was busy untying the MacKinnon boat from the dock. *Just you wait, Tripp MacKinnon,* she secretly promised him. *The next time you come around my house wanting me to go fishing with you, I'll show you how it feels to be ignored.*

Within minutes, Corey and her father had their boat out of its slip. The morning sunlight was beginning to peek through the tops of the trees as they chugged slowly along the canal. The familiar smells of stagnant water and gasoline followed them as they went. The water in the canal was smooth like glass except for the ripples radiating out from the back of their boat. In the distance, Corey could see the ocean waves crashing against the rocks at the canal's end. She held her breath in anticipation. Her dad had to turn the boat sharply into the oncoming waves and throttle up the power—or risk having the waves hit the side of the boat and push it back against the rocks. Corey knew that with her dad at the controls, she had no reason to be afraid. Nevertheless, her heart always beat just a bit faster as they approached the end of the smooth waters. She thought it strange that she was only nervous about going out of the canal, particularly as the ocean waves were usually much higher and rougher by the time they returned. Yet it was only the going out that made her nervous. She never gave a second thought to the dangers of the rocks when they were coming home.

CHAPTER 1

Corey Bennett paced back and forth and back and forth, like some errant schoolchild waiting for the principal. She looked at her watch once again. The minute hand was moving forward, but time within the large, mahogany-paneled, and heavily carpeted room seemed to be at a standstill. She had experienced this same sensation of timelessness during her job interview in this room. Barely twenty-six and just out of law school, she hadn't known if the interview was lasting minutes or hours. Perhaps this office had been designed so that important people making careful, deliberate decisions never felt pressured to hurry—very unlike Corey's small, cramped office where she was certain her waiting client was very aware of the time rapidly passing by. But what could she do? Larry Forrester, the managing partner of Landon, Crane, and Forrester, had asked to meet with her. An associate didn't refuse his invitation, although Corey had done her best to postpone it.

"Can't we do this later?" Corey had asked Larry's assistant, Barbara, upon discovering that Larry was running late. "Couldn't you just reschedule me for later this afternoon?"

"No, Ms. Bennett." Barbara's voice was as firm as the bun twisted tightly at the back of her head. "He said for you to go on in and wait.

He'll be here in a few minutes." Since Barbara had made a career out of enforcing Larry's directives, Corey knew there was no point in arguing with her further.

Now those few minutes had become thirty, and Corey's anxiety had grown with each one. She wished she knew what this meeting was about. It was unusual for Larry to call her to his office like this, so it must be important. Still, she was on the verge of leaving, regardless of the consequences, when the massive carved oak door swung open. "I'm so sorry," Larry said. He surged into the room with the air of a man much younger than his fifty-seven years. His salt-and-pepper hair was the only characteristic somewhat appropriate for a man of his age. "I've been downstairs in the lobby for half an hour talking to Jerry Sentell. And no matter how many times I said to him, 'Jerry, I've got an appointment, I've really got to go,' he just kept right on talking. I think he has some sort of problem. Have a seat."

"That's okay," Corey said in a voice that she hoped didn't sound as annoyed as she felt, "but I do have a client waiting for me in my office." Corey chose to sit in the upholstered wing chair by the fireplace rather than in the utilitarian leather chair in front of Larry's desk.

"This won't take long." Larry quickly looked at a note on his desk before sitting down in the wing chair opposite her. He cleared his throat. "Corey, the partners had a breakfast meeting this morning, and you were one of the topics we discussed."

Corey felt a tinge of anticipation. Were they about to make her a partner? On average, associates were either let go or promoted after five years. Since she was still here, perhaps it was finally her time. "I hope it was a good discussion," she said with a slight smile.

Pointedly ignoring her comment, Larry went on. "One of your clients approached Tom Crane at a wedding last weekend."

At the mention of Tom Crane's name, Corey's anticipation turned to apprehension. If Tom Crane, the firm's most senior partner, was the reason for this unscheduled meeting, it wasn't going to be good for her. She had three major faults, as far as Tom was concerned, and she could do nothing about two of the three. She couldn't change the fact that she was a woman. Tom might not voice his negative opinions about women openly, but the lack of women partners in a firm as large as theirs (and only a handful of women associates) spoke volumes about his feelings. Neither could Corey change the fact that she hadn't received either her undergraduate or her law degree from the University of Georgia. Tom knew she wasn't even peripherally connected to the "dawg" network through which a large amount of Atlanta business was conducted. Finally, and perhaps most damning for Corey, she didn't play golf. She'd heard Tom say on more than one occasion, "More business gets done on a golf course than in all the boardrooms in America." She'd been meaning to take up golf because she intended to be the first woman partner at Landon, Crane, and Forrester.

"Was this person upset about some problem with my work?" Corey asked curiously, but she felt confident about Larry's answer. She knew she was good at what she did. It was the one area of her life about which she had few doubts.

"No, no," Larry said matter-of-factly. "Your work is good. And you know you're one of the most productive associates at this firm. What the client said was that he's been meeting with you regularly for the past several weeks, and each time you've looked more . . . *haggard* was the word he used. Have you looked at yourself lately? You look terrible."

"Well, thanks a lot." Corey reflexively put her hand up to her temple, where a slight throbbing was beginning. It was midafternoon, and all she'd eaten so far that day was an apple—probably not a good idea. She wasn't sure how to respond to these charges that she didn't look good, so she just waited for what Larry was going to say next.

Larry's voice softened just a bit. "Although the partners certainly appreciate how much hard work you do, we've decided that it is in your best interest and ours for you to take some time off. You should have done it right after Luke's death."

Corey swallowed hard. Her heart, which had been quietly minding its own business, suddenly went into overdrive. She wondered if Larry could possibly see the rapid rise and fall of her chest as she experienced what her doctor had told her in a patronizing voice was merely a slight panic attack.

"I had to work," Corey finally managed to say. "I got way behind on my billable hours during Luke's illness." She didn't add that work seemed to be the only thing she was capable of doing anymore. She wasn't sleeping well, food had no taste, and she hated to be alone in her condo. The condo always seemed eerily quiet regardless of what electronic device she had on for company. She'd woken up two days after the funeral, the day after everyone had gone home, and she hadn't known what to do. Her life had revolved around Luke and work. Luke was gone. She'd decided she might as well go to work, reaching for that comfortable routine like a lifeline. Once at work, she'd faced stares of disbelief in the hallways and heard whispers after she walked by. "Didn't she just bury her husband?" Corey hadn't cared about the stares or the whispers—they were better than the nothingness that waited for her at home.

Larry interrupted her reverie. "Corey, you're the first person here in the morning and the last to leave at night, and you can't keep this up. No one could. So take the next two days and brief John on whatever you've got pending. After that, I better not see your face around here for two weeks. Go somewhere where you can relax. Get drunk. Sleep all day. Eat pasta and put some weight back on those bones. And those are orders."

"I don't know about this, Larry. I . . . ," Corey began.

"Corey," Larry stated unequivocally, "this isn't open for discussion. The partners made the decision this morning. I'm just the messenger."

Corey stopped in Larry's executive washroom to try to compose herself before heading back to her own office. After all, Mabel Johnson had been waiting for her this long. She could wait just a little bit longer. She stared at her reflection in the mirror as she took deep breaths. How long had it been since she'd really looked at herself? Gaunt cheekbones surrounded by dull, shoulder-length brown hair, dark circles under listless blue eyes, unusually pale skin. She supposed Larry was right. She did look sick. She looked much like Luke had during that last year—sunken eyes, pasty skin. Corey took a deep breath. What was she to do for two weeks?

She would go crazy if she stayed in her condo by herself doing nothing. Lately she'd been thinking that selling the condo might be a good idea. Luke had found the fixer-upper right before they'd married. Corey had thought the place was a dump—a 1950s apartment that had been converted into a condo sometime in the eighties and had unfortunately never left that era. Luke had convinced her otherwise. "It's got great bones, and we can't beat its Virginia-Highland location. We'll have fun renovating it. Just wait and see."

However, agonizing over paint and carpet colors at Home Depot had not been her idea of fun. Corey found it easy to leave those decisions to Luke. She much preferred when they went cruising yard and estate sales looking for that perfect piece of eclectic furniture for their new home. The last thing they'd bought at one of those yard sales had been a ficus tree. They'd paid a crazy woman five dollars for the plant after assuring her that they would provide it with a good home. It was the kind of quirky purchase she loved to make. However, once Luke was diagnosed with cancer, the house and the ficus tree hardly entered into their consciousness. And now that Luke was gone, the ficus tree's pale-yellow leaves fell in piles on the floor, accusing her of neglect. More and more, Corey wanted to sell the condo and take the plant back to its previous owner before it died.

Corey's heartbeat finally slowed to its normal pace as she silently repeated her mantra of the past nine months: *Focus on work. Focus on work.* It was what she said to herself each day in order to make herself get out of bed. It was why everyone had been telling her how wonderful she was doing. Without her work for the next two weeks, Corey might actually have to face the fact that Luke was gone. But not today. Right now she had a client waiting for her in her office, and Mabel Johnson was probably irate. Yet Corey knew that she could handle Mrs. Johnson's wrath a lot easier than she could handle what was left of her life.

By four that afternoon, when John Kowlowski stuck his curly brown head around the door of her office, Corey had already logged in eight hours of work, and her day was far from finished. She had e-mailed John and asked him to stop by her office before leaving.

"Is this a good time?" John asked, flashing his breezy, salesmanlike smile her way.

Corey waved him in. "Thanks for coming by." When the rest of John's body followed his head around the door, she wasn't surprised to see that he was already wearing a starched yellow golf shirt and crisp khaki shorts. "Going to the practice range?" Corey asked drily.

"No." His smile faded to a fake grimace. "I'm playing nine holes with Lester Inman this afternoon at the Country Club of the South. We're still trying to finalize that Cobb County deal, you know."

"Yeah, I'd heard it was taking longer than anticipated." Corey knew this golf outing would be primarily business for John. Still, it was hard to feel sorry for him when he would be spending the remainder of his afternoon out in the sunshine, drinking beer, and doing something he did every weekend for fun. Corey didn't dislike John, but she was wary of him. He'd been hired almost a year after Corey, and she'd been his mentor during his first six months of employment. Luke had jokingly called him "Eddie," after the *Leave It to Beaver* character Eddie Haskell, who was always sucking up to the parents while doing all sorts of bad things behind their backs. To the best of Corey's knowledge, John had never done anything to hurt her, yet she remained cautious around him. A sixth sense told her to be on guard.

Corey motioned for John to sit down. "I had a meeting with Larry earlier today, and the partners have decided I must take a vacation."

John's face showed no surprise, which Corey found interesting. Either Larry had already talked to John, or the partners hadn't been the only ones thinking she needed to take a break from work. "Larry said for me to brief you on what I've got pending that can't wait a couple of weeks."

"Sure. Just e-mail the files to me, and I'll go over them tomorrow. If I have any questions, I'll let you know. Anything else? I'm supposed to be at the club by five."

"No . . . except thanks." Corey hesitated for a moment and then felt like she needed to say something else, or maybe she just wanted to have the last word. "Don't beat Lester Inman this afternoon. I hear he's a real bad sport."

CHAPTER 2

Three hours later, Corey was finally in her car headed home, mentally checking items off her invisible to-do list. Her cell phone rang, startling her because it rang so seldom these days.

"Hey, sis." The cheerful voice of her sister, Diane, came through the cell phone when she hit the speaker button. "Just checking in. What's new?"

"Well, my boss ordered me to take two weeks of vacation today," Corey said.

"You are so lucky! Wish my boss would order me to take a vacation. So what are your plans?"

Corey couldn't help but smile at her sister's words. As a teacher, Diane wasn't exactly lacking in vacation time.

"I don't know what I'm going to do. I haven't had time to think about it yet." Corey saw the long line of traffic at a standstill ahead of her on Piedmont Road and felt frustrated. *Why wasn't rush hour over by now?*

"What a coincidence. I was just calling to pin you down on a date for coming to Mexico Beach, and for once you can't use work as an excuse. Marcy is at camp right now so we'll have plenty of time to relax.

We'll drink lots of red wine, lie out on the beach until we turn into crispy critters, and read a trashy beach book every day."

"Sounds like heaven," Corey agreed. How long had it been since she'd been to their family's beach house? Three years? Five years? She couldn't remember. The beach hadn't been Luke's favorite vacation spot. He preferred the excitement of a city. They had taken their vacations to places like Boston, Chicago, and San Francisco instead of Mexico Beach, Florida. But now, Corey suddenly realized that nothing sounded as wonderful to her as sitting on the sugar-white beaches of the Florida Gulf Coast and doing nothing. "Is Sunday too soon?"

"That would be great," Diane said excitedly, but then she retreated. "Oh wait, I've got that teachers' conference in Tampa starting on Monday. I can be back at the beach on Thursday, though. What if I get Fran to come stay with you until I'm back?"

Corey took her foot off the brake. The traffic was finally moving but still at a crawl. "You don't have to ask Fran to babysit me. I'm not sick. I'm just tired and overworked. I'll probably sleep for the first few days anyway. Besides, I haven't seen Fran since she gave that party for me right before I got married. Is she living at the beach yet?"

"No, not yet, but I think Mark's almost ready to take the plunge. They'll probably be living there by this time next year. Okay, I won't call Fran, but by the time I get there, you better be rested and ready to play."

The car in front of Corey stopped suddenly, and without her full attention on the road, she almost rear-ended it. "Damn it. Hey, I better pay attention to my driving. I'll talk to you later."

When Corey pulled up in front of her end-unit condo, Romeo, one half of the gay couple who lived in the unit next door to her, was standing on his front porch. He had a large manila envelope halfway out of the mailbox mounted beside his door, and he was carefully trying to extricate the rest without damaging it. Their mailman seemed to take perverse pleasure in wedging items into their tiny mailboxes that were way too large for the space.

"I'm going to report him this time," Romeo said with a huff, his smooth, round face flushed with anger as Corey approached him. "Any fool could see that this doesn't fit."

Every time Corey saw Romeo standing on his porch, she remembered the first time Luke had met him standing there. "Romeo? Really? Come on, guy, what's your real name?" One of Luke's most endearing or obnoxious qualities, depending upon whether you liked what he said or not, was that he usually said exactly what he thought.

Without a word, their offended neighbor had immediately pulled out his driver's license and thrust it at Luke. It read *Romeo Kermit Thompson*. "So . . . what . . . do you think . . . about that?" Romeo had asked, each word dripping with indignant sarcasm.

Without a moment's hesitation, and using his most adorable grin, Luke had said, "I think you chose the better of the two names. My apologies. Please come over for drinks after we get moved in so I'll know you've forgiven me."

Romeo struggled to hold on to his righteous anger. "Well, since we are going to be neighbors, I suppose it would help if we are friendly. My partner, Gary, and I will look forward to joining you."

Once inside their condo, Luke had dissolved into laughter. "Poor guy, his childhood must have been hell with two names like that." Despite the rocky start to their relationship, Luke had managed to charm Romeo and Gary with his honest, self-confident manner when they came over for drinks. Gary was a giant hulk of a man who sort of reminded Corey of Sean Connery in his later James Bond roles. Romeo was small and compact with a dry, sarcastic sense of humor. His wry comments delivered in a soft South Carolina twang often took Corey by surprise. Still, he'd cried more at Luke's funeral than Corey, who'd remained stoically dry-eyed. Corey had been cried out. Or maybe just shell-shocked. How many losses could one person stand?

The mailbox finally released the envelope in one piece, and Romeo turned to Corey. "You want to eat with us tonight? Gary's cooking at home for a change, and you know he always has plenty."

"You're sweet, but not tonight." Corey appreciated their thoughtfulness, she really did, but she often felt more alone while having dinner with the happy couple than she did when she was in her condo by herself. "I'm leaving for a couple of weeks on Sunday, so I've got a lot of packing to do. Would you mind getting the mail while I'm gone?"

"Be glad to. I hope this is a vacation and not work," Romeo said with an inquiring expression on his face.

"Definitely a vacation. I'll be spending two weeks relaxing on a Florida beach."

"Good, and don't waste one minute worrying about anything here. We'll have everything under control."

"I appreciate it," Corey said. "See ya later."

She put her key into the lock. Entering the dark, empty house was the worst part of her day. She turned on lights in every room as she went, and immediately turned on the television for noise. Her condo reminded her of a cave—cold and dank—even on a sweltering summer day like today. After shrugging off her work clothes and putting on her fuzzy blue bathrobe, she sank wearily to the sofa. She decided to order shrimp fried rice from the place on Tenth Street that delivered, but by the time it finally arrived, she wasn't very hungry. She added the Styrofoam container, still more than half-full, to the city of Styrofoam containers in her refrigerator, adding a mental note to her list to throw away all those leftovers before leaving on Sunday.

Her mother, if she were looking down at her from heaven right now, would be appalled. She had always considered throwing food away to be a sin. If leftovers weren't served again in their original form, they should be reconstituted into soup or casseroles. "I love leftovers," her mother always said.

Once, Corey had asked her dad how he ate her mother's dried-out meat loaf for the second day in a row with so much enthusiasm. "Do you really like it?"

Her father had winked at her conspiratorially. "To be honest, I don't. But I love your mother, and if it makes her happy, I guess I can put up with dried-out meat loaf every once in a while." Being a typical teenager, Corey had thought that if her mother loved them, she wouldn't ask them to eat dried-out meat loaf for the second day in a row.

Corey felt exhausted, but she always waited until midnight or later to get into bed because then she was likely to sleep for five or six uninterrupted hours. If she went to bed at ten, she was likely to wake up at two, and then she'd be unable to go back to sleep for the rest of the night. Her late-night bedtime ritual, as bizarre as it might seem, was better than taking the sleeping pills the doctor had prescribed for her. Those pills made her feel as if she were walking around in a haze for much of the following day.

The next few days were hectic, but by Sunday, Corey had managed to settle her affairs at work and had packed everything she could possibly think of, including the half-dead ficus tree, into her Lexus SUV. If her sister thought her strange for bringing her houseplant to the beach, she didn't care. Corey had realized over the weekend that if she left the plant for two weeks, it would certainly be dead when she returned. Corey hoped Diane, the earth mother, could bring it back from the brink.

She stopped for a brief visit with Luke's mother, Nancy, on her way out of town. Corey felt guilty that Nancy would probably have no visitors for the next two weeks. Nancy had sold her house in Buckhead after Luke's death and moved into a retirement home. Peachtree Wilden was advertised as the most prestigious retirement community in Atlanta, but it was far from Nancy's friends, and she seemed to have little interest in making new ones. When Corey arrived, Nancy held up her paper-white cheek for a kiss. She was slight, stooped, and brittle like fine china. Corey barely touched her face with her lips, afraid Nancy might bruise with any more force. Upon hearing about her vacation, Nancy seemed genuinely happy that Corey was taking some time off. "It is way past due, darling," she said before urging Corey to get on the road so that she would arrive in Florida before dark.

The almost nonexistent traffic on Interstate 85 made the trip out of Atlanta a pleasure, and once Corey was out of the city, the road felt like a long-lost friend. Immediately some of the weight she'd been carrying seemed lighter. It was hard to believe she hadn't made the trip home to Florida for so many years. But going back had been difficult after both of her parents died in a car accident while she was in law school. The massive coronary her father had suffered while driving had ended his life quickly. Her mother had hung on for a few more days before dying from the injuries she'd suffered in the accident. Now Corey's sister, Diane; Diane's husband, Jack; and their daughter, Marcy, were all the family Corey had left living in the small town of Marianna, Florida. With Corey's work schedule, and then Luke's illness, it had been easier for Diane and her family to come to Atlanta for holidays and visits. *Nancy was right,* Corey thought. *This trip is way past due.*

When Corey got close to her destination, she opened the car window so she could smell the salty air. The gray moss dripping from the pine trees seemed like decorations welcoming her back to the beach. She *had* missed all this. Every summer, she, Diane, and their mother had moved to their beach house—at Mexico Beach—an hour away from their hometown of Marianna. Her father would come down on Friday nights after work and go back on Monday mornings. A longing for her past swept over her as she approached the Overstreet Bridge, which had once been a floating bridge that was moved into or out of place by a large crane. She thought about the time she almost wet her pants while waiting for a huge boat to pass through. There was no waiting anymore. Corey cruised over the new, white-concrete bridge, made a right turn, then a left, and there she was at Mexico Beach. When she pulled up to their beach house, which had always looked exactly like a tan barn on stilts to her, she was surprised to see her sister standing on the wooden deck. Diane, with her frosted short hair blowing haphazardly in a stiff breeze, yelled down to her, "Glad you still know the way!"

Corey waved back at her as she stepped out of the car. Diane was eleven years older and had just turned forty-three. Since their parents' deaths, Diane had been more like a mother to her than a sister. And since Luke's death, Diane had been more like a Jewish mother, constantly worrying about Corey. Sometimes she wished her sister didn't call her quite so much. Sometimes she just wanted to be left alone. Most of the time, however, she felt lucky to have a sister who cared so much for her.

"I'm not sure I'm at the right place," Corey answered, looking up at a new wooden deck that wrapped around a glassed-in porch. "The old place looks a lot different than I remember it."

"These are the renovations you paid for but have never seen. Remember that check you mailed to me?"

Corey remembered arguing with Luke over the money. Luke had suggested they offer Diane her interest in the beach house instead of paying her the $20,000 she'd requested.

"Seriously, Corey," he'd said, "how often will you be able to make the six-hour drive down to Florida? It makes more sense for us to take the money and buy something at Lake Lanier that we might actually be able to use."

It might have made more sense, but Corey wasn't doing it. She'd taken the money from her parents' inheritance and sent Diane the check she'd requested. It was the first time she'd ever gone against Luke's wishes, and she was glad to finally see what she'd paid for.

"Let me look at you!" Diane squealed as she ran down the steps. "Perhaps I should send that boss of yours a thank-you present. Good grief, Corey, you're nothing but a bag of bones."

Corey's excitement about being at the beach and seeing Diane evaporated instantly. Her eyes inexplicably filled with tears, which took her by surprise because she couldn't remember the last time she'd cried.

"It's okay, darling." Diane shushed her. "Let's get your things in. What is that? Why in heaven's name did you drag a ficus tree down here?"

Corey smiled sadly through her tears. "I wanted it to live."

"Okeydokey, then," Diane said in her teacher voice as she looked at Corey curiously. "Let's leave it under the deck where it can get lots of indirect sunlight. In this heat, you'd better water it every day while I'm gone."

"What are you doing here anyway?" Corey asked. "I thought you were going to Tampa."

"Had to get you settled in first, didn't I? But since we're leaving Marianna at seven in the morning, I've got to go home tonight. I feel just dreadful leaving you. Won't you please let me call Fran to come spend the night?"

"I'm a big girl," Corey said. "You know, I do somehow manage to take care of myself in Atlanta."

"Not very well, I might say, now that I'm looking at you. Come on." After they'd finished carrying all of Corey's things up to the house, Diane showed her the renovations.

"You turned the old screened porch into a sunroom! How marvelous!" Corey exclaimed. "You've done a really good job of modernizing the house without losing its beachiness."

"Beachiness? Oh well, whatever, I'm glad you like it. I've felt like I should be paying you rent these past several years."

"It feels so good to be here that you may not be able to get rid of me."

"Nothing could make me happier," Diane said. "Are you hungry? The refrigerator's got the basics, so you should be okay for a few days. I also made some chicken salad and a breakfast casserole, which just needs to be reheated in the microwave."

Corey was overwhelmed by Diane's thoughtfulness. Although she wasn't terribly hungry, she pretended she was, and surprisingly, once she'd taken a few bites of Diane's incredible chicken salad, she found that she actually was hungry. Between bites she said, "Di, you don't have to hang around here with me. I'm fine, really. I'd rather you start for home before it gets any later. You know you aren't that great of a driver in the daylight."

Diane stood up from the sofa where she'd been sitting and stretched. "Yeah, if you're going to start insulting me, I guess I might as well leave. Call me if you have any questions about where anything is. And don't bother walking down with me."

After Diane's exit, Corey looked at the clock on the microwave. It wasn't quite nine o'clock, but she felt dead tired. She locked up downstairs and went up to her bedroom, where she heard the sound track of her childhood in the ceiling fan's clicking noise. In spite of the air-conditioning blasting away, she opened the bedroom window a crack so that she could add the murmur of the ocean to her playlist. She closed her eyes and let the sounds take her back. Her parents were downstairs—swinging on the old screen porch swing—talking and laughing. Corey remembered lying in that old iron bed, straining to hear what they were talking about, feeling secure in the knowledge that nothing could ever harm her while they were down there. She opened her eyes. What she wouldn't give for that feeling of security now. But it was gone—just like the scuff marks she'd made on the walls as a kid had been erased by a fresh coat of soft white paint so that everything in the room now looked shiny and new.

CHAPTER 3

Corey woke confused in the strange bed in the dark. After a few moments, she remembered where she was and saw on her cell phone that it was only three a.m. There was no television in the room, and without any mindless entertainment to occupy her, Corey's thoughts strayed immediately to Luke. How ironic that a runner who'd never smoked a day in his life had died of lung cancer.

For as long as Corey had known Luke, he'd suffered from a persistent, chronic cough. When Luke had gone in for checkups, his doctor had shrugged it off as an allergic reaction to an abundance of Atlanta pine pollen and smog. After all, Luke was young and healthy. In fact, he and his doctor had been planning on running the Boston Marathon together. However, the doctor's casual demeanor disappeared after Luke started coughing up blood. By that time, the cancer had already spread to his liver. Sitting in the doctor's office looking at the scans, Corey had known that Luke's condition was serious, yet she hadn't believed he might die. How could he? She couldn't imagine her future without him in it.

On each trip they made—to the Mayo Clinic, to Sloan-Kettering Memorial Hospital, to every cancer center anyone recommended—Corey thought that *this* was where they would find his cure. Every doctor, though, said basically the same thing: Luke had one to two years to live, depending on how well he responded to the chemotherapy treatments he'd started after his surgery at Emory Hospital. In the end, there was no miracle cure anywhere. Luke lived only one more year. Corey didn't want to think about that last year now. She got up and took one of her sleeping pills. She had nowhere to be the next morning, so it didn't matter how late she slept or how groggy she felt.

When she woke many hours later to bright sunlight streaming through her bedroom window, Corey realized she was hungry. She remembered the breakfast casserole Diane had left for her in the fridge, and she pulled her exhausted body downstairs to the kitchen. How could she still be this tired?

She made herself a little picnic of breakfast casserole, fruit, and cinnamon rolls on the coffee table and curled up on the sofa to snack and watch the classic Clark Gable movie *It Happened One Night*. Corey associated breakfast casserole with Christmas mornings, so eating it on a random Monday in early July made the day seem special to her. Curiously, she felt comfortable being alone there at the beach house, and not miserable like she did when she was alone at her condo. Here, she could almost hear her dad whistling as he repaired fishing tackle or did some other odd job. She could almost smell one of her mother's pies baking in the kitchen, and she could almost see Diane's angry face staring down at her after finding Corey listening through her bedroom keyhole to whatever secrets she and Fran had been hiding from her. Memories like those felt good.

She dozed on and off for the remainder of the afternoon on the sofa. Several times she awoke in a mild panic, with her heart racing, after having a dream in which she hadn't completed some work-related task.

Late that afternoon, Diane called. "How ya doing?"

"Great." Corey yawned. "I left the bed for the sofa and have barely moved all afternoon. I've been watching old movies and eating like a pig."

"Good, just what the doctor ordered. We've already checked in to our rooms, and our group is heading out for a swinging dinner at the Hard Rock Cafe. Don't you wish you were here?"

"Nah, not really. If I get energetic, I may open a bottle of wine, but that's about as much swinging as I want to do. You go and have some fun now, and don't call me anymore. I'm fine."

The sun was getting ready to set, so Corey decided to move her party out to the sunporch. Although the house wasn't on the beachfront, she could see the water in the distance and the sun hovering like some alien spaceship right above the horizon. She marveled at how much their sleepy beach community had grown in her absence. A brand-new yellow house had been built to the right. The contrast between the lush, green manicured lawn of the new house and the sparse brown grass surrounding Corey's beach house was startling. When did Mexico Beach attract the type of people who cared about their lawns? Who would spend time working on their lawns when they could be out on the beach or on the water fishing?

Across the street, and on the beachfront, Corey was pleased to see that the MacKinnon house—a faded, one-story, dark-wood house on stilts—hadn't changed one bit from how she remembered it. The tightly closed blinds let her know that no one was home, even though she couldn't see if cars were parked beneath it because of the trees. She wondered idly what Tripp MacKinnon was up to these days. Although she hadn't kept in touch with him over the last several years, he'd been an integral part of all her childhood summers. Diane and her friends never let Corey hang around with them too long, so unless she'd invited a friend to stay, the only other possibility for a playmate was Tripp. And if there were no other boys around for him to play with, he might just lower himself to play with her. Corey had never been able to understand why she wasn't good enough for him. She could fish just as well as he could, and when they raced their bikes down the back beach road to get ice cream, sometimes she won. When they'd grown older, he'd kissed her for the first time underneath the pier on the Fourth of July.

"Come on," he'd pleaded. "Don't you want to know what it's like?"

At eleven years old, Corey hadn't really cared. Finally, curiosity got the better of her.

"Have you ever done it before?" she asked innocently.

"Of course," Tripp said smugly. "How would I know what to do if I hadn't?" He approached her clumsily and stuck his tongue in her mouth.

"Ugh!" she said, pulling away immediately and wiping her mouth. "That's gross!"

"Yeah—with you, it is," he said angrily. "I never should have tried it with a kid."

Lost in her memories, Corey realized she'd missed the sunset. *Oh well, there will be another sunset tomorrow.* Of that one thing she felt reasonably sure.

Surprisingly, she was still sleepy after lazing around for most of the day. She decided to go to bed early again, but this time she slept like a baby all night. Unfortunately, she also woke up like a baby around six a.m. Corey stretched contentedly and realized she didn't feel tired anymore. Perhaps all she'd needed was twenty-four hours of sleep to begin to feel more like herself.

Today she'd get out. She'd go for a run and then spend the day on the beach. She felt excited, like a kid, and couldn't wait to get the day going. She enjoyed a few more bites of breakfast casserole and then dressed in her gym shorts, T-shirt, and Nikes. Sadness began to simmer as she tied her laces. She hadn't been running in a long time. Luke had been addicted to running, and they'd usually done it together. Corey shook off her memories and headed out toward the marina down the back beach road.

An hour later she returned, very sweaty in spite of the fact that she'd been forced to stop and catch her breath several times. Not so long ago, she and Luke had been able to run six miles without even thinking about it. Now, being unable to run only a couple of miles without stopping to rest, she realized how horribly out of shape she was.

Corey changed into her swimsuit and grabbed all the paraphernalia she'd need for a day on the beach. She found a small Igloo cooler just the right size for an apple, a turkey sandwich, and two bottles of water. She found an assortment of sunscreen tubes (no Coppertone), including one with an SPF of ninety-five. Corey hadn't even known they made sunscreen with that level of protection. She said a silent prayer of thanks to Diane for having it, because with her skin color right now, she would probably burn with anything less. A towel, an umbrella, a chair—she finally had everything she needed for the beach. It was difficult making her way, and about halfway down, she began to wish she hadn't brought so much junk. Pausing for a few minutes to rest by the MacKinnon house, Corey saw that she'd been right. There was no evidence that anyone was home.

Finally, she made it to the beach and looked around for a place to sit. A large tent was over to the left, where two grandparents sat watching a toddler playing in the sand. To the right, a man and a woman sat in folding beach chairs. Corey didn't think she recognized any of them, but her memory wasn't so good after being away from the area for such a long time. She smiled and waved just in case. A Frisbee landed right next to her feet.

"Sorry, lady," a young boy of probably ten yelled. "Will you throw it back?"

"Sure." She threw it, but a gust of wind took it out into the water. The boy looked disgustedly at her and then headed into the water to fetch it.

"I didn't mean to!" Corey shouted. But he didn't look back. She marveled at the emerald-green water, so clear that the boy easily found the Frisbee within seconds.

After setting up her umbrella and chair, she opened the mystery novel she'd found on one of the shelves in the beach house. Unfortunately, the romantic interlude at the beginning wasn't the sort of entertainment she'd been looking for, so she ate her sandwich and engaged in people-watching instead. An elderly man and woman plodding slowly down the beach holding hands brought unexpected tears yet again to her eyes. *How wonderful to still be in love at their age.*

She felt certain that, given the opportunity, she and Luke could have been like that little old man and little old woman holding hands, walking down the beach. Well, maybe not. Since Luke hadn't liked the beach, they probably would have been walking and holding hands along a street somewhere. Still, she ached for that lifetime of love and togetherness those people had shared and that she would never have with Luke. *Life just isn't fair!* The day that had begun with such excitement seemed dull and ordinary now. It was just another day, like so many other days, that she had to get through.

After a while, she began to feel drowsy from the cool breeze and the food she'd eaten. She spread her beach towel out on the sand and lay down. Coated in sunscreen, and under the umbrella, Corey let the sound of the surf lull her to sleep. She must have slept for a while, because when she opened her eyes, the families on both sides of her were gone, and thunder was crackling in the distance. She hadn't brought her cell phone to the beach, so she didn't know how long she'd slept, but either the sky had darkened because of the storm, or it had been a long while. If she didn't start hustling, she was going to be caught in the rain.

"Damn it!" Corey exclaimed as the umbrella suddenly blew ten feet or so down the beach. Quickly she gathered everything else together into a pile and went to chase the umbrella. Each time she got close, another gust of wind caught it and moved it a bit farther down the beach. *This is getting ridiculous. Why not just go buy another umbrella tomorrow?*

"Need some help?" a deep voice said behind her.

Corey whipped around to see Tripp MacKinnon standing on the beach in a business suit but with no shoes on. Thunder boomed again, seeming much closer this time.

He smiled in that boyishly familiar way. "Let's get your stuff up now, and we'll rescue the umbrella after the storm."

"Sounds good," Corey agreed. They didn't engage in any small talk but just grabbed her stuff and headed toward the path. Still, they were only halfway up the beach path when the raindrops started falling heavy and hard. They dashed under the MacKinnon house as lightning flashed close by.

"Drop your stuff here," Tripp commanded. "Let's get inside before we're electrocuted."

Corey nodded in a daze. She'd forgotten how intense these sudden afternoon thunderstorms could be at the beach. Quickly, she followed Tripp up the stairs and into his house. The cold air and her wet clothes made her start shivering uncontrollably. Tripp walked to the back of the house and came back with a large towel. Gratefully, she wrapped it around her body and felt some of the cold subside.

"I hope your suit isn't ruined," Corey said apologetically.

"I don't think a little rainwater will hurt it. But if you don't mind, I'm going to go take it off and let it start drying. You want some dry clothes? I can probably find a robe or something for you to put on."

"Save your suit. I'm fine." Corey watched Tripp disappear down the hall and then looked around at the house. It was like stepping back in time to her childhood, as nothing had changed—still the same pale-wood paneling, avocado-colored appliances, and brown shag carpet. She hated to think of how much sand might be in that carpet after all these years.

Tripp breezed back into the room. He'd donned a pair of well-worn khaki shorts and a faded blue T-shirt with pink-and-turquoise fish on the back. Corey thought Tripp was like the room: not much had changed in his appearance since the last time she'd seen him either.

Well, he might be a bit heavier, and he might have a bit less blond hair on top, but those sleepy brown eyes set in his deeply tanned face looked exactly the same.

"Did you recognize me down on the beach? Or were you just playing Boy Scout and doing your good deed for the day?" she asked.

"I recognized you, all right. How could I not remember that tall, skinny body of yours?" Tripp paused for dramatic effect. "Of course, it did help that Diane called a couple of days ago to tell me you were coming."

Corey felt her face flush. *Of course Diane had called him.* "It's been a while," she finally managed to say.

"Yeah . . . uh, and . . . I was real sorry to hear about your husband."

Corey felt the blood in her face drain away. For maybe ten or fifteen minutes, she'd been another Corey—not Corey the widow. With Tripp's few words, her reality snapped back into place. "Thanks," she said softly.

Tripp self-consciously tapped his fingers against the breakfast bar. "You want something to drink? A beer, or a cup of coffee, perhaps, to warm up?"

"Coffee would be nice if you've got it." Corey walked over to the bar. She felt dry enough to sit down on a bar stool across from him.

Tripp fiddled with putting the coffeemaker together. Finally, when he opened the refrigerator to pull out a container of coffee, Corey noticed that it was about as empty as her fridge in Atlanta now was, except that the bottom shelf of his was full of beer.

"Let's see. When was the last time we saw each other?" Tripp asked.

"I think it was at my parents' funeral, so I guess it's been a little more than seven years." Corey bit her lip, as she hated having to bring up yet another morbid topic. She had a sudden memory of Tripp and his now former wife, Martha Anne, in the receiving line at the funeral home that night.

"Yeah, that's right. Do you take cream or sugar?"

"Just Coffee-mate, or something like that, if you've got it." The coffee began to drip, and Corey savored the aroma. "Smells good."

Tripp placed two cups on the counter and turned to rummage through a cabinet behind him. He finally pulled a can of evaporated milk out of the cabinet. "I knew it had to be here somewhere." He opened the can, put it and a spoon next to Corey, and then poured them each a cup of coffee.

After she fixed her coffee, Corey turned her attention back to Tripp. "And what are you doing at the beach during the middle of the week anyway? Are you playing hooky from work to go fishing, like you used to skip school?"

Tripp smiled and shrugged. "I have grown up a little bit since high school. My territory with the bank stretches all over northwest Florida. When I have to be in Panama City or Port Saint Joe for meetings, I often spend the night here."

"I guess I'll give you a pass, then." Corey raised her cup and took several long sips of coffee, then held it in her hands, enjoying its warmth.

"It's good to see you at the beach again," Tripp said, still standing across the bar from her.

"I didn't realize how much I missed this place until I got here." Corey finished off her coffee, cocked her head, and listened for a moment. "I think the storm has blown over. It's looking a lot lighter outside, and I haven't heard any thunder in a while."

Tripp went to the sliding glass doors and looked out over the water. "You're right. It has stopped."

"I guess I'll go take a shower and put on some dry clothes. Thanks for the towel and the coffee." Corey put the towel on the bar and started walking toward the door. Without the towel, she was very conscious of Tripp's eyes on her and of the fact that her pool cover-up really didn't cover up very much. She stopped at the door to say good-bye. When she turned to look back at him, his inscrutable brown eyes met hers. Corey was the first to glance away.

"You wanna drive over to Port Saint Joe and eat at the Sunset Grill in a little while?" Tripp asked casually. "I don't have anything in the house, and I'm starving."

Corey thought of the refrigerator full of food Diane had left for her. She should invite him to come over and eat with her. But she was afraid it might be awkward, as their conversation already seemed stilted and sparse. A crowded restaurant would naturally provide topics for conversation. Plus, it would be fun to get away from the beach house for a while.

"I don't know what the Sunset Grill is, but sure, I'm game."

"Great. I'll go look for the umbrella and bring it when I pick you up. Will an hour be long enough?"

CHAPTER 4

While she showered and dressed, Corey reminded herself that she was just having dinner with an old friend. This was no big deal. The fact that the old friend was divorced—and that Corey had had a crush on him in high school and her freshman year in college—didn't really matter, did it?

Dothan, Alabama, where Tripp lived when not at the beach, was only forty miles from her hometown of Marianna. In high school, whenever one of them had an event and didn't have a date, the other would fill in. She'd gone to his junior prom, and he'd gone to both her junior and senior proms. They both liked to dance, so they were perfect partners for those kinds of events. When Tripp went to Auburn University and pledged the Kappa Alpha (KA) fraternity, Corey had gone to a couple of the football games with him his freshman year because pledges were required to have a date. Tripp's relationship with her was always playful and casual except when he'd drunk too many Jim Beams at the games. On those occasions, he'd wrapped her in his arms, kissed her sloppily, and told her she was his girl. Corey had been surprised by how much she'd enjoyed those kisses, and by how sad she'd felt, after he sobered up, when he seemed not to remember what had taken place.

Corey had followed her heart and Tripp's lead and gone to Auburn for college. She had imagined things would progress to the next level when she was there with him all the time. If her sorority had a social event and she needed a date, she called Tripp. And he always seemed more than happy to accept her invitation.

She'd also felt comfortable going over to the KA house uninvited to hang out with him and his friends. Corey had assumed she was going to KA's Old South event with him because he'd spent so much time describing in detail how the KAs rode their horses up to the dorms to deliver invitations in their Confederate uniforms. She'd assumed he was telling her so that she could prepare for the event. So on invitation day, she'd hung around the dorm lobby waiting for her name to be called to go outside and get her invite. Girl after girl went out and came back beaming, but Corey's name was never called.

Later, she learned that he had invited Martha Anne Ringson, a strikingly beautiful blonde cheerleader from Alexander City, weeks earlier. Corey supposed she had no one but herself to blame. Tripp had never actually told her he was going to invite her. Still, she felt certain he must have known how much she wanted to go.

After that, she stopped going to the KA house uninvited, and worked hard to separate herself from Tripp. Occasionally, while still at Auburn, they would grab a bite to eat and catch up with each other, as old friends do. But Corey never again fooled herself into thinking that Tripp considered her anything more than a friend. After Tripp graduated from Auburn, he and Martha Anne got married. Corey did run into him once or twice at the beach while she was still at school. But once Corey went off to law school at Ole Miss and then took a job in Atlanta, even those infrequent run-ins with each other at the beach ceased.

A car horn beeped outside the window and pulled Corey back to the present. She looked outside and waved to Tripp, who was standing by his white Yukon and waving the beach umbrella at her.

"Thanks for rescuing the umbrella," Corey said when she got downstairs. "You might have saved me from third-degree burns."

"No problem," Tripp said as he put the umbrella in the storage shed. Then he turned and opened the car door for her. This simple act took Corey by surprise. No one had opened a car door for her in a very long time.

As she climbed up into his SUV, she said, "Tell me about this Sunset Grill. The last time I was here, we had Toucan's Pizza Palace and the Wonder Bar."

"It has been a long time since you were here. Did you know the Wonder Bar burned down?" Tripp glanced at her as he was backing out of the driveway.

"Oh yes," Corey answered. "Diane had to call and tell me that important bit of news. They should build a shrine there to all of the underage drinkers who had their first drink at the Wonder Bar."

Tripp laughed. "That's not a bad idea. We certainly had a few experiences there, didn't we?"

"Yes, sir, we did. Do you remember the night I decided a sloe gin fizz was my signature drink?"

"I've tried to put that night out of my mind," Tripp answered with a smile. "It isn't a memory I want to hang on to."

"I still can't stomach Hawaiian Punch, or really anything with that particular color of red."

Their conversation remained light and casual, mostly focusing on other beach landmarks that had changed since their childhood, until they pulled up in front of the Sunset Grill. It was an old warehouse on wooden pilings that had been painted sapphire blue and decorated with netting and rusty anchors.

"I know it looks a bit touristy," Tripp began, "but if you still like fried oysters and shrimp, you're going to love this place."

As they were walking into the restaurant, Corey saw a tall, thin, dark-headed man in the distance, and something about him reminded her of Luke. A sliver of guilt washed over her as she realized she hadn't thought of Luke for the last couple of hours. When she looked down, the wedding ring she still wore on her ring finger seemed to be shining more brightly than usual. The hostess seated them in front of a large window overlooking the water. The sky was a collage of purple, pink, and blue streaks—an aftermath of the storm and a picture-perfect setting for lovers. Corey's guilt raised its head again.

"I'm Tonya. I'll be your server tonight." Corey recognized Tonya as the quintessential beach waitress—a bleached blonde with leathery skin who was closer to forty than she'd ever admit to being. Her slightly wrinkled white blouse was straining to contain her Dolly Parton–size breasts. "Can I get you folks something to drink before I take your order?"

"A glass of your house pinot grigio," Corey said, hoping it would make the guilt go away and return her mood to what it had been in the car. She wondered idly if northwest Florida had the monopoly on women of Tonya's type. In all her time in Atlanta, she'd never run into anyone who looked quite like her.

"How about let's get a bottle?" Tripp asked, looking at the wine menu. Corey nodded in agreement.

"Here's to old friends," Tripp said, holding up his glass after Tonya had made quite a production of opening the bottle.

"Old friends," Corey repeated, clicking her glass against his, and then, regardless of good wine etiquette, she took a very large gulp. In a few minutes, the wine began to take effect, and Corey felt herself start to relax.

"So . . . what kind of lawyer are you?" asked Tripp. "The kind that follows an ambulance to the hospital?"

Corey smiled slightly. "That sounds exciting, but no, I do mostly trusts and occasionally real estate transactions."

"Your husband—he was a lawyer, too, same kind of law?" Tripp asked.

Corey felt that pang of guilt once more. "Yes, he was a lawyer. But trust law was too boring for him. He worked for the district attorney downtown at the federal courthouse. Did you hear about that prisoner who escaped and shot up the courtroom and killed the judge?"

"Yeah . . . I did," Tripp said.

"Luke was in the courtroom that day."

"Wow . . ." Tripp shook his head. "Do you ever get bored doing your kind of law?"

"Bored? Me? No way. I get a perverse thrill out of knowing that Mabel Johnson's ne'er-do-well kids are never going to break the trust I just set up for her. They'll get their allowance for the rest of their lives, but they'll never get their hands on that principal."

"Y'all ready to order?" Tonya was back, and they still hadn't looked at their menus.

"How about you bring us another bottle of wine?" Tripp suggested. "And we'll be ready by then."

Corey started to say that she rarely had more than two glasses of wine, but then she decided she had way too good of a buzz going to stop.

"Going with the specialty of the house? Fried oysters and shrimp?" Tripp asked after Tonya had departed.

"I haven't put a piece of fried food into my mouth in years, so sure, why not? I guess it's about time."

After taking their orders, Tonya was back immediately with their house salads—iceberg lettuce, large wedges of tomatoes, and a few croutons sprinkled on top. Corey had gone all out and ordered regular Thousand Island dressing on her salad, and she didn't even ask for it on the side, as she usually did.

"Okay, enough about me. Tell me about you." Corey tried to spear one of the tomato wedges dripping with dressing, but her fork wouldn't go in, and it scooted across the plate and onto the table right in front of Tripp's plate. "Whoops," Corey said.

Tripp scooped it up immediately and plopped it into his mouth. "Five-second rule, right?"

Corey couldn't believe what he'd just done. "Right." She grinned, wondering if he followed that rule when he attended bank luncheons. "Are you still working for the Gulf Coast Bank? And how are your parents? I bet your Mom still bakes cookies for you every afternoon, doesn't she?"

Tripp looked suddenly sad. "Yes on the bank, but no on the cookies. Mom has dementia. They tell us it's not full-blown Alzheimer's, but I don't know what the difference is. We found out a couple of years ago and just recently had to put her in an assisted-living home. Dad goes and sits with her every day and doesn't do anything else. I wish I could get him to come down here for a few days and go fishing. But he won't hear of it. He has to be there, he says, whether she knows him or not."

"I'm sorry, I didn't know." Corey wondered if Diane had told her about Tripp's mom during Luke's illness and she'd forgotten. Luckily, their dinner arrived just then. Corey had never seen anything, even in the finest restaurants, that looked as good as the fried perfection placed in front of her. Upon her first bite, her taste buds remembered what fried food was all about and rejoiced. They both ate heartily for a while in silence.

"You were right. This is really good," Corey finally said with her mouth full of food, not wanting to stop long enough to talk.

"I told you so," Tripp said smugly, in a voice she remembered all too well from when they were kids.

"You've always been so sure of yourself," Corey said. "You never could stand it when I beat you at something."

"Well, you were just a girl, and younger than me too!" Tripp exclaimed.

"Only two years."

"But still a girl!"

Corey kicked his leg hard under the table.

"Aww . . . that hurt. What are you, like ten years old?"

Corey was surprised at her instinctive childish response, but Tripp had always been able to push her buttons. "My esteemed law partners in Atlanta would be shocked, thoroughly shocked," Corey said, trying to make a joke.

Tripp refilled their wineglasses. "Seriously, do you like your work?"

Corey paused to think carefully. "I'm good at what I do."

"And Atlanta? Somehow I never pictured you as a big-city girl."

"Maybe not at first, but Luke was definitely a big-city guy, and I loved him," Corey said honestly.

"And now?"

Corey thought for a minute. How did she feel about Atlanta now that Luke was gone? She'd never given it much thought. "I love Atlanta," she finally said.

Tonya cleared their plates. "How about some dessert?"

"Looks like you could use a little fattening up," Tripp said.

Corey started to decline, as she'd already eaten more than she normally would have in a day. But then the night would be over, and she was really enjoying herself. "Sure, why not?"

"As I remember, your desserts always had to have chocolate in them, right?"

"Of course!"

"We have chocolate bread pudding," Tonya offered.

"Great. Bring us one, and how about two coffees?" Tripp asked, looking at Corey.

"Decaf, please. I feel like we've been talking about *me* all night. Come on, catch me up with what's going on in *your* life."

"You know Martha Anne and I are divorced, right?" Tripp asked. Corey nodded her head that she did. "It's not something I'm too proud of," he continued. "We wanted different things. My idea of fun is coming here and fishing or going to Auburn for a football game. Hers was flying to New York for a play. She lives in Atlanta now and is going to design school. Apparently, she loves Atlanta too. Who knows . . . maybe she can decorate your house for you one day."

"I don't see that happening in the near or distant future. Martha Anne and I never hit it off too well, if you didn't know. She was beautiful, though. I will give her credit for that."

"Funny, the longer I knew her, the less beautiful she was. I guess the silver lining is that we didn't have any children."

Corey wasn't sure how to reply to that comment, but luckily their dessert and coffee arrived. Tonya definitely wasn't one to disappear for too long. She was probably anxious to free up their table for one of the groups of people milling around the hostess stand. "I've really enjoyed dinner. Why don't we go dutch on the bill?"

"Why, ma'am, I don't know how they do things up there in Atttt-lanta," Tripp said in his best southern drawl. "But down heah, when a gentleman invites a girl to dinna, he pays the tab."

Corey laughed. "Okay, okay. Still a Kappa Alpha gentleman to the core, right?"

"Of course," Tripp said with mock humility. "Once a KA, always a KA. Hey . . . do you by chance remember our old KA chant?"

"Yes!"

Tripp smiled. "So, how many damn Yankees were there?"

"Ten thousand," Corey answered without hesitation.

"And how many Rebel soldiers?" Tripp continued.

"Ten."

"And what did the Rebels do?"

Together, and rather loudly, they both said, "Charge!" just as Tonya arrived back at their table with the check.

"Well, of course I'll charge it," Tonya said, looking confused, and Corey and Tripp burst out laughing, which made Tonya look just that much more confused.

As they stood up to leave, Corey placed her hand on Tripp's arm. "I haven't laughed like that in a very long time. Thanks."

Tripp said nothing in reply, but Corey thought his brown eyes that suddenly reminded her of chocolate seemed to darken just a bit.

CHAPTER 5

As Corey began to maneuver around the tables in the restaurant, she realized she was more than a little bit tipsy. And she found the big step up into Tripp's Yukon to be a bit of a challenge.

"Need some help?" Tripp asked from behind her. "I can give you a little push from the rear."

"You leave my rear alone," she replied. She grabbed the handle above her head and managed to pull herself into the seat. She felt exhausted from her efforts and stretched her head back and closed her eyes as the car started moving. When she felt the car stop, she opened her eyes to find that they were sitting at a red light.

"Welcome back," Tripp said, looking over at her.

"I wasn't asleep."

"Yeah, yeah, whatever you say."

When they passed the pier, Corey thought of their first kiss, and she couldn't help but bring it up. "Tell me the truth. You'd never kissed anybody before you kissed me under that pier, had you?"

"Of course not. Couldn't you tell I was scared to death?"

"All I can remember is how awful it was," she said with a cheeky smile.

Tripp stopped at another red light. "I can do better now," he said with an evil grin on his face. He challenged her by leaning in toward her. Surprised, Corey started to turn her head away, but his hand reached out for her face and stopped its progress. Then his face followed his hand toward her face. Corey's first thought was, *He smells good, like the outdoors, or maybe sunshine.* His lips touched her closed mouth, soft and timid. When she started to protest what he was doing, his tongue seized upon the opening of her lips and moved in. That sudden warmth, and the intensity of her emotions in response, was overwhelming. His hand moved to the back of her head, pulling her in closer, and the kiss became deeper. Corey felt as if she were literally melting right there in the car seat. A beep sounded from the car behind them, and they quickly disengaged, like two teenagers caught necking by their parents.

With what sounded like a sigh, Tripp turned back to the steering wheel. "Not so awful now?"

Corey was so stunned she couldn't think of anything smart to say back to him. They drove in breathless silence for another minute. Corey thought each seemed to be waiting for the other to say something. Finally, Tripp cracked and said, "It's still early. Do you want to go home or back to my house?"

Corey knew he wasn't asking her back to his house to watch television. Going home was the safe choice. They could shrug off what had just happened in the car. *What had just happened?* Things would remain the same between them. *Whatever that was.* Going to his house was taking a step into the unknown. Was she ready to take that step? Corey saw they were almost to their street; she needed to make a decision fast—stop at his house, or go on to hers. *Why not take a chance?* She hadn't been kissed like that in a very long time either. "Umm . . . sure, your house would be nice."

His house was dark when they entered, and he didn't turn on the lights. Once inside, he immediately pulled Corey into his arms. She made no effort to stop him this time. She feasted on his lips as eagerly as she had the fried shrimp and oysters back at the restaurant. When he suddenly pulled away from her and said, "I'll be back in a moment— too much wine, I think," she felt disoriented and unsure of what she should do next. The chill of the air-conditioning replaced the warmth of his arms. Corey saw the beach towel still on the bar where she'd left it earlier, grabbed it, and curled up on the sofa. Without Tripp's nearness, she had the clarity of mind to wonder, *What am I doing here?*

Before she found an answer, Tripp was back. Then she found it hard to concentrate on anything but what he was doing. He went to the kitchen and turned on a dim light and a classic-rock radio station. When Led Zeppelin's "Stairway to Heaven" started playing, Corey felt the years fall away.

"How many times did I have to listen to you try to play that on the guitar?" she asked.

"*Try* is the operative word there. I never could actually play it. You want something else to drink? A beer or a glass of wine? I think I've got a bottle of pinot here." Tripp opened a small lower cabinet and peered around, carefully shifting bottles as he searched.

"I think I've had more than enough for one night." She was beginning to feel drowsy again. She closed her eyes, put her head back against the sofa, and let the music wash over her, leaving a thousand memories in its wake. She remembered Tripp letting her drive his Chevy Bronco before she had her license, and how he'd taken the blame when she hadn't put it in park and it had rolled into a telephone pole. She remembered her senior prom, and how they'd won the dance contest after outlasting all the other contestants.

"Don't you dare go to sleep on me," Tripp said, walking back toward the sofa.

"Let's dance," Corey said, offering her hand to him.

"Okay." He grabbed her hand and hauled her up from the sofa. He pulled her in close and wrapped his arms around her tightly.

As Corey put her head down on his shoulder, she said dreamily, "Do you remember how we won the dance contest at my senior prom?"

She felt Tripp nod his head as they continued to sway around the room. Corey suddenly realized that the cold air was causing goose bumps to form on her exposed arms. "Have you ever heard about this thing called an energy crisis that we're in?"

Tripp looked confused. "And . . . you are asking me this now because . . . ?"

"I can't imagine how much you spend on electricity keeping this place this cold all the time."

"Ah . . . but don't you like snuggling in the cold? It's so much nicer than snuggling in the sweaty heat."

"But so environmentally irresponsible," she said, smiling up at him.

"I like being irresponsible," Tripp whispered next to her ear. "You ought to try it—you'll like it too."

His breath on her ear was enticing. Corey turned just enough in his arms so that he could kiss her neck, should he want to. To her delight, he did. As Robert Plant crooned his last *"and she's buying a stairway to heaven,"* she felt different types of chills radiating through her body from the spot on her neck where his lips touched. When she moaned softly, his arms tightened, and his lips moved to her lips. His hands began to move down her back, pulling her in closer to him, and Corey began to feel that same melting sensation she'd experienced in the car. Then, abruptly, he wrenched himself away from her. "Let's go lie down where we can be more comfortable?"

Corey felt abandoned standing there alone in the middle of the floor without his arms around her. Tripp stood in front of Corey with his hand outstretched, waiting patiently for her to make a decision. Directly behind Tripp, Corey could see the sliding glass door. A part of her wanted to say her good-byes, go through that sliding glass door, and head for home. It was the smart thing to do. After all these years, did she even know this man? Yet another part of her wanted desperately to stay. After all, this was Tripp, her Tripp, not some stranger she'd picked up at the Sunset Grill.

Being back at Mexico Beach, and being in Tripp's beach house, Corey felt like she was that younger version of herself—the one who did impulsive things and didn't worry about the consequences. She pushed all logical thought about what she was doing out of her mind. These feelings were intoxicating, as much as or more so than the wine she'd drunk earlier. Without saying a word, she put her hand in his, and they walked arm in arm to his bedroom.

Later, much later, they lay in his bed intertwined, not speaking. Unfortunately, Corey's brain was once again beginning to override her emotions. What had she done? She felt guilty, as though she had cheated on Luke. Yet even those feelings of guilt didn't stop the electric tingling in her arm where Tripp's fingers lightly stroked in a rhythmic motion. Then his hand slid up the side of her leg, and she felt an urgency that caught her by surprise. Corey's brain was on the verge of shutting down once more when Tripp's cell phone rang. She couldn't help but look down at it on the nightstand beside her. She saw that someone named Lucy was calling. She glanced at the clock on the nightstand. It was almost eleven—too late for a casual caller. Corey felt a cold rush of reality sweep over her as Tripp reached over her, picked up the phone, looked at the name, and put it back down on the nightstand. He rolled over onto his back beside her, placed his hands behind his head, and stared at the ceiling.

"Who's Lucy?" Corey asked in a soft, steely voice.

Tripp took a deep breath, still looking at the ceiling. "She's a friend. We go out sometimes."

Corey felt her breath catch in her throat. Yet on some instinctual level, she realized she wasn't surprised by his words. "You mean . . . she's your girlfriend?" Corey turned to stare pointedly at him. "How come you failed to mention Lucy at dinner tonight?"

"Come on, Corey." Tripp sat up in bed. "I've been divorced for two years. Did you think I was a monk?"

"You didn't answer my question." Each word came out terse and tight.

The house phone rang in the living room. Tripp looked relieved. "I was going fishing tonight. Lucy's probably worried, since I haven't called her to let her know I'm back safely."

This last statement acknowledging that his relationship with this woman had advanced far enough that she would check up on his safety infuriated Corey. When she spoke, her words were like icicles, sharp and pointed. "Well, by all means, then . . . please go answer the phone. I should have been gone a long time ago anyway."

Corey gathered her clothes from the floor and scurried into the bathroom. She heard him say, "No, I didn't go fishing. I went to dinner in Port Saint Joe with an old friend, Corey Bennett. We sort of grew up together here at the beach. No, you've never met her. I don't know. She's just here for a couple of weeks."

His evasive statements fed the clear, crisp anger swelling within Corey. Suddenly she was ten years old again, and Tripp had just abandoned her because someone he thought would be more fun had appeared unexpectedly. She dressed quickly. When she opened the bathroom door, he was sitting on the side of the bed in his boxer shorts, holding his head in his hands. He looked up when she entered the room.

"I don't know why I didn't tell you about Lucy. I really don't. I've been dating her for several months, but I don't know where it's going. She's a sweet girl. I guess I just didn't want to make more out of it than there is. And I just . . . I mean . . . I didn't—"

"Yeah, I know," Corey interrupted him. "Why should you complicate things with Lucy? After all, I'll be gone in a couple of weeks, and she'll never have to know about this little"—Corey paused, looking for the right word—"*fling* with me, will she?"

Tripp's face turned red. "Now wait a minute. I'm not like that, and you know it."

"I haven't laid eyes on you in almost a decade. I really don't know you that well."

Tripp challenged her with angry eyes. "Well, you should know me just a little better after tonight."

Corey felt a sudden urge to kick him like she had at the table. Instead, she turned and stomped to the door.

Tripp's anger seemed to evaporate instantly. "Wait, don't leave like this." Corey opened the door. "I've got to be in Panama City for an early meeting tomorrow morning. Why don't you stay awhile longer, and let's talk this thing through?"

"There's nothing to talk through. You haven't changed a bit since . . . since the fifth grade." Corey noticed the blank look on his face, but she wasn't going to stay and explain. "Just leave me alone, Tripp. Just leave me alone!" And with those words still hanging in the air, Corey went down the stairs and out into the dark night.

The house phone was ringing when she unlocked the beach-house door. *Probably Tripp,* she thought, and she let it ring. She went upstairs and started the shower and brushed her teeth. Corey wished the hot water could wash away the memories of what had just happened. She also wished she could blame everything on the alcohol. But in all honesty, she had to admit she'd known exactly what she was doing. It had felt good, and it had been so long since she'd felt much of anything at all. No, she couldn't blame what had happened on the alcohol.

She also had to admit that curiosity had played a role in what had happened. Somewhere deep inside of her, she had always wondered what it would be like making love with Tripp. Now she knew. It was fantastic. She could cross that off her bucket list and move on. Corey wasn't going to play the role of Tripp's always available friend, particularly a friend with benefits, ever again. It had taken her a long time in college to realize that Tripp didn't feel what she felt for him. It had taken even longer to let go of the hope that one day he might. But eventually she had. Tonight, a few of those long-dormant feelings had sparked to life. Lucy had been the cold water that had finally snuffed them out for good.

CHAPTER 6

The incessant ringing of the house phone woke Corey up the next morning. When she looked at her cell phone to see what time it was, she realized it was dead. As the ringing continued, she made her way downstairs to answer the phone.

"Are you okay?" Diane asked when Corey picked up the phone.

"Yeah, I'm fine," Corey replied grumpily.

"Where were you last night?" Diane's voice was eerily reminiscent of the voice their mother had used when they were in trouble. "I called your cell phone and the house phone like a hundred times."

Corey thought about making something up, but she wasn't that quick. "I went to dinner in Port Saint Joe with Tripp MacKinnon last night. Oh, and I haven't charged my cell phone since I've been here, so the battery went dead."

"Well, how was it?" Diane's voice had an immediate change in tenor.

"Dinner was great," Corey said brightly. "But before you go getting any ideas, he has a girlfriend."

"I used to think you two would end up together," Diane continued. "You are so much alike."

"Really," Corey said. "Because last night, I realized how very different we are."

"Okay, okay," Diane said. "At least you got out and did something fun. Have you been watering the plant?"

"Of course," Corey lied. She hadn't thought about the plant one time since she'd been there. "I'll see you tomorrow." Corey went downstairs to water the ficus tree and noticed a white piece of paper under the windshield wiper of her car.

I'll be away for the next two days. Please call this number after 5:00 p.m., and let's talk.

She tore the paper into pieces and threw them in the trash can. She was done thinking about Tripp MacKinnon, and that was a fact! The weather seemed to mirror her emotions as dark clouds swirled overhead. No beach today. She guessed she would stay in her pajamas and watch old movies. Somehow that didn't seem as appealing as it had just two days ago.

A tiny yellow MINI Cooper pulled up as she started to go up the stairs. An almost entirely gray-headed woman was waving at her from behind the steering wheel. After a moment, Corey realized it was Fran, and she walked over to the car. "I've been calling all morning to see if you wanted to go to the mall in Panama City. I've got to get some makeup and take the boat cushions to get them restitched. It's supposed to rain all day, and I'd love the company."

"I'm not dressed," Corey said, pointing down to her pajamas and thinking how wonderful it was that someone whom she hadn't seen in years still cared enough about her to invite her to spend the day with her.

"I'm not leaving right now. I've got to go to the marina and get the cushions off the boat. I'll be back in twenty minutes or so. Go get dressed."

Why not? Corey thought. "Okay, I'll be ready." And just like that, the empty day that had stretched before her was full. She was glad, because if she'd had too much time on her hands, she might have started trying to put those pieces of paper back together again.

Diane arrived the next day and brought the sunshine with her as well as a ton of groceries. "Look at your tree! It has tiny green nubs forming. I think it's going to make it, and I had my doubts. Come on and help me carry all of this stuff up."

After what felt like a hundred trips up and down the stairs, Corey sat in amazement and watched the whirling dervish that was her sister simultaneously put up groceries, put a ham in the oven, and talk non-stop about her trip to Tampa. After a while, Diane paused long enough to look critically at Corey. "You know, the ficus isn't the only thing that's looking better around here, though you still need some work on your tan. Come on, I'm done here. Let's go to the beach."

Diane and Corey were drinking margaritas on the beach. "It doesn't get any better than this, does it?" Corey asked. They'd spent almost two full days lounging on the beach—reading, eating, and drinking. Corey couldn't remember ever being so lazy in her adult life.

"No . . . but unfortunately, I need to go up and shower. Jack will be here in a couple of hours, and he might appreciate a clean wife. It's the least I can do since I left him alone all week."

"I'll go up too," Corey said, after picking up one bikini strap and looking at her slightly pink shoulders. "I think I've had enough sun for the day. Thank God for sunscreen."

They gathered their stuff and started to walk up the beach path. Corey's stomach quivered in some weird way when she saw the white Yukon just pulling up under the MacKinnon house. Tripp got out, waved, and waited for them to approach. Corey thought the dark aviator sunglasses he wore with his black business suit made him look like an FBI agent.

"Hey, Tripp, thanks for entertaining my sister during my absence," Diane said cheerfully.

"It was my pleasure," Tripp replied without a hint of sarcasm and without looking at Corey. "Glad to see the umbrella is okay."

"What?" Diane looked at Corey questioningly.

"I forgot to tell you. The wind blew it away, and Tripp saved it for us." Corey's voice was expressionless.

"So I owe you double?" Diane gave a little laugh. "I guess the only way to pay you back is to invite you to dinner. Jack is going to grill steaks when he gets here. Come on over about seven and we'll have cocktails."

Tripp still hadn't looked at Corey. "Sounds great. I'll see y'all at seven."

Corey had known she was going to have to face him sooner or later. She'd stupidly hoped that he might stay away from the beach for the remainder of her vacation. But of course that would have meant that he had some consideration for her feelings.

Jack and Tripp were downstairs by the grill, drinking beer and telling stories. Corey could hear them laughing, which really irritated her. She supposed it was because Tripp seemed to be experiencing no awkwardness over what had happened between them. He had arrived promptly at seven, not long after Jack, greeted all of them as casually as could be, and since then, he and Jack had been downstairs supposedly getting the charcoal started. But the smoke plume billowing up the side of the house indicated that the charcoal had long ago passed the starting point.

"I'm done here. Do you want to go downstairs and join the guys?" Diane asked from the kitchen.

"And fight the heat and the horseflies? Nah, let's just sit on the sunporch and be comfortable," Corey answered lightly.

After a while, Tripp came up as carefree as could be to get the steaks and some more beers. He teased Diane about hiding the pepper shaker, and while he was looking in the cabinet for it, Corey tried hard not to look at him. For when she did, she felt too much. Looking at his lips, she remembered how they tasted. Looking at his hands, she remembered how they felt. Then she'd remember Lucy, and her anger blocked out every other feeling, except for the guilt that was interwoven through all her feelings. How could she have gone to bed so casually with Tripp?

"Let's eat," Jack announced, putting the steaks on the breakfast bar along with Diane's potato salad, freshly sliced tomatoes, lady finger peas, and sweet tea. "Look at this feast. Has any man ever had a better wife? Come here, woman, and give me a great big kiss. I've missed you!"

"You're drunk," Diane said. But Corey could see from Diane's smile as she raised her face for his kiss that she was pleased by the attention. Corey and Tripp looked everywhere but at each other while Jack and Diane were kissing.

"Mmm-mmm, good!" Jack exclaimed, before folding his large frame into the chair at the end of the table and motioning for everyone else to join him.

"So . . . Tripp," Diane said as they were eating, "Corey tells me you have a girlfriend. How come I haven't seen her with you down here? Must not be that serious."

Corey felt her face grow warm. She noticed that Tripp's face seemed to have a slight tinge of red as well. Without addressing whether it was serious or not, he said, "She's a nurse at Dothan General. She works weekends."

"What's her name? Where's she from?" Diane sounded like a police sergeant grilling a prisoner.

"Lucy Conroy," Tripp answered tonelessly. "She's from Ohio. She moved to Dothan about a year ago."

"Oh no, not a damn Yankee!" Diane said with mock horror.

"Okay, let's leave Tripp alone," Corey interrupted. "I think he's had enough of the inquisition for one night." She wondered idly what Lucy might think about Tripp's KA chant as they finished up dinner in a companionable manner. Diane ushered them out to the sunporch for coffee and some of her famous triple-chocolate delight.

"That was a fabulous dinner," Tripp said. "I hate to call it a night, but surprise, surprise, I'm going fishing in the morning, and six comes awfully early. You want to come, Jack?"

Jack looked at Diane like a hungry puppy begging for food. "Go ahead," Diane said laughingly.

"You and Corey could come too?" Tripp offered casually.

"That's a bit early for me," Corey said quickly before Diane could accept for both of them.

"And Marcy's coming home from camp tomorrow anyway," Diane added. "Corey, why don't you see Tripp out, and you can water that plant of yours, which we forgot to do today." Diane turned without waiting for an answer and started stacking the dishes.

There was no way to gracefully avoid going outside with Tripp, so Corey rose and followed him out the door.

"Why didn't you call me?" Tripp asked as soon as the door closed behind them.

"There's nothing to talk about," Corey said bluntly, continuing to walk down the stairs.

"Damn it, Corey. I don't want a one-night stand with you. Let's try to see how this thing between us might play out."

Corey's anger, simmering below the surface all night, exploded. She turned to him halfway down the stairs. "You want to know how this will play out? Well, let me tell you right now. In seven days, I'm going back to Atlanta. That's where I live, where I work. Oh sure, we could make plans to get together in a few weeks. We might even pull it off once or maybe twice. But I'm a city girl, and didn't you already have one relationship go bad with a city girl? And what about sweet Lucy? Are you going to keep seeing her as well? I'm not much for sharing. Have you forgotten that?" Corey paused to catch her breath and tried to finish more calmly. "The best thing for us to do is to forget about what happened the other night. Chalk it up to too much wine or whatever, and let it go."

Even in the dim moonlight, Corey could see that Tripp was stunned.

"Can I at least kiss you good-bye? You know . . . like for old times' sake?" Tripp asked.

"No," Corey answered firmly.

Tripp nodded and headed down the stairs. Corey turned and started walking back up. She'd water the ficus tree later. Right then, she didn't want Tripp to see how her eyes were suddenly teary, and for no good reason that she could tell.

CHAPTER 7

Marcy was delivered from camp the next day around lunchtime. Diane had taken her daughter and her best friend, Beth, to camp; Beth's mother, Carol, had been responsible for picking them up. Diane had invited Carol and Beth to stay at the beach for a few days, and Corey was glad for the distractions that the two thirteen-year-old girls provided. From the moment they'd walked through the door, it had been nonstop action. "Let's go swimming, Aunt Corey. Let's play cards." Also, Corey was glad that Diane finally had some other people around to nurture. She loved her sister, but her constant hovering was beginning to drive Corey crazy.

Jack came home from fishing late that afternoon with a slightly sunburned face and an ice chest full of red snappers. He reported that, unfortunately, Tripp had gone back to Dothan. "Probably a hot date with Lucy," he said, winking at Corey. *She works weekends,* Corey wanted to remind him.

The next week was as active for Corey as the first week had been restful. Jack, who was a pharmacist, had arranged to take a few days off from work. On Monday, they took the boat out to Hurricane Cut, an area that only the locals knew about. They picnicked all day, floated for hours in the pristine water of their own private paradise, and hunted for seashells on a beach that appeared untouched by human hands. On Tuesday, they took the boat up the Intracoastal Waterway to Apalachicola and ate oysters at a pier-side restaurant that advertised their oysters had been swimming in the bay just hours earlier. Unfortunately, the memory of the incredible fried oysters Corey had eaten with Tripp made these pale in comparison.

Much to Corey's surprise, she discovered she was still as agile as a cat on the boat. Skills she hadn't used since before the death of her dad came back to her the first time she tried. She automatically climbed out on the front of the boat to keep it from hitting the dock's piling without anyone asking her to do so. She grabbed the hook and brought in the fish Beth had floundering on the side of the boat. And when Jack asked her to drive the boat while he worked on getting a hook out of a fish, it seemed like days instead of years since she'd last done so. It was as if her body remembered the familiar warmth and smells and rocking of the boat, and she acted automatically, without any need for conscious thought.

And the beach house, brimming over with people and echoing with happy noises, seemed just right. Corey was sincerely sad when it was time for Carol and Beth to leave. She, Diane, and Marcy spent two more days just relaxing on the beach, and then it was time for Corey to start thinking about heading back to Atlanta. Corey had to admit she felt a certain excitement about getting back to her life. Her office had managed not to contact her during the first week. But during the second week, she'd had to handle several emergencies using the e-mail on her phone. Corey supposed it felt good to be needed.

On Friday night, Corey loaded her car so that she could leave early the next morning. She glanced occasionally over at the MacKinnon house as she went up and down the stairs. By ten, when she had yet to see a light on in the house, she realized Tripp wasn't coming for the weekend. She felt a strange mixture of disappointment and relief. It was probably better this way.

"It's hard to believe the changes in you in just two weeks," Diane said as Corey came up from taking the last load to her car. Corey knew that Diane was right; she had changed both externally and internally. Her hair was now streaked with blonde from the sun, and her body glowed with a soft golden tan. But more important, Corey had rediscovered how to find pleasure in simple things like eating a good meal or feeling the sun on her skin.

"Don't forget your tree," Diane continued. "Put it someplace where it can get a lot of indirect light, and don't forget to water it every day if it's outside, and once a week if inside. A few more weeks here and it wouldn't fit in your car."

"If I kill it now, I'm going to feel really bad. Maybe I should leave it with you?" Corey offered.

"Not on your life. Just give it what it needs: sun, water . . . and maybe talk to it now and then."

"Talk to it? You really are an earth mother, aren't you?" Corey laughed.

"You need to take care of yourself, too, okay? A little sunshine every day wouldn't hurt you either. And promise me that you aren't going to wait three or four years before you come back to the beach again."

"I promise," Corey said. Once again, tears filled her eyes unexpectedly. "I'm going to bed now. Love you."

For two weeks, Corey had been able to sleep anytime she put her head down. Now, on this night, the night before she was to leave, she couldn't sleep. After tossing and turning for hours, she got up at sunrise, left a note for Diane and Jack, and headed out. The MacKinnon house looked sad all shuttered up. Or maybe Corey just felt sad looking at the

MacKinnon house without Tripp in it. However, the long drive reaffirmed everything that Corey had said to Tripp. The distance between Atlanta and Dothan was too far to try to build a relationship with him, even without a Lucy in the picture.

Corey looked at her condo when she arrived home as if she were seeing it for the first time. It was dreary and full of wallpaper and colors she didn't like. She hated red, and the kitchen had red cabinets and beige wallpaper with red cherries on it. One of the bathrooms was wallpapered in floral patterns of pink, and the other in floral patterns of baby blue. And it was no wonder that the ficus had been dying; she rarely remembered to open the heavy damask curtains in the great room to let in any light. Her condo would be a depressing place for anyone to live regardless of her mental state.

Renovating the condo had never crossed her mind after Luke died. When faced with the enormity of his death, did it really matter what color the walls were? Also, Luke had been the one with all the plans. She really hadn't known what she wanted to do. Now, Corey suddenly felt motivated to get started on renovating the condo as soon as possible. She had money from both her parents' and Luke's life insurance. All she needed was a plan. Corey decided to find a decorator and get started on creating a home where she might actually want to live. Hopefully, the decorating firm wouldn't be associated with Martha Anne, Tripp's ex-wife.

CHAPTER 8

On Monday morning, Corey walked into the sprawling lobby of the law offices of Landon, Crane, and Forrester and went straight back to Larry's office. "Hi, Barbara. Can I stick my head in for just a moment?"

"Certainly, Ms. Bennett. Did you have a nice vacation?" Barbara was actually very nice when she wasn't acting as Larry's policewoman.

"It was perfect."

Larry was drinking a cup of coffee while looking over some papers on his desk. "Hey, Larry, I'm back." Corey walked over to his desk and laid a perfectly shaped scallop shell on top of his papers.

Larry looked from the shell up to Corey, and his eyes widened. "I don't know where you went, but given what it's done for you, I think I'm planning my next vacation there."

Corey laughed. "I just wanted to thank you. I really did need a vacation."

"Well, it's nice to see the girl, I mean, woman, I used to know," Larry said. "Now, get back to work and make up for all those billable hours you missed during the past two weeks."

At lunchtime a couple of days later, Corey walked downstairs to the first floor and joined the fitness center. She knew her condo wasn't the only thing that needed some work done on it. It was time she started taking better care of herself, and exercising was an important part of that process. Corey knew that running was no longer a viable option for her everyday exercise. She would never go running alone in the dark around her neighborhood. The fitness club was a good alternative. Corey spotted a couple of guys who worked for her firm. *How did they find time to work out on their lunch hours?*

Thinking about the guys at the health club, she decided at five thirty to pack up a couple of documents in her briefcase and head for home. Since somehow the male associates managed to get their work done without living at the office, Corey decided she was no longer staying late unless there was a bona fide emergency. Besides, she was having dinner that night with Romeo and Gary. She'd offered to take them out as a thank-you for getting her mail. Instead, they had insisted she eat with them.

"I'm the best chef in Atlanta, darling," Gary said while batting his long, dark eyelashes at her with fake modesty. "Why waste your money? But do bring lots of good wine." Remembering that, Corey stopped on the way home and bought a case of the couple's favorite wine.

Gary's dinner was as good as advertised. The stuffed manicotti was probably the best that Corey had ever put in her mouth. Instead of comparing this dinner with other evenings that she and Luke had spent with them, she just focused on enjoying her dinner that night, and for once she didn't feel like a third wheel while eating with the couple. She laughed at their expressions when she described Mexico Beach.

"Is it like Destin? We've been to Destin before." Romeo arched one eyebrow at her questioningly.

"Not quite," Corey said. "Mexico Beach has one grocery store, a fishing marina, a gas station, and an ice-cream shack. For everything else, you have to drive fifteen minutes to Port Saint Joe, or forty-five minutes to Panama City."

"That sounds dreadful. Isn't it boring there?" Gary asked earnestly.

Corey tried to think whether she had ever been bored at the beach. "Nope," she said. "Doing nothing there is more fun than doing nothing here. I don't know why."

"But I want to do stuff when I go on vacation—like clubbing, shopping, and eating in good restaurants," Romeo said dramatically.

"Simple solution, then—don't go there," Corey said.

"I don't think you'll have to worry about that," Gary promised.

Corey's life was suddenly very full. Work was hectic after being on vacation, but not so hectic that she didn't make it to the gym at least three mornings a week before work. She visited with her mother-in-law on Sunday afternoons, and in between everything else, there was now Kathryn, the interior designer, who practically lived with her. Kathryn had been the second interior designer Corey interviewed. She was about Corey's age, and they had clicked so well that Corey had hired her on the spot.

Kathryn had a plan for practically every room in the condo. New skylights were to be installed in her bathroom and in the great room to brighten up the place. The kitchen cabinets and walls were to be painted a glossy white, and new black-granite countertops would be installed. The master bath and a small extra room next to it would be combined and turned into a master suite with a spa tub and walk-in closet. New hardwood floors would replace the carpet, and there would not be a hint of wallpaper anywhere in sight. Corey thought it all sounded heavenly.

As Labor Day approached, and the one-year anniversary of Luke's death passed, Corey felt a semblance of normalcy again in her life. Not that she didn't still miss Luke, because, of course, she did. However, the overwhelming sadness she'd felt for so long seemed gone. Now the sadness took her by surprise in unguarded moments, like when one of Luke's favorite songs came on the radio, or when Nancy made a facial expression that seemed so very Luke-like. And if Corey still thought about her night with Tripp occasionally, she found more and more that it seemed like a nice dream rather than a part of her reality. Corey finally felt ready to move forward with her life.

On a bright morning in early September, the day that demolition was to start for the master bathroom, Corey woke up nauseated and then threw up. She was still holding her head over the toilet when Kathryn arrived, using her front-door key to let herself in. Kathryn, a petite five-foot elfin brunette, came breezing into the bedroom announcing her presence by yelling loudly, "He . . . lll . . . ooo!" She stopped abruptly at the bathroom door.

"Big night last night?" Kathryn asked drily.

"Must be a stomach bug," Corey groaned. "Don't get too close. Do we have to start the demolition today? I kind of need my bathroom right now."

"You need crackers and ginger ale," Kathryn said brightly. "Here, let me help you to the guest bathroom, and then I'll go get some for you. We can't hold up the subcontractors."

Much to Corey's relief, after a few crackers and a can of ginger ale, she felt much better. She got up, dressed for work, and arrived at her office at a respectable time.

After the same thing happened several days in a row, Corey began to worry that maybe something was seriously wrong with her. She'd seen firsthand how quickly a medical anomaly could mushroom into a medical crisis. In between appointments at work, she logged on to WebMD. The first question that came up after she'd entered her symptoms into the system was: Could you possibly be pregnant?

Corey stared at the words on the computer screen until the screen saver kicked in. *No, I couldn't possibly be pregnant!* She and Luke had tried to get pregnant for almost a year with no luck. Being five years older than Corey, Luke had been eager to start their family right away. But Corey had put him off, wanting to become more established in her job first. They had only seriously begun trying ten months or so before Luke's cancer was diagnosed. At the time, Corey had felt thankful that she wasn't also pregnant. Then, immediately, she'd felt guilty for feeling that way. *No, I couldn't possibly be pregnant! That would be just too ironic!*

"Ms. Bennett, your three o'clock appointment is here," her assistant, Erica, said from the doorway. When Corey didn't reply, Erica added, "Are you okay?"

After an afternoon of trying to focus on the peculiarities of the Winston estate, and not doing a very good job of it, Corey started for home. She stopped on the way and bought a pregnancy test and then picked up a salad. It was late. Kathryn and all the workmen were long gone by the time she arrived home. Corey wiped a layer of fine dust off the kitchen table and sat staring at the EPT box while she ate her salad. When she finished, she put her fork in the dishwasher and walked into the great room. Everything in the house had a layer of dust from the demolition. Kathryn had said the contractors would seal off the master bedroom, but it hadn't seemed to have mattered. Corey wondered if the dust might be harmful to a baby. Despite the sweltering heat, she walked outside to her small, enclosed patio area and sat down. She noticed the ficus tree standing under the eave of the condo. Corey had put the plant outside after returning from the beach and had been faithful in watering the plant every day—or at least almost every day. Its lush green leaves were now a testament to the good care she'd been giving it. She remembered Diane telling her that she should also talk to the plant, and since no one else was around, she thought, *Why not?*

"You see, plant, it's like this. I'm in a bit of a dilemma. On the one hand, I'm thirty-two years old. My biological clock is ticking. If I'm pregnant, a part of me will be really excited because I do want to have a baby. I mean, it would have been nice for it to have happened with Luke. But then, it would have been nice if Luke hadn't died, right?"

Corey paused for a moment and took a deep breath.

"If I'm pregnant, I want to keep this baby. But should I tell Tripp? If I do, things will get complicated. I know he will want to be involved. He might even want to marry me just to give the baby his name. Southern men often have rather old-fashioned views about that kind of thing. But the thought of joint custody, and shuttling a baby back and forth to Florida, isn't very appealing.

"On the other hand, the clients of Landon, Crane, and Forrester aren't the kind of people who will accept an unwed and pregnant lawyer as their counsel. The partners might not be able to fire me, but I'll never become their first woman partner. And who knows? They might even make my life so unbearable that I'll have to quit. If I'm pregnant, perhaps I should look for another job, at a different type of firm, where a woman wanting a baby and going it alone wouldn't raise any eyebrows. But I've put in a lot of time at LCF, and I really don't want to start over somewhere else."

Corey paused and waited, as though there might be a response from the tree. *Okay, ficus, you've been a great listener, but I really could use some advice now.* When nothing seemed to be forthcoming from the ficus tree, Corey went inside, grabbed the EPT, and went to the bathroom. When the plus sign appeared in the little round window, indicating she was pregnant, Corey didn't know whether to laugh or cry. She couldn't help but remember how anxiously Luke had waited outside the bathroom door each month to see if she was pregnant, and his obvious disappointment when she wasn't. Crazily, she then thought about her eighth-grade health teacher. She'd been right. You *could* get pregnant after doing it only once.

She wanted to share her news with someone but quickly realized there was no one. Luke had been her best friend. She had some casual friendships with people at work and, of course, with Romeo and Gary.

But that was it. She and Diane were close, but Corey knew her sister would want her to go straight to Tripp and tell him about the baby. Heck, Diane might even tell Tripp about the baby if Corey didn't. So she was just going to have to figure this thing out herself. At least the next day was Saturday, so she wouldn't have to try to focus on work as well.

After her ritualistic early-morning throw-up, Corey grabbed the newspaper and decided to go out to a deli for some breakfast. She wanted to stay out of that potentially unhealthy house as much as possible. She was nibbling on a cinnamon-raisin bagel and skimming the front page of the metro section when she came across a headline that read: *Chemotherapy Patients Can Still Be Parents by Going to the Bank.* It was a feel-good story about how more and more cancer patients were freezing their sperm or eggs in order to have children after chemotherapy.

Corey's heart started pumping rapidly, not exactly like a panic attack—but something similar. She remembered how Luke's doctor had suggested that Luke might want to do such a thing. He hadn't. Luke had said if he recovered, they would adopt. But Corey was sure that no one knew that he hadn't. What if she told everyone that she was artificially inseminated with Luke's sperm? That way, the baby would be cloaked in respectability. The firm could pass Corey off as a pregnant widow carrying her late husband's baby, and Tripp would never have to know that he was the father.

Of course, there was the ethical issue of denying Tripp his rights as a parent. And there was Nancy to consider. How could she let an eighty-seven-year-old woman believe that a baby with no biological connection to her was her grandchild? But, Corey rationalized, if they had adopted, the child would have had no biological connection and still would have been her grandchild. The artificial-insemination story was beginning to seem more and more plausible to her. Also, for some strange reason, she had a feeling that Luke wouldn't object to her actions. They had tried for so long to have a baby that somehow her pregnancy felt more connected to Luke than the distant and faint memory of her night with Tripp.

Corey went to the library to learn everything she possibly could about artificial insemination. People would ask questions, and she must know exactly how to answer. She even researched obstetricians and found one who appeared to be good and was conveniently located close to her office. With the next day being Sunday, Corey decided she might as well start the ball rolling with her mother-in-law. In some ways, Nancy would be the hardest person to tell, but in other ways, she would be the easiest. If Corey could get over the guilt, and actually get the words out of her mouth, she knew Nancy would not ask a lot of questions about the process. *Luke, please forgive me for lying to your mother.*

The next day, Corey felt as though she were on a racetrack as the Sunday-afternoon drivers flew by her on I-75. It was a good twenty-minute drive out to Peachtree Wilden, which gave Corey plenty of time to think about what she was about to do. Corey imagined Nancy sitting in her tiny one-bedroom apartment, watching television, and waiting for her to arrive. The resident director had expressed concern to Corey that Nancy never took advantage of any of the many social and recreational activities that she was paying for by living there. Each time Corey visited her, Nancy seemed less like herself in some way than she had the week before. Last week, as she was leaving, the director had informed Corey that Nancy wasn't coming down to eat in the restaurant anymore but had started taking her meals in her room.

The entrance to Peachtree Wilden seemed more like the entrance to a country club than a retirement home, with its crystal chandeliers and expensive oil paintings. As Corey rode the elevator up to Nancy's apartment, she felt as if she were standing on the edge of a cliff. Lying to Nancy would be like stepping off the edge, and there would be no going back. She couldn't say, "Oh, my mistake, I'm actually pregnant by someone else and not your son." Did she really want to do this?

She knocked on Nancy's door several times before it finally opened. Nancy's disheveled appearance shocked Corey because she had never seen Nancy's hair looking anything but perfectly groomed. She supposed that this week Nancy had given up on going to the hairdresser. Corey gave her a light kiss on the cheek.

"Hi, darling," Nancy said, welcoming her. The room was extremely warm and smelled strongly of something that Corey couldn't identify but which made her feel slightly queasy.

"Sit down, dear. Can I get you something to drink? I've got some iced tea made."

"Thank you," Corey replied. "That would be nice. How have you been this week?"

"I can't complain. How are your renovations coming along?" Nancy walked slowly into her little kitchen nook and came back carefully, carrying two crystal glasses of iced tea.

"The skylights and kitchen counters are in, but they've just started on the master bath, and dust is everywhere."

"Renovations can be so trying," Nancy commiserated.

Corey took a deep breath. "I have some big news."

"Are you dating someone, dear? Oh, I knew it was about time. You are so young. You know you have my blessing."

Corey was surprised. "No, I'm not dating, but I hope I will have your blessing anyway. Do you know what artificial insemination is?"

"Of course." Nancy looked confused and somewhat embarrassed.

"Before Luke began chemotherapy," Corey said, looking down at her hands in her lap, "his doctor recommended he freeze some of his sperm so that he might be able to have children afterward. I decided I wanted to have a child, so I underwent artificial insemination. I just found out I'm pregnant."

"Do you mean you're having Luke's baby?" Nancy asked incredulously.

Corey finally looked up. She was disturbed to see that tears were beginning to drip down Nancy's face. "Yes." Corey prayed lightning wouldn't strike her for such a bald-faced lie. "Please don't be upset. Please don't cry."

"Oh, my dear, can you not tell that these are tears of happiness? I've been sitting in this place for a year with nothing to look forward to, just waiting to die. Now you've given me a reason to live. How far along are you?"

"About six weeks," Corey lied. "I probably should have waited until I was farther along to tell you about the pregnancy, in case something happened. But I was too excited."

"Do you have morning sickness?"

"Yes."

Nancy's face suddenly brightened with a look of gladness that Corey hadn't seen there for at least two years. "Then everything will be fine. Morning sickness is a real good sign. Now, you need to start eating lots of eggs and drinking milk. I know you don't like milk, but drink it anyway—maybe ice cream if you can't bring yourself to drink milk. Let's go downstairs and get you some ice cream now. I think I'd like some too."

A couple of hours later, and after they'd both eaten an ice-cream cone, Corey started to leave. At the door, Nancy hugged her with a strength that belied her tiny stature. "You do not know how happy you have made me today. I wish I hadn't moved so that I could be close by to help you with the baby."

As Corey drove home, she prayed that the happiness she'd brought to Nancy that day would negate the wrongness of the lies she'd told.

With a sigh, she recognized that she'd made it over the first obstacle. Telling Diane tonight was going to be an even bigger challenge.

Corey waited until she felt sure that Diane would be finished with dinner before she called.

"Hello, Di, it's Corey. How's everybody doing?" After a minute or two of idle chitchat, Diane began to be suspicious.

"Okay, sis, you never call just to chat. What's going on?"

"Are you sitting down?" Corey's mouth went dry, and she felt almost dizzy.

"Is this bad news?" Diane's voice quivered just a bit. They'd had more than their share of those types of calls in the past.

"I don't think so." Corey hoped she sounded more confident than she felt.

"Are you dating someone?" Diane asked with sudden excitement in her voice.

Corey wondered why everyone expected her to be dating. "No, but there will be someone new in my life in the near future."

"Okay, what gives?"

"You know how I've wanted to have a baby for a while. Well, Luke's doctor recommended that he freeze some of his sperm before he started chemotherapy. So right after I came back from the beach, I was artificially inseminated, and I just found out I'm pregnant."

"What are you talking about?" Diane sounded exasperated. "Don't kid around about stuff like that."

"I'm not kidding. I'm pregnant."

"If you'd been thinking about doing this, why didn't you say something to me at the beach?" Diane asked in disbelief.

"I . . . I was afraid you'd talk me out of it," Corey stammered.

"Why?" Diane challenged her.

"Because I can't even keep a plant alive, so you might not think me fit to be a mother." Now that the lies were flowing, they seemed to be coming easier and easier.

"Wow, I'm speechless. You know, Corey, having a baby can be pretty tough, and having one alone is going to be twice as tough."

"I'll hire a nanny. Come on, Di, can't you be happy for me?"

"I just don't understand it, Corey," Diane said harshly, "You show up at the beach looking like some concentration-camp refugee. You seem barely able to take care of yourself, and now you're having a baby? It just doesn't make sense. Did you consider going to grief therapy instead?"

Corey suddenly longed to tell Diane the truth. But fear of what would happen next stopped her. "I'll talk to you later," Corey said abruptly, and she hung up the phone.

CHAPTER 9

When the alarm went off at five thirty the next morning, Corey wanted to hit the "Snooze" button and go back to sleep. But she'd missed several days of exercise already, and she felt so much better when she was exercising regularly. The saltines she kept by her bed and snacked on immediately upon waking seemed to help with the morning sickness. And she knew exercise couldn't hurt the baby because she'd known some women who exercised right up until the day they delivered. Once dressed in her exercise clothes, Corey actually felt pretty good. She grabbed some work clothes and her makeup bag and headed out for the fitness club.

As she left the ladies' locker room, Corey was surprised to see John Kowlowski come out of the men's door.

"Hi, John," she said in greeting. "I've never seen you here before."

"Oh, I'm usually long gone by now."

Corey looked at him closely to see if he was trying to be funny, but as best she could tell, he was serious. She made a face indicating how impressed she was and stepped up on a treadmill. She was surprised when John stepped onto the treadmill beside her, as there were several other treadmills available a little farther away. Corey felt compelled to make small talk with him, so they chatted about the Inman deal while they were walking at a slow pace and warming up.

After a while, they both adjusted their speeds to running, and their conversation stopped. Corey was thinking about the best way to break the news about her pregnancy to Larry, when she noticed that John had increased his speed so that his pace was somewhat faster than hers. She reached down and adjusted her speed to match his. When John moved his speed into a gallop, the competitiveness within Corey made her ramp up her speed as well. Corey felt as though she and John were actually in a race next to each other. She began to feel breathless and realized she should probably stop, but she didn't. Corey wasn't going to let John beat her. She could feel her heart hammering against her chest, and she was having more and more trouble catching her breath. Then, all of a sudden, everything went dark.

The next thing Corey knew, she was lying on the floor behind the treadmill. John was leaning down next to her, and several other people were standing around her. She tried to sit up, but someone put a restraining hand on her; it was the guy who worked the front desk at the fitness club. "You need to wait for the EMTs to get here."

"What happened?" she asked hesitantly.

"You blacked out." John's face was close over her. "Just suddenly collapsed on the treadmill and then rolled off the back."

Corey felt ridiculous. Of course she'd fainted. Didn't pregnant women do that all the time? She tried to sit up again, but the fitness guy still had a death grip on her arm. "I'm fine, really. I don't need to go to the emergency room."

"Sorry, but it's club policy," the guy said. "Here's the EMTs now."

Two guys with a gurney came hurrying up to Corey. One looked hardened, as if he'd done everything and seen everything. The other looked about twelve years old. "Everything's going to be okay; just relax," the younger of the two reassured her.

"Listen," Corey said to the older guy, who was feeling her legs, "just let me sit up and make sure nothing is broken. I don't need to go to the emergency room."

"We need to figure out why you fainted. Could be just blood sugar, or it could be something more serious," he said.

"Or," Corey said, exasperated as the younger guy put a blood pressure cuff on her, "it could be because I'm pregnant." The moment the words came out of her mouth, Corey wished she could pull them back in. She looked at John. His eyes were wide with shock.

"Pregnant?" John repeated, as though he hadn't heard her correctly.

"Yes, I'm pregnant. I was artificially inseminated with my husband's sperm while I was on vacation. I'm four weeks' pregnant."

"In that case, we'll make sure nothing's broken and then let your doctor take it from here," the older EMT said.

"Thank you."

"Who's your doctor?" The young guy had picked up a clipboard and was writing furiously on it.

"Uh . . ." Corey was thankful that she'd done her research. "It's Dr. Byrne. Dr. Pat Byrne." She needed to call his office as soon as it opened and make an appointment.

After a few more minutes of prodding and poking, finally the EMTs helped her stand up and watched her walk around a bit. "You're probably going to have some bruising," the old guy warned, "but nothing's broken." He looked at John. "You a friend of hers?"

John nodded yes.

"How 'bout you drive her home?"

"I'm not going home. I'm going to work," Corey said adamantly.

"So I guess you want us to take you to the ER, after all?" the old guy asked facetiously.

"No," Corey answered. The old EMT was a tough nut, and he wasn't going to go away easily.

"Then go home until after you've seen your doctor."

"Okay, I'll go home," she muttered.

"And you'll take her home?" The old guy turned back to John. "Sure."

"Okay." The EMTs started packing up their bag and, after one last look at Corey, rolled their gurney toward the door.

Corey turned to John as soon as the door closed behind them. "I'm not going home."

"I know, but are you sure that's wise?"

Corey thought John seemed genuinely concerned about her. "I'll be smarter than I was on that treadmill. I was running so hard because I didn't want you to beat me, you know."

John looked at her curiously for a moment or two. "I know. I was running so fast because I wanted to beat you."

An understanding silence hung between them. Corey realized that the competition they'd disguised for years was finally out in the open. Corey studied John's face carefully. "I haven't told Larry about my condition yet. Can we keep this between us for a little while?"

"I won't say anything, but you can't keep news like this a secret for long. I wasn't the only person from the firm who saw you collapse this morning, you know."

"I'm going to tell him today. I had planned to tell him today anyway," Corey explained.

"Good luck," John offered, and for once Corey sensed that he was being completely sincere. "You've really surprised me today, Corey. I thought the firm was your life."

Corey suddenly realized that John's concern about her and his openness with her was because he no longer considered her a threat. In his mind, she'd dropped out of the race to become a partner.

"Yeah . . . well . . . it is a big part of my life," Corey stated tersely, "but I decided I needed more in my life than just a job. Thanks for your help, John." Corey turned and walked into the ladies' locker room. She figured she had about thirty minutes until Larry would be in his office, and she needed to be there when he showed up.

Barbara wasn't at her desk when Corey arrived. Corey tapped on Larry's office door just in case he'd come in early. When she heard him call, "Come in," Corey entered tentatively. Larry was bent over, looking into a minifridge that had been cleverly designed to hide behind a wall panel. He glanced over at Corey but didn't stop his search.

"Got a few minutes?" Corey asked, her voice strained.

"Sure, come on in. You want a Coke or some water? Seems there's everything in here except a Diet Coke."

"No, I'm good." Corey's voice quivered. She was more nervous about telling Larry than she had been about telling Diane.

"What's up?" he asked, finally pulling out a Diet Coke and holding it up like a trophy.

"I have an exciting announcement," Corey said with the widest smile she could muster.

Corey suddenly had Larry's full attention. "You better not have taken a job with another firm."

"I wouldn't do that to you," Corey said honestly, and then bluntly, "I'm pregnant."

Larry looked thoroughly confused. "What did you say?"

"I was artificially inseminated with Luke's sperm during my vacation, and I'm pregnant."

Larry stared at her unblinkingly for a moment or two. "I don't know what to say."

"How about saying you're happy for me?" Corey suggested.

"No, I'm thinking more like, have you gone crazy? I don't understand. Why would you do something like that?" Larry asked incredulously.

"I want a baby. Why is that so hard for you to understand?" Corey's eyes flashed, and her voice went up a notch.

"You don't understand," Larry said grimly. "I love my two girls, but parenthood is tough. Sherri doesn't work; she has full-time help, and yet we eat out two or three nights a week because she doesn't have time to cook. How can you possibly handle your career . . . and motherhood . . . alone?"

"I'll have full-time help, too, and I already eat out every night, so I'm ahead of the game." Corey tried to lighten Larry's decidedly somber mood.

Larry wasn't taking the bait. "It's no game we're talking about here. I probably shouldn't say this, but I've always had a soft spot for you, so I'm just going to put it all out there. You've had more shit happen to you than any one person deserves. So why you brought this on yourself, I just don't understand. You know, Tom Crane and every other misogynist in this firm are going to be saying that this is why we shouldn't hire women."

Corey couldn't believe what she was hearing. "You mean because I want to have a family, just like you and Tom and every other man in this firm?"

"I'm going to be honest with you, Corey. I've been the managing partner for almost ten years. During that time, I've had three *married* women associates resign after having children to be stay-at-home moms. We had invested three or four years in those women, and poof, one day they just left with no warning. Guess how many male associates have done that to us?"

"Well, I can't be a stay-at-home mom. I'm going to have to work to support my baby."

"If you had become pregnant, with a husband, with Luke, there still would have been speculation about whether you were coming back from your maternity leave, or maybe about how long you would stay after the baby was born. But . . . this . . . I mean . . . those old codgers are going to have a field day with you deciding to have a baby on your own. They're going to be looking for any excuse not to promote you, or worse."

Corey was shaken by the vehemence in Larry's voice. "I guess I'll just have to make sure I don't give them any excuse."

Larry shook his head wearily, and his tone became calmer. "You don't understand. The nanny will get sick, the baby will have an emergency, there *will* be something that happens that is out of your control. And when it does, Tom Crane will be the first person in my office to say, 'I told you so.'"

Corey stubbornly refused to agree. "There's a first time for everything. I'll just have to be the first."

"I hope so," Larry said in a not-so-very-hopeful voice. The phone on his desk rang. "I've got to take this. I've been expecting this call."

CHAPTER 10

Amazingly, when Corey got back to her office, she was able to get an appointment with Dr. Byrne for the next day. She supposed telling the receptionist about her fainting episode at the gym had made her an emergency of sorts. She must have landed on her right arm when she fell because it was extremely sore and was already turning black-and-blue in several places. But other than the arm, she felt fine. Still, she wanted to make sure as soon as possible that she hadn't harmed the baby.

When she finally made it home after the day from hell, Kathryn was talking to a carpenter in Corey's bedroom. As best as Corey could tell, the carpenter had made the shelves too short for the closet and was going to have to redo them. She supposed it was just that kind of day. She didn't interrupt Kathryn. She just gave her a weary wave as she went to the guest room, where her clothes had been transferred, and changed out of her suit. When she came out, the carpenter was gone, and Kathryn was sitting on the sofa, drinking a glass of wine.

"I took the liberty of opening one of your bottles of wine. I figured from the look you gave me when you walked in, and from the way I feel, we could both use a drink."

Corey shook her head. "None for me, thanks. I'm gonna be off the wine for a while."

Kathryn looked at Corey curiously. "Um . . . what does that mean?"

"I'm pregnant. I had artificial insemination right before I hired you, and I just found out that it worked."

"Well, I guess your 'stomach bug' makes sense now. But if you were artificially inseminated, why didn't you suspect you were pregnant?"

"Too busy to think, I guess." *What a lame excuse,* Corey thought, but Kathryn didn't ask any more questions; she just looked at Corey even more curiously.

Later that night, Corey had to add Romeo and Gary to the growing list of people who were unhappy about her pregnancy.

"It's bad enough that we've had to endure all of that noise with your renovations," Gary complained, "but now a baby too?"

"Did you not read the condo covenants before you moved in?" added Romeo sarcastically. "This is an upscale, trendy midtown neighborhood. Babies don't belong here; they belong in the suburbs."

The only good thing about the entire day was that Diane had called while Corey was next door with Romeo and Gary. The message on her machine was brief: "I love you, Corey. If you are happy about this baby, then I'm happy too. I'll call you tomorrow."

It was a small ray of hope, which Corey clung to desperately. For perhaps the first time in her life, she was on her own. She didn't know much about babies, and she was afraid of having a baby alone, but she knew with certainty that having the baby was the right thing to do. The rest she would just have to figure out as she went along.

Corey began to feel her first twinges of happiness about the pregnancy as she walked to her appointment with Dr. Byrne the next day. His office was located in the building next to hers, so she wouldn't have to waste time in traffic going to appointments. Still, Erica had been frantic all morning trying to reschedule two hours of Corey's day so that she could go to this appointment. After a thorough examination, Dr. Byrne determined that everything was fine, and that her due date was tax day—April 15. Corey decided to tell everyone that her due date was May 10. If she didn't have a nine-pound baby on April 15, no one would ever suspect a thing.

For several days, Corey was once again the focal point of the firm's gossip. She tried to avoid being in the hallways at work as much as possible. However, when one of the partners was found to be having an affair with an associate, the news about her pregnancy fell off the office radar. And when the irate wife threatened a nasty public divorce, Corey's pregnancy was all but forgotten.

By the end of September, Corey was completely over her morning sickness and feeling better than she could ever remember. She was eating healthy food, exercising, and sleeping for at least seven or eight hours every night. She awoke energized each morning and ready to take on the world.

By mid-October, Corey was beginning to think that the work on the master bathroom would never end. As much as she loved having Kathryn in and out of the condo all the time, she was anxious for everything to be finished before Thanksgiving so that it would be perfect when Diane, Jack, and Marcy got there.

The Wednesday before Thanksgiving, Corey's guests arrived just after the painter had finished putting the final touch-ups on the cream walls of the master bathroom. The blue-and-green tiles gave the bathroom a bit of a tropical feel, as did the now massive ficus tree, sitting under a skylight in the corner.

"This doesn't even seem like the same place," Jack said, walking around and around in the large closet in awe.

"If I had a bathroom like this, I'd never get anything done around the house. I'd just float around in my pool . . . uh, I mean, bathtub, all day," Diane said.

"Yeah, I can't believe it's finally done. It will be so nice to have my house back to myself."

"Well, it won't be just your house for too much longer," Diane reminded her.

"I haven't forgotten about the baby, if that's what you're trying to say," Corey laughed. "As a matter of fact, y'all need to give me a moment in here alone. How can I forget there's a baby when it's making me pee all the time?"

The next morning, Corey and Diane cooked while Jack and Marcy rode out to Peachtree Wilden to pick up Nancy. Taking some chopped onions from Corey, and adding them to melted butter in a saucepan, Diane said, "You really seem happy, and you certainly look healthy."

"I am happy, and I'm taking these prenatal vitamins that look like horse pills, so how could I not be healthy?"

"It's just a really big step you're taking." Diane added tiny bits of flour to the butter/onion mixture. "I wish you had started out with a dog or something."

"What about the ficus? It's doing great!"

"Babies are a little bit more labor intensive than plants. I guess mainly I just wish you lived closer so that I could help you more. I had mom helping me all the time that first year after Marcy was born."

Corey didn't say anything. However, a feeling of sadness swept over her as sharp and as fresh as the day she and Diane had said good-bye to their mother at the hospital. Corey's eyes filled with tears, and her face started to collapse into itself. These emotions surprised her. She had thought she was done grieving over her mother and father. Suddenly she realized that grief was a chronic condition. The symptoms of grief might diminish over time, but you never fully recovered from it. She wished their mother could have been here to help her with her new baby too.

"Oh sweetie," Diane began, "I didn't mean to upset you." Then, wanting to change the subject, she said, "Hey, guess who I saw the other day?"

Corey managed to pull her facial muscles back down into some semblance of normalcy, and she wiped the tears away with the back of her sleeve. "I don't know. Who?"

"Tripp." Diane offered the word carefully, watching to see if Corey might have any more unusual reactions. Seeing none, she continued, "I told him we were coming here for Thanksgiving, and he wanted to know how you were doing. He seemed real surprised to hear that you're pregnant."

"Well, I guess artificial insemination isn't exactly the norm." Corey wiped the tears from her face with her sleeve. "Is he still dating Lucy from Ohio? I'm sure you asked."

"Yes, he said he was." Diane turned and started pouring chicken broth into the saucepan.

"Good for him. I hope it works out this time."

"Honey, we're home!" Jack yelled from the front door.

"You okay?" Diane gave Corey a quick, assessing glance.

"Sure . . . I guess my pregnancy hormones are making me a bit crazy."

When they sat down to eat, Corey thought the difference between last year's Thanksgiving table and this year's was remarkable. Last year they'd gone through the motions of having Thanksgiving even though everyone would have probably preferred just to skip it. They had sat stiffly in their little circle of chairs at the dining-room table. Jack had eaten more than his share and gushed over Diane's cooking. Diane's conversation had been the social glue holding their tiny group together and covering all awkward silences. Marcy had been an uncomfortable preteen, unsure of how to proceed in the uncharted waters. And Corey and Nancy had sat with zombielike calm, thinking about the void at the table, which was as obvious as if a place had been set for Luke.

There was a different vibe this year. Conversation ebbed and flowed naturally around the table. Out of the corner of her eye, Corey watched Nancy chatting with Marcy. Nancy seemed much more robust than she had even a month ago, and she stunned Corey when she asked for second helpings of the dressing. As they were enjoying thick slices of pecan pie with ice cream, Nancy asked Diane what she thought about being an aunt. Diane pondered it for a moment before answering. "I'm thrilled as I can be about Corey having Luke's baby, but I am a little concerned about my baby sister being up here so far away from me when she has a baby. She needs to have her family around her."

Nancy seemed to tense for a moment before replying, "I am family and will be here to help her in whatever way I can."

"I could quit school and move to Atlanta to help her," Marcy offered. And just like that, the tense moment was gone, and the atmosphere at the table went back to one of congeniality.

CHAPTER 11

December brought the melancholy feelings back to Corey that had been gone during the fall. Suddenly she had to struggle to keep her emotions in check. The twinkling Christmas lights that sprouted on houses and lampposts almost overnight brought tears to her eyes, and she found herself sobbing whenever a cheesy Hallmark commercial came on television. Even Romeo and Gary's Christmas Elf Extravaganza didn't cheer her up. Corey decided that if watching adults partying in elf costumes didn't lift her spirits, there was no hope for her.

She thought it wasn't so much her grief that had her feeling blue these days—but Christmas looming ahead of her, empty and lonely. Going to Florida was out of the question. Corey had mounds of work that had to be finished before the end of the year. Besides, she wasn't going to leave Nancy to suffer alone through her second Christmas without Luke. She had proudly refused Diane's offer to come to Atlanta for the holidays. Diane's family had spent the previous Christmas there with Corey and Nancy—that first Christmas without Luke. But Corey knew that Diane enjoyed being in her own home for Christmas, and she wouldn't allow her to do it again this year.

The only silver lining to her cloud of gloom was that she and Kathryn had become fast friends. Kathryn was recently divorced and always available to go out to dinner or to a movie whenever Corey could make it. Because Kathryn lived in Norcross, it was often easier for her just to stay over at Corey's condo when they did things at night, particularly if Kathryn had an appointment in Atlanta the next day. For the first time since college, Corey spent time just hanging out with a girlfriend, watching television and doing the kinds of things that girlfriends do—snacking on popcorn and talking until the wee hours of the morning. Kathryn admitted to knowing very little about childbirth, but she promised Corey she would go to the childbirth classes with her and be her labor coach during delivery. And after the Christmas holidays, Kathryn would start transforming an extra bedroom into a nursery.

To help Corey out of her doldrums, Kathryn insisted she have a Christmas tree. "It will make you feel better. I promise."

"Okay, you handle it," Corey said. "Get one and decorate it for me. I don't have the time, nor do I really care to decorate one."

"It's not the same if you don't have a hand in it. Plus, you need to do something other than work."

Which was why, on the second Saturday afternoon in December, they were at a Christmas-tree lot, looking over every tree. Corey had liked the first tree they saw, but it didn't suit Kathryn, nor had the last twenty trees. "Just pick a tree," Corey said, her frustration clearly evident as her cell phone rang. The glare of the sun made it impossible to see who was calling.

"Let it go," Kathryn ordered. "No work today." Corey looked at Kathryn defiantly, pushed the green button, and answered the call.

"Corey?"

Corey was surprised that she recognized Tripp's voice instantly. "Hey," she said as she walked away from Kathryn toward the empty corner of the lot, where the Christmas music pouring over loudspeakers wasn't quite as loud.

"Sounds like you're busy."

"Just shopping for a Christmas tree." Corey's heart, which had been minding its own business for weeks now, suddenly made its presence known.

"Well, I won't keep you. I got your number from Diane because I'm going to be in Atlanta next week, and I want to take you out to dinner one night."

"Which night?" She hoped her voice didn't sound as panicky as she felt.

"Any night is fine," he answered.

A part of her really wanted to see him, and a part of her was afraid to see him. *What if he suspects something?* "How about Thursday?" she finally asked when she realized the silence was stretching a bit long.

"That would be great. Is seven o'clock okay?"

"Sure."

"I'll call that afternoon and get directions."

"Okay."

Corey walked back to where Kathryn stood waiting for her. "Well . . . ?" asked Kathryn. "The way your face turned red when you answered that call, I'm thinking it wasn't a business call."

"It was just a friend who's going to be in town next week and wants to go to dinner." Corey hoped her voice sounded light enough to disguise the panic she was still feeling.

"A girlfriend?"

"No, a guy friend."

"Mmm," said Kathryn. "Does he know about your pregnancy?"

"My sister told him."

"Well, let's get you a dress that will make him forget about it."

"Kathryn, it's not that kind of a dinner," Corey argued.

"Honey, you can tell yourself that if you want to, but I saw your face." Kathryn waved the tree man over to where she was standing. "We'll take this one," she said to the man with an imperious wave. "We've just had a bit of an emergency. Can we speed this up?" And then back to Corey. "When is he coming?"

"Thursday."

"We've got a lot to do in a short period of time. Come on, come on, we've wasted half the day already."

As they were driving home, Corey contemplated what Tripp's appearance might mean to her. She'd given no thought to any sort of Tripp complications.

When they reached her condo, Kathryn didn't get out. "The tree will be delivered before five o'clock. You make sure they put it in the space across from the foyer. I'll go shopping for decorations and be over tomorrow to decorate."

"Don't you think you're going a bit overboard?" Corey asked as she got out of the car.

Kathryn didn't reply, but just shook her head no as she drove off.

Kathryn arrived full of excitement early on Sunday afternoon with a car full of shopping bags containing all sorts of Christmas decorations for the house and the tree. Corey was afraid to find out how much all that stuff was going to cost her, since none of the bags had been from Walmart.

Corey discovered that decorating a tree with Kathryn was unlike any Christmas-tree decorating she'd ever done. First, Kathryn wrapped almost every tree branch in white twinkling lights until it was one huge blaze of white light.

"But I thought the lights went around the tree," Corey complained as she assisted Kathryn.

Kathryn gave her a disgusted look. "This way the light seems to come from within the tree itself."

Placing the wide, gold taffeta ribbon on the tree took almost as much time as the lights. The ribbon had to be carefully placed so that it looked like it had just been carelessly thrown on the tree without any thought. When it was finally time for hanging the ornaments, Corey quit.

"I could have decorated three trees by now!" Corey exclaimed in frustration. "I've got work to do, and I really don't care whether the tree has ornaments or not."

"Fine, I'll finish it myself. I'd rather do this part alone anyway. You'd probably just put the ornaments on the tree without any thought about placement, and then I'd have to move them."

When Corey returned to the great room to see the finished product, she had to admit it was a work of art. Still, it was a work of art, she reminded herself grumpily, that would be disassembled and thrown away in a few weeks.

On Monday when Corey got home from work, Kathryn was waiting in her bedroom with an assortment of outfits spread out on the bed. "I knew you didn't have time to shop." Kathryn's eyes sparkled with anticipation.

"I think it's about time you turned over my house key and MasterCard," Corey said, unable to keep the excitement out of her voice. She'd been wondering lately what she was going to wear—not just on Thursday night, but to work as well. Most of her clothes were getting tight, and she'd been intending to go shopping. *Maybe this is what it's like to have a personal assistant—or a wife.*

"Can't get them back until I do the baby's room. I'm already shopping for those pieces right now. Let's try this black pullover and pants first."

"Are those maternity pants?"

"Yes . . . can you believe it? You can't even tell. Not that you really need maternity pants yet, but when they're this stylish—and you *will* need them soon—why not?"

Corey ran her hand over her stomach. She supposed it was because she'd been so underweight when she got pregnant, and also because she'd continued to exercise during her pregnancy, but she only had a slight baby bulge even though she was five months pregnant. Yet there had been changes. Her face had lost its gaunt look, and she finally had breasts. Overall, she had probably never looked better in her life.

"This does suit me," Corey said, standing in front of the floor-length mirror and turning from side to side. "Thanks Kathryn, I don't know how I survived before I met you."

"Not very well, I know," Kathryn informed her with a cheeky smile.

The next decision Corey had to make was where to go for dinner. She wanted Tripp to see the real Atlanta, which could easily be done by walking to Capo's Café, a neighborhood bistro. But Capo's had been one of Luke's favorite restaurants, and one they had frequented almost weekly. Going now with another man whose baby she happened to be carrying seemed wrong on so many levels. Yet the closer it got to Thursday, the more Corey felt like Capo's would be the best place for them to go. She supposed it was time for her to face her memories of Capo's as she'd faced so many other memories.

Once all the preparations had been completed, Corey finally had to think about Tripp and what his sudden appearance in her life might mean. What if he suspected something? If so, should she just tell him the truth? And if she did, what would happen next?

After what seemed like a month, Thursday finally arrived. Corey left work a bit early so that she would have plenty of time to get ready. Kathryn stopped by unexpectedly to approve her hair and makeup. It was fun to have someone to discuss the pros and cons of hairstyles with. Did her hair look better pulled back or left loose? In the end, they decided that pulled back looked more elegant, and more appropriate for Corey's new outfit.

"I feel like I'm going to the prom or something," Corey laughed. "Actually, I never spent this much time getting ready for any of the proms I went to with Tripp."

"Oh my gosh, you never told me you went to proms together. This really is serious! Can I stay and meet him?"

"No, you may not."

"Please?"

"No! I'm not sixteen, and my date doesn't need to meet my parents. In fact, it's time you were leaving." Almost as if on cue, the doorbell rang. *It's only six thirty. Could he be this early?*

"I'll answer the door," Kathryn said, heading toward the door, "on my way out."

"Wait!" But it was too late. Kathryn was already opening the door. The good thing about Kathryn opening the door was that Corey was able to observe Tripp for a couple of minutes without his knowing. Her first impression was that his blond hair contrasted very nicely with the dark-brown coat he was wearing, and the confused look on his face was really adorable. He stared at Kathryn blankly, obviously wondering if he was at the wrong address. *Here is my baby's father,* Corey thought, and something inside her tightened.

"Hello, Tripp. I'm Kathryn—a friend of Corey's." Tripp's face noticeably relaxed at Kathryn's words. "I would love to stay and chat with you, but unfortunately I have a prior commitment. Maybe next time."

Tripp looked beyond her, toward where Corey stood. "Yeah, okay, nice to meet you."

"You two kids have fun," Kathryn said breezily as she put on her jacket. Then, with a brief wave, she walked out the door.

Corey walked forward to greet Tripp. "You have any trouble finding the place?"

"Not too much." They stood in the foyer looking at each other sort of awkwardly.

"Here, let me take your coat."

He slid out of his coat, then noticed the Christmas tree behind her. "I see you did get a tree the other day." He walked over to it. "This may be the prettiest Christmas tree I've ever seen." He looked around the room appreciatively. "And what a great place you've got. I'd never suspect that a traditional redbrick apartment building on the outside could be so spacious and modern on the inside."

Corey laughed. "I wish I could take credit for all of it—the condo, the Christmas tree—but my friend Kathryn is a decorator, and all the credit goes to her."

Tripp turned from the tree to look at Corey, and his eyes stopped obviously at her stomach. Corey felt her face reddening in embarrassment.

"Pregnancy suits you. You look beautiful."

Corey felt her face flush even more. "Thanks."

"And very sophisticated," he added.

"Thanks," she said again. Suddenly, she was anxious to get out of the condo. "If you're up for a short walk, I thought we would go to a neighborhood restaurant."

"Not too cold for you?"

"What are you talking about? This is practically a heat wave," Corey said.

"Well, then, let's go. I'm hungry."

The night couldn't have been more perfect. The moon was full, and lit up the night like a large overhead street lamp. The unusually mild December temperatures had brought tons of neighborhood people outside. A lady dressed in a very expensive-looking white woolen suit walked in front of them with a very expensive-looking small white dog on a silver leash. When the dog stopped to do its business, Tripp and Corey scooted around them on the sidewalk as a man and woman jogged by them on the street.

"This is a real neighborhood you live in," Tripp said appreciatively. "I've never thought of Atlanta being like this."

"A lot of people only think about the horrible traffic on the interstates when they think about Atlanta. But there's a lot more to it than that."

"Yep, that would have been me." Tripp grinned at her. "That's why I'm so early tonight. I wanted to allow a lot of extra time in case I got stuck in traffic."

Corey smiled back and felt herself relax. It was fun to be the one showing Tripp something for a change. He paused in front of the local hardware store window. "This is like taking a step back in time. I thought the warehouse stores had run these places out of business." They stopped to window-shop at a bookstore and a pottery shop, and then they were standing in front of the restaurant. The hostess directed them to the bar because their table wasn't quite ready.

"What'll it be?" the bartender asked as they approached. There were a couple of guys at the other end of the bar drinking beers and watching a football game on a small television mounted on the wall in the corner.

"You go ahead," Corey offered as she sat down. "Just because I can't drink doesn't mean that you shouldn't get something." She noticed that her baby bump was a bit more obvious when she sat down.

"Congratulations, guys," the bartender said. "When is your baby due?"

Corey felt her face grow warm. They looked like a married couple, she supposed, and she did still have her wedding ring on. "May 10," she lied. Tripp ordered a beer and then seemed to be thinking hard. Corey could almost picture his mind working, subtracting backward from the date she'd just given.

"I hope you like this place," she said lightly. "The food is really wonderful, not a lot of fried foods, but I'm sure you can find something you like just as well."

The hostess told them their table was ready, and they followed her through an almost-empty restaurant to a corner in the back. "Don't worry," Corey said as they walked by the empty tables. "The place will fill up in a few minutes. We're just a bit ahead of the crowd."

After they were seated, Tripp seemed oddly uncomfortable. He took a sip of his beer and then looked directly into Corey's eyes. "I had this idea that maybe you'd gotten pregnant at the beach." His directness took Corey by surprise. Before she could think of how to respond, he continued, "I had to come see you for myself."

"And what do you see?" Corey asked, in order to stall for time so that she could think about what she wanted to say next. *Is it time to tell the truth?*

"I see a woman who seems to have it all. You have a fabulous house in a great neighborhood. You have good friends who decorate your Christmas tree for you. And I see a woman who barely looks pregnant at all, and who certainly doesn't look five months pregnant."

"Are you relieved?" Corey asked hesitantly.

"I suppose so."

The sadness Corey had held at bay for almost a week hit her hard once again. What had she expected from him? That he would tell her he hadn't been able to stop thinking about her since their time at the beach? Is that what she really wanted?

"Oh . . . I meant to give this to you at your house. I brought you a Christmas present." He took a small box out of his coat pocket and set it on the table in front of her. "Go ahead, open it now."

Corey felt confused as she studied him for a moment and then looked at the small green box wrapped with a red satin ribbon.

"It's not much, really . . . go on," Tripp urged.

She opened the wrapping paper slowly and carefully so that she wouldn't have to look up at Tripp for a few more moments. Finally, when she could stall no longer, she took the top off the box and saw a small piece of wood. She looked up at him curiously.

"I was passing by the Wonder Bar the other day. They were clearing what's left of the burned building. When I saw part of the old bar out by the road, I had to stop and preserve a piece of our teenage history. I picked up a small piece for each of us."

Tears suddenly sprouted from her eyes unexpectedly. "I'm sorry," she said, looking at Tripp's bemused face. "Pregnancy seems to make me very emotional. I even cry at Hallmark commercials these days. This is great!"

"Well, I'm glad you like your present. Are you hungry? I'm starved. How about we order now?" Tripp picked up the menu and began studying it like a student cramming for an exam.

Corey gathered her emotions while she pretended to study the menu as well. By the time Dylan, their young, blond, buff server, arrived to tell them about the specials, Corey felt back in control. Dylan was the prototypical Atlanta waiter. "Tonight the chef has prepared three extraordinary dishes that aren't on the menu." Dylan continued to describe the specials with more superlatives than Corey thought humanly possible. Many of the words he used Corey barely recognized, and she wondered what Tripp was thinking. After Dylan left to give them some time to ponder their many and varied choices, Tripp said, "Did you bring a dictionary? I'm used to simple orders.

You know, I'll have the steak, medium rare. Or, I'll have the shrimp, fried."

Corey smiled, wondering why she'd never before noticed how pretentious the servers at Capo's were. "If you can figure out what to order, I promise you whatever you get will be really good."

After what seemed like an excruciatingly long time, Dylan came back to take their orders, and Tripp found that he could, after all, order just a plain fillet, cooked medium rare. Once the ordering was complete and Dylan was gone, Tripp seemed thoughtful, and then hesitantly said, "I don't want to upset you again, but I really want to know what made you decide to become a single mother."

Corey fiddled with her napkin nervously. "Luke and I had been trying to have a baby before he got sick," she said, deciding to, at least, start out honestly. "And, you know, I'm not getting any younger."

"Yeah, thirty-three in March, I know."

Of course he would know. His birthday was in April. How many times had she reminded him that for one month, he was only one year older than she was? How ironic would it be if she had the baby on his birthday?

"Weren't you afraid? This is a really big step to take on your own."

"I was, and still am, afraid. But I'm mostly happy. And I've already contacted this highly recommended nanny service for help after the baby comes."

Tripp didn't say anything for a few minutes. He was uncharacteristically serious when he said, "I don't want to be an old man trying to teach my son to play baseball. And my mother's condition is making my dad's health go downhill fast. I'd like for him to see a grandchild before he dies." Corey felt a pang of guilt stab at her. How could she deny him his rights to this child?

Dylan arrived with their salads, effectively breaking up their intense moment. For the remainder of dinner, they both made a concerted effort to keep the conversation casual. Tripp caught her up on the local gossip, and she told him about an interesting case she had going on at work. When they left Capo's to head back to her condo, the temperature seemed to have dropped a few degrees, or maybe it was just from leaving the warm confines of the restaurant. "Brr," Corey said with a smile. "I'm afraid I'm going to have to take back what I said about the heat wave."

"Here, let me warm you up," Tripp offered, pulling her into his coat in a bear hug and rubbing her back roughly to create some heat. He could have skipped the rubbing. As soon as he pulled her next to him, Corey felt her temperature go up several degrees. Oddly, he still had that outdoor smell she remembered so vividly from last summer, which instantaneously brought memories of that night rushing back to her.

"Thanks," she said, pulling away quickly. "I'm fine now." They walked along for a while in silence.

"You know, Corey, sometimes I think about that night," Tripp began. It was almost as if he'd been reading her mind. "And I wonder what might have happened if you had stayed the rest of the night, if we had gone fishing that next Saturday, if we had spent some more time together."

Corey's heart started racing while she waited to see what he would say next.

"I mean, it would have been nice to have given it a chance to see where it might have gone." Corey felt her heart speed up a notch more. "But coming here makes me realize you were right about us. You are a different person than the one I grew up with. You are so much smarter and more sophisticated than I am. I wasn't around you long enough at the beach to see it. You've got it all here. You're living the life you were meant to live, and I'm really happy for you."

Corey felt her eyes fill with tears. They were almost back to her condo, and she needed to do something that would keep the tears at bay. "Yeah," she said in her best Humphrey Bogart imitation, "but we'll always have Mexico Beach, right?"

Tripp looked confused and perhaps a little hurt. "I guess I better head on now. Take care of yourself and that baby."

"Thanks," Corey said sadly. "You too." She stood in the open doorway feeling thoughtless and cruel. He'd been baring his soul to her, and she'd been plagiarizing lines from *Casablanca*. She stood there long after the taillights of his car were out of sight. Why were things always so complicated between the two of them?

CHAPTER 12

Kathryn called while Corey was on her way to work the next morning, but she didn't answer the phone. Unable to sleep, Corey had already rehashed the night plenty of times in her mind. Should she have told him the truth? Well, she hadn't, and it was too late now, and she didn't feel like going through it all one more time with Kathryn.

As usual, she took solace in her work, and in spite of everything, the day passed rather quickly. When Corey got home, she wasn't surprised to see Kathryn curled up on the sofa watching television.

"I'm dying to know. Tell me every little detail," Kathryn said, sitting up on the sofa as Corey walked in.

"Not much to tell. We had a nice dinner."

"Oh come on, and afterward? Did he stay the night?"

"No, he didn't even come in after dinner."

"Mmm, that's not good. So what happened at dinner?"

"Nothing happened. He's an old friend who was in town. We had dinner, period, the end."

Kathryn looked as though Corey had just told her there was no Santa Claus. Corey was trying hard to be strong and not let Kathryn see how upset she was. But suddenly the strain of the secret she'd been keeping for so many months was too much for her. She sat down on the couch, put her face in her hands, and started sobbing.

"Now, now," Kathryn said soothingly as she rubbed Corey's back. "You know, decorators are just like therapists. We never air our clients' dirty laundry, and anything they tell us must be held in the strictest confidence."

Corey looked up and gave Kathryn a weak smile. "I guess I do need to tell someone. I can't keep this secret by myself any longer." Rather calmly and without hesitation, Corey said, "Tripp is the father of my baby."

"I knew it," Kathryn said excitedly. "I never believed all that malarkey about artificial insemination. After all, when did you have time to do that?"

Corey nodded silently in agreement.

"And you told him last night, and he doesn't want to have anything to do with you and the baby. That bastard! He—"

"No," Corey interrupted her, "he doesn't know."

Kathryn seemed to deflate right before Corey's eyes. "You didn't tell him? Why?"

"I don't know . . . scared, I guess. I'm just so afraid about what might happen next. I want this baby, but I can't see how Tripp can fit into the picture. And nothing he said or did last night made me change my mind. At one point, he started talking about how perfect my life is here, and it seemed like a sign. Besides, this isn't 1959. A woman doesn't have to have a man to raise a baby anymore."

"I don't know about this, Corey. You may not need Tripp to raise a baby, and it might be less complicated not to tell him, but doesn't he have a right to know? Aren't there certain paternal rights that exist regardless of how the parents feel about each other? Hey, I'm sounding like the lawyer around here, which is kind of scary, don't ya think?"

Corey stopped and thought about what Kathryn had said. It was as though the fog that had been clouding her mind for the past five months lifted, and she realized clearly for the first time that Kathryn was right. Tripp did have a moral and legal right to know he was the father of this baby, which trumped whatever uncertainty she had about her feelings for him.

"You're right," Corey said. "I need to tell him. But he's already back in Florida, and I can't tell him something like this over the phone. As soon as the holidays are over, I'll drive down to Dothan and tell him to his face."

"Why not earlier?"

"I've got a lot of work that has to be finished by the end of the year. No way can I take a couple of days off before then."

"Okay, the first of the year. I don't know how *we* are going to survive until then."

Corey smiled. Kathryn was certainly "all in" as far as Corey's life was concerned.

Just as she'd predicted, work was horrendous up to and including Christmas Day. Corey drove out to Peachtree Wilden on Christmas morning to spend the day with Nancy, and was pleasantly surprised to see how well she looked. Corey found Nancy waiting for her in the lobby. She was dressed elegantly in a red suit with matching red heels. She was chatting pleasantly with some other women and looked happier than Corey had seen her look in years. *At least some good has come out of my lies,* Corey thought. She didn't want to think about what the truth about the baby's paternity might do to Nancy. Corey was going to do everything in her power to keep Nancy thinking that Luke was the father of her baby.

"Merry Christmas, my darling," Nancy said, smiling at her. "You remember Claire and Nina, don't you?"

"Of course. Merry Christmas, ladies. Shall we go in for lunch? It smells divine."

"Our families aren't as prompt as you. But they should be here shortly."

"Okay, we'll see you in the dining room." Corey reached out for Nancy, and they walked hand in hand into the dining room past the largest Christmas tree Corey had ever seen.

"How are you feeling?" It was always Nancy's first question these days. Corey smiled. "Fat, but other than that, good."

"Don't be silly. You barely look pregnant. I remember when I was pregnant with Luke; I had gained thirty pounds by now. Of course, I never exercised like you do, and I took those cravings very seriously! It was nothing for me to eat a whole pint of ice cream every day. What did the doctor say at your last appointment?"

"The doctor said the baby is growing just fine and that my mother-in-law should stop worrying so much."

Nancy smiled at her. "I have some presents for you and the baby upstairs."

"Nancy . . . ," Corey said accusingly, "I thought we'd agreed to do just a little something this year. I'm going to feel terrible if you've gone all out and I just have one little present in my purse for you."

"Ah . . . but you are giving me the best gift of all. How could I ever top that?" The nagging guilt that was never far away when Corey was with Nancy made its presence known.

After lunch there was sing-along Christmas caroling, but Corey and Nancy decided to skip it. When they entered Nancy's apartment, Corey was stunned. The biggest white wicker basket she had ever seen sat on the coffee table, with pink-and-blue bows cascading down from the handle. It was stuffed with individually wrapped presents. "It's like an instant baby shower!" she laughed. "How in the world am I going to carry this out?"

"I've already arranged for Tyler who works at the front desk to come and help you when it's time for you to go. And you need to get

Romeo or Gary to help you at your place. Can't have you straining anything now, can we? The basket is for the baby, but I also have a little something for you." Nancy opened a jewelry box, and Corey recognized Nancy's exquisite eighteen-inch strand of pearls. "These were given to me by Luke's father when Luke was born. I want you to have them now. Things will be so hectic later."

"Oh no," Corey objected vehemently. "I can't take your pearls. I wouldn't feel right. You love these pearls, and they are perfect on you."

"I will love them much more when I see them on you, the mother of my grandchild."

Corey felt as if she were the worst person in the world. But recognizing that refusing the pearls would only hurt Nancy's feelings, she took them with a heavy heart. Corey gave Nancy her small gift, a locket with one of her favorite pictures of Luke in it, and then she apologized for having to leave so soon. And she honestly did have work waiting for her back at the condo.

Corey threw herself into her work because it was necessary, and also in the hope that it would make the time pass more swiftly. Finally, the day before New Year's Eve, Corey could see that the end was in sight. One more day of burning the candle at both ends and she'd be able to go to Dothan on New Year's Day and tell Tripp the truth about the baby. She wouldn't allow herself to think too much about that conversation now or about what might happen afterward. However, regardless of what happened with Tripp, she thought she'd spend a couple of days in Marianna. Corey needed time to tell Diane and Jack the truth as well.

Ironically, Diane called that night, and she seemed to be in one of her chatty moods. Corey cut her short. "Di, I really can't talk right now. But I promise I'll have some time to catch up soon." Corey decided it would be better to tell her in person in just a few days.

"Okay, but first let me tell you one more bit of news. I saw Tripp yesterday, and he told me that he and that girl Lucy got engaged at Christmas. They're planning on getting married in June. I thought you would want to know."

Corey felt stunned. "Uh . . . yeah, thanks for letting me know. I really have to go now."

After she hung up, Corey sat in disbelief. How could she tell Tripp about the baby now? Everyone would wonder why she'd waited until after he was engaged to Lucy to break such important news. What was the moral and right thing to do now?

Corey called Kathryn. "I've had something come up," she said in a deadpan voice.

"Is it the baby? I'll be right there."

"No, it's not the baby. It's Tripp. He's getting married."

"Oh . . . no . . . I'm on my way."

Despite Corey and Kathryn talking everything through again and again until they both felt exhausted, there appeared to be no good solution. If Corey went to Dothan now and told Tripp, it would look as if she were trying to break up his relationship with Lucy. And even if Corey convinced Tripp that she had no designs on him, Lucy might be a little upset that her boyfriend had slept with Corey a little more than five months before proposing to her. Lucy might ditch him anyway. After going through everything for the hundredth time, it seemed that the best solution was to just leave everything as it was. Tripp would likely have other children with Lucy, and he couldn't be hurt by something he didn't know.

CHAPTER 13

The remainder of January was bitterly cold and dreary. Corey hated cold weather during the best of times, and her situation certainly didn't qualify as the best of times. Yet the baby had finally started making its presence known, so for once the cold weather couldn't bring her spirits down. At first she'd been unaware that the light fluttering she felt in her stomach was the baby. When the movements became more pronounced and Corey realized what they were, she had to stop every time it happened and marvel over the life she carried within her. The novelty never wore off. And she joked happily with Diane that the baby would likely become a gymnast, for it was definitely doing somersaults inside her belly.

In early February, Atlanta got a couple of inches of snow and ice, and predictably the city shut down for two days. Corey was thankful for this unexpected time-out and actually enjoyed spending the days alone at her condo. She'd been working as hard as she could to finish up some cases before her maternity leave. The weight she'd finally gained was making her feel awkward, and she had to be conscious of staying off her feet as much as possible or they were likely to swell. For two days, Corey remained stretched out in front of her fireplace reading the dozen or so child-rearing books Diane had sent her. It reminded her in many ways of cramming for a final exam, and that gave Corey confidence because she'd always done really well on finals.

At the end of February, Corey and Kathryn started going to the natural-childbirth classes. They watched some pretty graphic films and talked about breathing a lot, but Corey wasn't sure she was getting much out of the classes. She did make a couple of new friends, Ralph and Judy, who happened to live down the street from her. They lived on Morningside, not too far from her condo on Rock Springs. When the weather wasn't too cold and Corey was home at a decent hour, they would all go for a walk. Ralph and Judy were in awe of her decision to have a baby alone. "I'd be too scared to do this by myself," Judy had said on more than one occasion. And each time, Corey had to remind herself that they thought she'd made a conscious decision to get pregnant and have a baby alone, rather than just trying to make the best of a difficult situation.

In March, Kathryn organized a combination birthday party/baby shower for Corey. She invited a few of her work friends, Judy and Ralph, and as a special surprise, Diane came up from Florida.

"This is gorgeous," Diane complimented Kathryn during the tour of the nursery. Since Corey didn't know whether she was having a girl or a boy, the nursery had been decorated in shades of white and yellow. "It's too perfect to use."

"I hope not." Kathryn laughed. "Otherwise, your sister just wasted an awful lot of money."

After everyone was gone, Diane and Corey sat on the floor of the nursery. Diane grabbed a pillow off a chair and threw it at Corey. "I can't believe my baby sister is thirty-three years old today and is about to have a baby."

Corey took the pillow and held it to her chest. "Sometimes I can't believe I'm about to have a baby either. It seems so unreal to me."

"It doesn't seem real until you're sleep deprived from getting up every two hours to feed that baby. Then it will be all too real."

"Hush, no negative talk. Misha, the natural-childbirth instructor, says to focus on what is good and positive."

"I'm just telling you like it is. There's a reason Jack and I only have Marcy, you know," Diane said sarcastically.

However, Corey knew that it had been their parents' car accident that had made Diane and Jack postpone having a second child, until after a while they'd decided Marcy was all they needed. "Do you ever think about how different our lives would have been if Mom and Dad hadn't died?" Corey asked carefully.

"Of course. Although, honestly, mine probably wouldn't have been that different because I was already married and had a child. But I think your life might have been incredibly different."

"What do you mean?"

"You seemed to get serious with Luke real fast. And he was so domineering."

"Luke wasn't domineering," Corey disagreed. "He was just confident."

"Yeah . . . confident that he always knew best."

Corey thought for a moment. She supposed it had been Luke's confidence that had attracted her to him. When he believed something, he was capable of making others believe it too. After her law-school graduation, she'd stopped in Atlanta for a visit with a sorority sister on her way back to Florida. Corey had never thought about moving to Atlanta. In fact, Atlanta wasn't even on her list of possibilities until that night when she was sitting next to Luke at a bar, waiting for her friend to return from the dance floor. Somehow she and Luke had started talking, discovered their common interest in the law, and before she knew it, she was considering interviewing at Landon, Crane, and Forrester, where Luke had a connection. And then she was moving to Atlanta. Yes, Corey supposed, things had moved rather quickly once she met Luke, but when something was right, you knew it, didn't you?

"Hel . . . lo." Diane interrupted Corey's thoughts. "You still with me?"

Corey nodded her head yes, and then her thoughts went off in a different direction. "Diane, I really want you to be here when the baby is born."

"Call me when you first think you might be in labor, and I'll get here as fast as I possibly can."

Tax day came and went, as did Tripp's birthday a few days later. A very lethargic Corey continued to waddle into the office and do paperwork, even though she hadn't scheduled any more client appointments. When she went to see Dr. Byrne, he wanted to induce labor, but she stubbornly refused. "Only if the baby is in danger," Corey stated firmly.

Finally, early in the morning on May 1, two weeks after her real due date, she woke to a feeling of wetness in her bed and knew that her water had broken. Corey felt thankful that she'd made it into May. She called Dr. Byrne, who told her to go on to the emergency room even though she hadn't felt a labor pain yet. She called Kathryn, who was planning to take her to the hospital, and woke her up. And then, because she had twenty minutes or so before Kathryn could get there, she called Diane and Nancy and woke both of them up as well. After the excitement of those calls, she sat down next to the overnight bag that had been so carefully packed, and she realized how depressingly quiet the house was. *This is not a time to be alone,* Corey thought. She wished her mother were still alive. She wished Luke were still alive. She even imagined for a moment calling Tripp and breaking the news to him over the phone that he was about to be a father. However, when her first labor pain suddenly radiated through her abdomen and into her back, the only thing she could think about was that maybe she should call a cab rather than wait for Kathryn to take her to the hospital. By the time the pain had passed, Kathryn was there and they were on their way.

At the emergency-room entrance, a nurse whisked Corey and Kathryn up to the maternity ward and assigned them a birthing room. Corey was extremely thankful that the room included a rocking chair, because when a labor pain hit her, rocking seemed to be the only thing that helped—so much for all those breathing exercises she'd been practicing for months. Kathryn served admirably and enthusiastically as her labor coach. But after several hours, Corey broke down and asked for an epidural. She irrationally made Kathryn promise not to tell Misha, the natural-childbirth teacher, that she'd failed at natural childbirth.

Stella Louise Bennett was born at eleven that night. It had been a long day for Corey, but at least Stella had waited until her Aunt Diane and Uncle Jack arrived before making her appearance. She was a respectable seven pounds, two ounces—not too big and not too small. No one questioned her birth date coming a little earlier than expected. Cleaned and swaddled tightly, Stella was placed in Corey's arms, and tears fell freely from her eyes. She couldn't help but imagine how different this day would have been if Luke were still alive and this had been their long-anticipated baby. How excited and confident he would have been about the future—unlike Corey, who felt scared of what was next. All she knew for certain was that her life had changed, and she prayed she was ready for it.

CHAPTER 14

The next day, Sunday, Diane drove Corey and Stella home from the hospital in Corey's Lexus. Diane was a nervous driver in the small town of Marianna, and now driving in Atlanta, she alternated between hitting the brakes and the gas in such a brutal cycle that Corey was beginning to feel carsick. Jack had left early that morning to go back to Florida and would return the following weekend to pick Diane up. Although Diane had taken a leave of absence for a week from school, she would have to return to finish up the remainder of the school year.

"When will the nanny start?" asked Diane.

"Next Monday," Corey answered, carefully concentrating on the scenery outside the car to help fight off her feelings of nausea. "I had thought about having her start this week but decided I'd rather it just be you and me for these first few days."

"What do you know about her?"

"The nanny service I hired thoroughly investigates the background of each candidate, so I don't have to worry about her being a psycho or anything."

"But do you like her?"

"I only met her once. She's German. She seems very efficient and very no-nonsense. She has impeccable references."

"Not exactly like Ethel."

"Not anything at all like Ethel." Corey thought fondly of their old housekeeper, who'd practically raised Diane and Corey. Ethel was a tall, imposing black woman with very little education, who cooked and cleaned and ran the house in Marianna as if it were her own. In many ways, Corey supposed, the house in Marianna had been Ethel's, and the beach house had always been their mother's.

Corey was very thankful as they pulled up to her condo that she'd made it home without becoming sick. Nancy, Kathryn, and Gary were waiting there to welcome Stella and her home. Corey was happy that Romeo and Gary had gotten over their initial antipathy toward Stella and were now proudly promoting themselves as her new uncles. Her heart warmed to the sight of her pseudofamily welcoming this new addition.

During the next few days, Stella was the best baby ever. She slept almost all the time, waking only to eat, have her diaper changed, and look around in a bemused manner at whoever might be holding her. Diane took the lead in caring for Stella, but Corey tried to do her share. However, if she hadn't been breast-feeding, Diane likely would have taken over completely. Corey gradually began to relax. Perhaps it wasn't going to be that difficult to be a mother, after all.

One afternoon about midweek, Corey and Diane stood watching Stella as she slept in her bassinet. Corey was thinking that she'd never realized how good babies smell, when Diane interrupted her pleasant thoughts.

"Babies almost always sleep like this for the first few days." Diane's mind was obviously on less benign thoughts than Corey's.

"Well, I didn't think she would sleep around the clock for the rest of her life, you know," Corey said with a slight smile. Diane always seemed to be focusing on the negatives, and Corey was determined to keep the conversation light. "I may not have a lot of experience with babies, but I did know that," she added.

"What I meant is . . . it's not always going to be this easy," Diane began. "I just want—"

"I know." Corey stopped her. "You just want me to be prepared. Let me enjoy her right now, Di, and have faith that I'll be able to figure out the other stuff as I go along."

Unfortunately, the week passed all too quickly, and Jack was back to take Diane home before Corey felt she was ready for her to go. Then, exactly thirty minutes after Diane and Jack pulled away that Sunday afternoon, Stella stopped being the best baby that ever was. It was as though she recognized that the experienced caregiver was gone. Stella opened her eyes and rooted around as if hungry even though she'd eaten only an hour earlier.

Corey had intended to go down the street to visit Ralph and Judy, who'd just come home from the hospital with their new son, Alex. But Corey decided she'd better try to breast-feed Stella again. Stella nursed for a while but still seemed fretful and not that interested in eating. In fact, Stella only seemed content when Corey was walking her or rocking her. They spent a difficult night walking, rocking, and feeding.

By the time Mildred, the German nanny, arrived at eight the next morning, Corey was near tears. The night had passed excruciatingly slowly, with Stella only napping for short periods—thirty minutes or less. After explaining about their sleepless night, Corey was more than happy to hand Stella off to Mildred and head for a shower. Hot water had never felt so good, and Corey stayed in the shower for an extremely long time. As she was drying off, she thought she heard Stella crying. Corey finished quickly and pulled on a clean pair of sweatpants and a T-shirt. When she opened her bedroom door, she could hear Stella screaming loudly from her room. Corey went into Stella's room and saw her lying on her back, red-faced, crying angrily. Corey picked her up, and Stella immediately calmed down. Corey carried Stella into the den where Mildred was sitting on the sofa watching *The Price Is Right* on television.

"Why did you let Stella get so worked up? Couldn't you hear her crying?" Corey asked angrily.

"You said she'd been fed and was just being fussy. You have to get babies on a schedule. She would have eventually cried herself out and gone to sleep."

"You know, Mildred," Corey said, "I'm not much for letting a baby cry itself to sleep. One of the books I read said that you can't love, hold, or feed a newborn baby too much during the first six weeks of life."

"Pooh on that," said Mildred haughtily. "You need to get a baby on a schedule right from the first. It's better for the baby, and it's certainly better for you."

"I'm sorry, Mildred, but I want to take a more flexible approach to raising Stella."

"You can't do that," Mildred warned. "Babies need a schedule."

Mildred's superior attitude was too much for Corey's already frazzled nerves. "Mildred, I don't think it's going to work out between me and you."

"Well, I never! Do you realize I've got over twenty years of nannying experience, and you've got what? Eight days of experience in being a mother?"

Corey walked to the front door and opened it. "Thank you, Mildred, for coming today. I'll call the service and suggest that they find you another more suitable placement."

Mildred grabbed her purse and stomped out of the house, shooting daggers of hatred as she went. Corey didn't care. She wasn't leaving her precious Stella with anyone who would just leave her to cry when she was upset. Corey's exhilaration over sending Mildred packing was short-lived. *Now what?* The day stretched endlessly before her, and Stella was beginning to root around again. Corey called the nanny service. The exasperated woman on the phone said that they would do their best to find her a suitable replacement, but she could make no guarantees about how long it would take. They also reminded her that she owed Mildred two weeks' pay since she was supposed to have given her two weeks' notice before letting her go. "What kind of nanny do you think would be more suitable?"

Someone like Ethel, Corey thought. "I want someone different from Mildred, someone more loving, more motherly, more southern."

"We'll see what we can do." The woman didn't sound very hopeful.

Corey laid Stella down on the bed and quickly tried to comb out her still-wet and tangled hair. Stella looked at her angrily, as if to say, "What do you mean putting me down on the bed?" Before she could start squalling again, Corey decided it really didn't matter if her hair was a tangled mess. She picked Stella up and walked with her into the great room where *The View* was now on. Corey sat down, still rocking Stella back and forth, and proceeded to watch Barbara Walters bring the other hosts down a notch or two. Whenever she thought Stella was sound asleep and tried to put her down in her crib, Stella would start screaming again. "What is wrong with this baby?" Corey wondered after a while.

During the brief times that Stella would sleep, Corey lay on the sofa and tried to nap. But it always seemed as soon as she drifted off, Stella would begin to cry. It wasn't a whimper but a loud, piercing cry. By two o'clock that afternoon, Corey was convinced there was something seriously wrong with Stella. It couldn't be normal for a baby to sleep so little and cry so much. Corey was in tears when she called Kathryn.

"There's something wrong with this baby. Can you drive us to the pediatrician's office?"

"Of course I can. I'm over on Peachtree Industrial, but I'll be there in thirty minutes. What's wrong?"

"She won't stop crying, no matter what I do. She does better when I'm holding and rocking her. But if I put her down, she just starts the scream cycle all over again."

Once in her car seat and on their way to the doctor's office, Stella immediately fell asleep and slept through the entire trip. Sitting in Dr. Carrington's office, waiting to be worked in as an emergency, Stella continued to sleep peacefully, and Kathryn looked at Corey as if she were crazy. "Maybe she just has her nights and days mixed up."

"Then she would have been sleeping all day, right?" Corey replied defensively. "I'm telling you, this is the first time she's slept in almost twenty-four hours. I know there's something wrong with her."

Finally, when Corey stood before the doctor with the still-sleeping baby in her arms, she burst into tears. "I promise you she has been fussing and crying for over twenty-four hours. I'm not crazy."

As the doctor examined Stella, he said, "Does she draw up her legs as if she's in pain? Does eating not seem to satisfy her?"

"Yes, yes," Corey said worriedly. "That's exactly what she does. What's wrong with my baby?"

"I'm afraid your baby has colic."

Corey thought she remembered reading about that in one of her baby books, but it hadn't sounded anything like what she'd been going through. "I don't think so."

"It's a fairly common condition in which babies become fussy for no reason. There's some thought that it's a milk allergy, so let's try Stella on soy milk."

"But I want to breast-feed!" Corey sobbed.

"Well, the soy milk might help the colic. And I'll give you some drops that you can put in the bottle at night to help her sleep."

"I'm going to drug my baby?"

"It's not really a drug; it will just relax her. And you only give it to her for as long as you feel that she needs it, or when you really feel like *you* need it." He smiled at her with a fatherly expression as he handed her a tissue. "She's a beautiful baby, and she will be fine. You just need to give her a little time to grow out of this colic, and try to relax. Babies can sense when the mother is feeling stressed."

"Thank you, Dr. Carrington. I appreciate the counseling."

"Part of being a pediatrician is counseling new moms. I promise you, everything will be fine. Just hang in there."

Corey handed the still-sleeping Stella over to Kathryn while she paid the receptionist. She felt really foolish, but also greatly relieved that Stella didn't have appendicitis or some other more severe condition.

Later, Corey felt like a failure as she mixed the soy milk for Stella that Kathryn had bought on the way home from the pediatrician. Kathryn insisted on staying the night and taking care of the night feedings so that Corey could get some sleep. Corey accepted her offer and then went to take a shower, where she cried until the hot water ran out. What had she gotten herself into? Taking care of a baby was a big job. No wonder there were two parents.

After several uninterrupted hours of sleep, Corey did feel better the next day. Kathryn looked at her apologetically. "I hate to leave you, but I've got an appointment in Norcross that could be worth thousands to me."

"Of course you have to go; don't be silly," Corey said, trying not to feel panicky at being left alone again.

Three hours later, when Corey had yet to take a shower, she started fantasizing about having Kathryn move in with her. Around lunchtime, Judy called and wanted to know if Corey could bring Stella down for a bite of lunch. Corey was embarrassed that Judy's baby was a week old and she had yet to go and see him. Corey should have been bringing her lunch rather than being invited to lunch. "Stella and I are about to take a nap," Corey lied. "Let's do it another day."

Finally, Stella did go to sleep, and Corey went to take that much-delayed and much-desired shower. She hoped the hot water would relieve the pain in her breasts, which she assumed came from stopping breast-feeding. Corey had just shampooed her hair when the baby monitor sprang to life. "Wah . . . !" Stella cried out intensely. Corey hurriedly rinsed her hair and washed the remainder of the soap off her body. She longed desperately for the peace of the law office and the life she used to have.

After only a few days on the soy milk, Corey noticed a change for the better in Stella. And the one drop of medicine Corey put in Stella's bottle at night guaranteed that they both could get several hours of uninterrupted sleep, which also seemed to be improving both of their dispositions. When Corey talked to Diane at night, she stressed these positives and tried to sound more upbeat than she felt. But she had a feeling she wasn't fooling Diane because she could hear the anxiety in her sister's voice as she promised to come back as soon as she could. When Corey talked to Nancy, she tried to sound even more positive because she didn't want her mother-in-law to get a taxi, as she'd been threatening to do, to come and help her. Nancy would require nearly as much care as Stella, and she just couldn't do any more than she was already doing.

On Friday morning when Corey woke up for Stella's six a.m. feeding, she didn't feel so well. Her right breast was hard and swollen, and Corey thought she might be running a fever. It was seven a.m., much too early to call Dr. Byrne's office. Corey took some Tylenol after feeding Stella and then put her back in her crib. Corey lay down on the floor next to Stella's crib because she didn't have the energy to go back to her own bed, and then she promptly fell asleep. She woke up to Stella's fidgeting and realized she felt dizzy. She grabbed her cell phone and called her obstetrician's office. Frantically, she described her condition to the doctor's answering service and asked to have the doctor call her immediately. It seemed like an hour, but was probably only minutes, before the phone rang again.

"Ms. Bennett?" Dr. Byrne's familiar voice asked.

"Yes," she said anxiously. She felt so dreadful that she thought she must have the flu or something worse, and she worried about infecting Stella.

"You likely have an infection in your breast. It's fairly common among mothers when they stop breast-feeding. I'll call you in some antibiotics. Use cold compresses on the breast, and take Tylenol every four hours. If it isn't substantially better by tomorrow, come to the office first thing in the morning. However, I'm sure this will take care of it."

Corey tried calling Romeo and Gary to see if they could pick up her prescription, but neither answered their cell phones. So she had no choice but to call Kathryn once again, desperate for help. An hour later, Kathryn arrived with Corey's medicine and a pile of groceries. "Okay, I'm moving in until this nanny situation gets fixed."

Corey burst into tears. "I really don't know what I would do without you."

"I know, I know," Kathryn said. "Just call me Florence Nightingale from now on."

By the next day, Corey knew that the antibiotics were clearly working, as she felt much better. The good news continued when the nanny service called and said that they'd found someone for Corey to interview on Monday. They warned her that the woman was probably not suitable to be Stella's long-term nanny, as she had to maintain a rather fixed schedule. But for the short term, she was all that was available.

"The cavalry is arriving to rescue us on Monday," Corey said to Kathryn when she put down the phone. "And I promise you, if this woman isn't an ax murderer, I will welcome her with open arms."

On Sunday, it was hard for Corey to believe that it had been just a week since Diane and Jack had left her. She felt as if she'd lived through an eternity since then. However, Stella was doing much better on the soy milk, even if she continued to be somewhat fussy at times, and was beginning to develop a schedule of sorts with her eating and sleeping. With help from Kathryn, Corey finally felt able to make the walk down to Ralph and Judy's on Sunday afternoon to see Alex. When she saw Ralph proudly holding up his son, she felt uncomfortable. *Didn't Stella deserve to have a father hold her like that as well?*

She convinced Kathryn to go home Sunday night. Corey didn't want to abuse Kathryn more than she already had, and she knew Kathryn had an installation out in Norcross the next day. Once she was gone, the condo echoed with emptiness. Corey put Stella on the sofa with her, and they both dozed off and on, with the television keeping them company. It wasn't a practice encouraged in all the good parenting books Corey had read, but it felt good to her, and obviously to Stella as well, because she slept contentedly on Corey's chest.

When Corey opened the door the next day to the new nanny, she felt an immediate connection with the slender black woman standing on the steps. "I'm Millie Simpkins," the woman said in a soft southern voice that Corey knew must have come from Alabama, or south Georgia, or maybe even Mississippi, but definitely not from Germany.

"I'm so glad you're here," Corey said. "Come on in and let's get to know each other." As if on cue, Stella's cries could be heard on the baby monitor in the great room. "I think Stella is eager to meet you too. I'll go get her and be right back."

When Corey returned, Millie was seated on the sofa, looking nervous but very proper, with her feet crossed at the ankles. Her eyes warmed as they rested on Stella. "My goodness gracious, she's a little one."

"Stella's just a little over two weeks old."

"Can I hold her?" Millie asked, stretching her hands out toward Corey. "I just love holding newborn babies. I could hold them all day long."

Without realizing that she'd been holding her breath, Corey exhaled as she handed Stella over. Stella looked curiously at this new person, but she didn't cry. Millie, on the other hand, looked as if she might start crying as she looked down at Stella. "She's just a little angel!" Millie exclaimed. A sliver of hope was born in Corey. *Millie might just be the answer to my prayers.*

"Can you drive?" Corey asked.

"Yes, ma'am. I have a license, but I don't have a car."

"I'm going to need you to drive us to doctors' appointments for the next week until I'm allowed to be driving."

"Does that mean I've got the job?" Millie asked in disbelief.

"I know a good thing when I see it." Corey decided it was time she started trusting her own instincts, and her instincts told her that Millie was the right nanny for Stella. Besides, she would be here with Millie for the next few weeks to make sure that her good feelings about her were right. It really was a no-brainer.

"Did they tell you about my daughter?" Millie asked hesitantly.

"No . . ." Corey was suddenly afraid of what Millie was going to say. She remembered that the service had mentioned something about Millie probably not being good for the long term.

"Deborah was born . . . uh . . . you know . . . slow. Now she's growing up." Millie paused and gave Corey a shy smile. "She's sixteen. I heard about this school here in Atlanta that could teach girls like her to do a job and to take care of herself. So we moved here from Cairo so that Deborah could go to that school. The school bus picks her up at seven thirty in the mornings and brings her home around six at night. I looked at the MARTA bus schedule on my way here, and I won't be able to get here any earlier than eight in the mornings, and I have to be on the five-thirty bus in the afternoons to get back to our apartment before she gets home. She wouldn't know what to do if she got off her school bus and I wasn't there." Millie looked worriedly for Corey's reaction.

"Um . . . ," Corey said, finally understanding what the service had meant when they mentioned that Millie had a fixed schedule. Since Corey's schedule was anything but fixed, she realized Millie wasn't going to work, after all. Corey felt devastated. "I'm a lawyer who works a lot of hours," Corey began. "I'm rarely home by five thirty, and even if I tried to be home by then, in all honesty, I couldn't guarantee you that I would be able to do so."

Millie's face fell. "It seems like no one can. You're about the tenth person I've interviewed with."

Corey felt touched by the look of despair on the woman's face. Suddenly Corey had an idea. Maybe Millie could help Corey while she was on maternity leave until she found someone else more suitable.

"I've got six more weeks of maternity leave, and I'd really love to hire you to work during that time. You see, I'm an inexperienced single mother who is desperate for some help. Of course, I'll have to find someone who can be more flexible when I go back to work. But for now, I'd really love it if you could help me out."

Millie appeared frozen for a few minutes, and then finally she said cautiously, "If the service finds me another job, I'll have to interview for it."

"Of course," Corey said.

"Well, when do you want me to start?" Millie asked.

"Can you start right now? Like I said, I'm desperate!"

Millie nodded her head yes and gave Corey another shy smile, and that was that.

CHAPTER 15

By the end of that week, Corey realized she was falling in love with Millie. Like most love affairs, it started a bit awkwardly. Millie was hesitant and quiet, not sure how to act around Corey.

She was always asking permission before doing anything; she even asked permission before going to the bathroom. So Corey had spent much of that first day trying to make Millie relax and feel comfortable around her. Millie had no trouble feeling comfortable around Stella.

By midweek, Millie had begun to unwind a bit. When she volunteered that she loved to cook almost as much as she loved babies, Corey declared, "I hate to cook. Well . . . actually, I don't really know how to cook. While my mother was teaching my sister to cook, my dad was teaching me how to bait hooks and clean fish."

"Cooking's not hard," Millie said. "It just takes a little practice. I'll be glad to teach you if you like. Actually, I'd love to cook for you and Stella if you'll just tell me what you like."

"Really? You'd cook for us?" Corey asked incredulously, and it was official: Corey was in love with Millie.

"Sure, I would. When you feel like it, why don't we go to the grocery store and do some shopping?"

"Maybe you could go by yourself. I've never taken Stella out any-where, except to the pediatrician's office."

Millie shook her head as though she didn't understand. "Stella won't break. You can take her to the grocery store."

"I worry about her crying. You've heard her when she gets wound up."

"So what? Everybody's heard a baby crying in a grocery store. Come on, Ms. Corey, I think it's time we went grocery shopping."

Corey was sure they presented quite a picture going through the gro-cery store. Millie placed Stella in her carrier in a grocery cart, and then proceeded to push the cart and lecture Corey as they went along on the finer points of cooking. At first Corey could hardly listen to anything Millie said because she was too busy looking at Stella, waiting for her to explode into one of her crying jags. But Millie kept asking Corey questions, forcing her to look at this or that, until Corey began to focus more on the grocery shopping than on Stella. They started in the deli, where the smells of the rotisserie chicken made Corey want to buy one.

"No, let's buy some chicken and I'll roast it for you," Millie argued. "It will taste better and be cheaper."

"But I want to eat it now," Corey objected. "It smells heavenly."

Millie gave in. "Let's still buy some chicken, though, and I'll fix it for another day. Do you like chicken and dumplings?"

Corey hadn't thought about chicken and dumplings since she was a child. Ethel had made wonderful chicken and dumplings. "Love them," she said, remembering how good they tasted.

"Okay, what about some hamburger? I can do a lot with that. I can make meat loaf, lasagna, or spaghetti?"

"No, meat loaf, ever!" Corey exclaimed.

On and on they went down every aisle in the grocery store, Millie learning about the things that Corey liked and didn't like to eat, and Corey learning what ingredients you needed to cook lasagna. When they got to the fruits and vegetables, Millie happened to mention that Deborah loved bananas, and Corey insisted they get some for Millie to take home to her daughter. Then Corey learned how to pick out a ripe cantaloupe, and how to tell which tomatoes were the best. Corey realized later that it had actually been fun grocery shopping, which was a first for her. Or perhaps she'd just been delighted that Stella hadn't whimpered one time during the entire shopping event.

By the end of the second week, Corey had learned how to cook a few basics like lasagna, a chicken casserole, and green beans. Millie was in the process of teaching Corey how to frost the seven-layer cake they'd just baked when the doorbell rang. Corey ran to the door before it could ring again, as Stella was sleeping. Romeo, who'd already changed from his work clothes, was standing at the door.

"Good news. We have a new postman," Romeo stated, totally oblivious to Corey's distress over the doorbell.

"You've got to remember to knock rather than ring the bell," Corey fussed at him. "If you wake up Stella, and Millie has to leave before I finish icing this cake, I'm going to put you in charge of Stella."

"Oh my gosh, is that yellow cake with chocolate icing?" Romeo ignored Corey and walked straight back to where the one iced layer sat on a platter on the island that separated the great room from the kitchen.

"If you promise not to ring the bell anymore, I'll let you lick the spoon," Corey offered.

"I'll promise you anything for a piece of that layer cake—it's my favorite kind."

"Ms. Corey, I didn't realize it was already after five. I better get myself together so's I can head on to the bus. Besides, you know what you're doing now. You can ice this cake just fine."

Corey nodded worriedly. "What if I break one of the layers? They look awfully thin."

"Put the pieces on, put the icing on the pieces, and believe me, it will still taste just as good." Millie washed her hands, grabbed her purse, and within five minutes she was out the door.

"Okay, Romeo, we've got to get this finished before Stella wakes up and wants her bottle. Come on, you can help." Together they managed to stack and ice the remaining six layers. The cake slanted a bit on one side, but overall it didn't look too bad. "I'll cut the slanted part out for you to take home; then it will look perfect."

"That Millie is a gem. You sure are lucky you found her," Romeo said, taking one final lick from the spoon in his hand.

"I know . . . I just wish I could keep her." Corey sighed as she washed the icing bowl. The thought of losing Millie was almost more than she could stand.

"What do you mean?" Romeo asked curiously.

"Didn't I tell you? I'm only using her until I can find someone else. She has to catch the five-thirty bus to get home in time for her daughter. And you know I'm hardly ever home from work before then."

"That's terrible!" Romeo exclaimed. "She's so perfect."

"I know . . . I love her, and Stella loves her. I just wish she could be a bit more flexible." Corey got out a knife and plate and started cutting the cake. When she placed the large piece of cake on the plate for Romeo to take home, she had to admit it looked pretty darn good.

"Um . . . you know, having a government job like I do, I'm home every day by four or four thirty." Romeo arched his eyebrows toward Corey. "Are we talking like . . . fifteen or twenty minutes between hand-offs, or are we talking about an hour or two while you work until who knows what ungodly hour?"

Corey looked at Romeo in surprise. "You know, I was doing better about not working late at the office before Stella was born. And I'm determined not to work late now. Oh Romeo, if you're suggesting what I think you're suggesting, I promise you, I will do my best to get home most days before Millie has to leave. Oh, and I'll make you a yellow layer cake with chocolate icing whenever you want one."

Romeo contemplated her words in silence for a few moments. "Let me talk this over with Gary and sleep on it. I'll let you know tomorrow."

Corey walked over and gave him a kiss on the cheek. "Pleeeeasse . . ."

In mock anger, Romeo said, "You stop that right now. You know I'd never fool around on Gary."

The next night, Romeo and Gary came over just as Stella was getting ready to have a bottle. Corey thought Stella looked particularly adorable in a brown-and-white polka-dot sleeper that Corey had chosen for her to wear after the guys had called to see if it was a good time for them to visit.

Gary began, "That seven-layer cake is incredible—so moist and rich. Baking is one area of cooking that I've never done a lot of, so I'm envious of someone who can do it well."

"Not too bad for my first cake ever," Corey bragged.

"I'll hold my verdict on your baking until after you fly solo," Gary retorted.

Corey couldn't beat around the bush any longer; she had to find out Romeo's answer. "What are your thoughts about keeping Stella?" Corey looked at them hopefully.

"We're thinking you can't let a cook like Millie get away," Romeo said with a grin.

"Do you mean it?" Corey asked excitedly.

"Besides, we are Stella's uncles. What kind of uncles would we be if we didn't help out when needed?" Gary added.

Corey felt as if her heart might burst with happiness as tears filled her eyes. Gary shifted uncomfortably, looking at her. "No waterworks," he commanded.

"Yeah, otherwise, I'll start thinking I've gotten myself involved in something I don't want to be involved in," Romeo added.

"I'd kiss you both, if I could get to you," Corey laughed, wiping her tears away with her left hand while holding the bottle with her right. "Stella, you have the best uncles in the whole world."

Corey was waiting for Millie at the front door when she arrived the next day. "You can stop worrying about interviewing for another job. Romeo has volunteered to keep Stella if I'm running late. And it was your seven-layer cake that did it!"

Millie exclaimed, "My prayers have been answered!"

"Mine too," Corey added with a grin, feeling amazingly light-hearted. She hadn't realized how anxious she'd felt about losing Millie.

CHAPTER 16

After another week, Corey felt so much more in control of her life that she decided she ought to go in to her office for a few hours to check on some things. When she called her assistant to tell her to gather some papers for her, Erica begged her to bring Stella in with her. Corey considered her request for just a moment. She really wanted to show Stella off to Erica and Larry and a handful of other people at the firm. However, the thought of running into Tom Crane in the hallway with Stella, particularly if Stella was having one of her crying fits, was enough to squelch that idea. *What a scene that would be!*

Erica was on the phone when Corey arrived, so she just waved to her as she went into her office. She flipped on the light. No great transformation had taken place during her absence. It was still tiny and overwhelmingly beige. As soon as Corey sat down, Erica—looking fresh and perky, as most twenty-five-year-olds look—entered her office.

"You look great, Ms. Bennett. No one would imagine that you'd just had a baby. I wish you had brought her in."

"Thanks," Corey replied. "I didn't want to make this a big production, and I wouldn't have gotten much accomplished if I had brought

Stella. As a matter of fact, since my time is limited, I guess I better get started. Can you bring me the Morris files?"

"Sure thing. Be right back."

Thirty minutes later, Corey's head was bent over the Morris files when Larry stuck his head in her office. "Why did I have to hear through the office grapevine that you're here?"

Corey looked up, embarrassed. "I was going to stop by your office before I left."

"Okay, as long as you weren't trying to avoid me. Sherri and I have a present for you and were wondering if we could bring it by your house next Saturday."

Corey was touched that they wanted to stop by for a visit with her. "Sure. Why don't y'all come for a light lunch, like maybe chicken salad?"

"Are you sure you're up for that?" Larry asked, amazed. "We were just going to do a quick drop-by."

"I wouldn't have invited you otherwise. Really, I'd love for you and Sherri to come for lunch."

"Okay. Around twelve?"

"That'd be perfect." Immediately, Corey started wondering, *What in the world have I done?*

On Saturday, Stella woke up unexpectedly early. Corey had started Stella's morning routine before it crossed her mind that it was Tripp's wedding day. Diane and Jack were going to the wedding, and Corey knew she would eventually hear all the details, whether she wanted to or not. How did she feel about Tripp getting married? She wasn't sure. She felt oddly out of sorts. Was she sad? Was she disturbed? She'd slept with Tripp. She'd had his baby. Of course she had feelings for him. But he seemed somehow disconnected from her current life. Besides, after today he'd be a married man, so perhaps it was best if she just didn't think about him at all.

Although Tripp's wedding hadn't crossed her mind at the time she invited Larry and Sherri to lunch, Corey realized now how fortunate she was to have something to keep her mind occupied. Millie had basically prepared the lunch—chicken salad, an assortment of fruits, strawberry shortcake, and iced tea. All Corey had to do was straighten the house, take a shower, and set the table. A challenging list, for sure, but Corey felt that with Stella's more regular routine, it was certainly doable. When Stella went down for her midmorning nap, Corey jumped to work and felt almost like her old self when she stood dressed in pre-pregnancy clothes, with makeup on, surveying the table decorated with fresh flowers. The house looked warm and welcoming, and Corey felt that for the first time in a long while, she had everything under control.

The doorbell rang, and Corey remembered too late how she'd intended to put a sign outside asking people not to ring the doorbell when Stella was sleeping. She listened intently while she walked to the door. *Maybe it won't wake Stella this time.*

"Welcome," Corey said as she opened the door, trying to look calm, as if she had her boss and his wife over for lunch every day. Larry and Sherri were standing on her step awkwardly, with a bright-red stroller wedged between them. The stroller was sleek and streamlined, and Corey realized immediately that they'd bought her a running stroller. "Oh . . . how did you know I've been coveting one of those?"

With a warm smile, Larry said, "Well, I know how much you enjoy running, and I thought it might be difficult now that you have Stella. This way you can get back to running sooner rather than later."

Corey was truly touched. "What a great gift for both me and Stella." She noticed Sherri shifting uncomfortably between the stroller and a holly bush located beside the step. "I'm so sorry." Corey hurriedly opened the door. "I don't know where my manners went." Corey took the stroller, pulled it inside, and ushered the two of them into the foyer. Sherri looked every bit the Dunwoody housewife—sleek and toned in tightly creased slacks and a casual silk blouse. She was in that nebulous age range: somewhere between forty and who knew what. Corey always felt nervous around Sherri and her type of woman. At their office Christmas parties, Corey always gravitated toward the men rather than the stay-at-home moms, who were talking about car pools and orthodontists and things she knew nothing about. As a result, she really didn't know Sherri that well.

On the baby monitor, she could hear Stella moving around, which wasn't a good sign. Corey supposed Stella had heard the doorbell ring, after all. "Can I get you a glass of iced tea, a soft drink, or a glass of wine?" Corey offered.

"Just some water for me," Sherri said.

"Tea would be great," Larry added.

Corey walked to the kitchen, and they followed her. "Your house is just lovely," Sherri said. "Sometimes I wish we still lived in town."

"Yeah, right," Larry laughed. "Like you would ever move from Dunwoody? You look great, by the way, Corey. Motherhood agrees with you."

"Thanks." Corey could hear Stella beginning to become more active, and she felt her stomach tightening in response. She wished Stella would go back to sleep, because if she didn't get in her full nap, she was liable to be very fussy. Corey tried to look relaxed and concentrate on the small talk that Larry and Sherri were making while keeping one ear attuned to the baby monitor.

"Wahhhhhh!" Stella's voice came loudly through the baby monitor. *So much for wishful thinking.*

"Would y'all excuse me for a moment? Stella never wants to miss a party. Please make yourselves at home." Corey remembered before she left the room to turn off the baby monitor.

While she was changing Stella, she heard her cell phone ringing. It was probably just Diane, but if it was important, whoever it was would leave a voice mail. "You've got to be good now, Stella girl. This is your mommy's boss, and I'd really like for him to think I'm a superwoman."

In answer, Stella's face tightened into a grimace, and she let out another cry. *Probably not a good sign,* Corey thought. Praying desperately that Stella would be good, Corey picked her up, wrapped her in a blanket, and went forward to face whatever was going to come next.

Larry and Sherri were sitting on the sofa, sipping their drinks, but they immediately put them down and came toward Corey as she entered the room. "Well, hello there, little princess," Larry said in that tone that adults always use for babies. Stella looked up at him wide-eyed, but thankfully without crying.

Sherri reached out. "Can I hold her?"

"Of course. Just don't get your feelings hurt if she starts fussing. She didn't take her usual nap." Corey handed the baby off to Sherri, and watched in surprise as Stella settled into her arms comfortably and even cooed a bit as Sherri rocked her back and forth. *Perhaps miracles do happen!*

"I just love infants. Unlike teenagers, they don't talk back to you, and you always know where they are."

"Don't go getting any ideas," Larry said. "If you need an infant fix, I'm sure Corey would be glad to share Stella with you anytime."

"Definitely," Corey agreed. "I must admit that I am not quite as enamored as you are with the infant stage. If you don't mind, I'll get lunch on the table while you've got Stella occupied." When she walked into the kitchen, Larry followed her.

"So how are things really going?" he asked as he plopped one of the grapes off the fruit platter into his mouth.

"I'd be lying if I said it was easy. But I've found a wonderful nanny, and I'm beginning to get my life back under control."

"Good! We miss you at the office. I've told them to leave you alone these past few weeks. But if you think you could handle it, I'd really like for John to call you about a few things."

Although Corey still had two weeks of maternity leave left, what could she say other than, "Of course. Let me refill that tea glass for you before we eat." She took his glass and turned to get the ice and tea out of the refrigerator. She put the crackers on a tray with cheese and placed the bowl of chicken salad and the fruit tray on the table.

"Sherri, let me see if Stella will play in her bassinet for a bit so we can eat." Corey reached for Stella, who immediately started fussing when Corey placed her in her bassinet.

"Why don't you just let me hold her while we eat?" Sherri suggested. "I used to be quite good at holding a baby and eating at the same time."

"Are you sure?" Corey asked in amazement. "I haven't quite mastered that skill yet."

"I'd love to."

So Corey handed Stella back and watched as Sherri deftly pacified Stella and still managed to eat her lunch. Corey was in awe. Probably not the best etiquette for treating a guest, but since Sherri seemed to be enjoying herself, Corey supposed it was okay. After lunch, when Stella was starting to fuss in earnest, Larry and Sherri said their good-byes so that Corey could get Stella down for her afternoon nap. "Thanks so much for coming," Corey said.

"I really enjoyed it," Sherri said. And Corey could tell she meant it. Corey felt like she and Sherri had bonded because she was now a member of the motherhood club. Corey's feelings were verified when Sherri leaned over and gave her a hug. "I know this infant stage can be stressful," she said soothingly to Corey, "but try to relax and enjoy it. Babies grow up so fast."

"Everyone keeps telling me that, but I must say the past six weeks seem like six months. It must be because I miss my work so much." Corey gave Larry a grin and then turned back to Sherri. "Please come back anytime you feel like you need another infant fix."

CHAPTER 17

Stella seemed exhausted after being the center of attention and went right down for her afternoon nap. Corey looked at the clock. It was 2:20. The afternoon stretched long and empty. The weekends were the worst time for her. Having Millie during the week, Corey was free to go for a run or do an errand. She felt so trapped on the weekends because she just didn't feel comfortable taking Stella out alone. As a result, Corey spent most of her weekends at home, reading or watching old movies. She remembered the call that had come earlier, and she picked up her cell phone. Great, she had a message from Kathryn.

"I know this is Tripp's wedding day, and I thought you might be feeling a bit blue, so I've got a surprise for you. I've arranged for my favorite client's daughter to babysit for you tonight. Don't argue. She's got lots of experience—more than you, definitely. So get all dolled up, and I'll be there around seven to pick you up."

Corey called Kathryn back immediately. "I thought I was your favorite client."

"You've moved up to the friend category," Kathryn explained.

"Does that mean I don't have to pay you anymore for your services?"

"Darling, we'll never be that good of friends. So, what do you think of my surprise?"

"Um . . . I don't know about leaving Stella with an unknown baby-sitter," Corey said.

"What? I was there when Stella was born. I've taken her to the doctor. I've been there for you and for her every day of her life. Do you really believe I would leave her with someone who wasn't one hundred percent capable of taking care of her? I'm hurt. I really am." Kathryn's voice wasn't kidding for once.

"No, no, of course, I know you wouldn't," Corey apologized. "It's just that I'm not sure I'm ready to go out."

"Ah . . . so now we get to the real heart of the matter. It's time, Corey. It's been over six weeks since you've been anywhere except the doctor's office and the grocery store. Listen, we'll go to Capo's and get something to eat. If the babysitter has any problem, you can be home in five minutes."

"I guess that sounds okay."

"Well, don't sound too excited. I guess I'll bring Annie over at six so she can get to know Stella, and you can feel more comfortable with her before we leave for dinner."

Corey cleaned the kitchen and thought about what she might wear that night. She didn't want to wear any of her maternity clothes, but the pre-pregnancy clothes that she could wear were somewhat limited. Even though she'd only gained seventeen pounds while pregnant, things seemed to have shifted around into different places. Thinking about this displacement, she vowed to try out the new running stroller as soon as Stella woke up.

Later, she strapped a fidgeting Stella into the stroller, and once outside, Stella seemed perfectly happy. So happy that Corey ended up taking a much longer jog than she'd anticipated, and she even paused to visit with Ralph, who was working in the yard, when she ran by his house.

At six, Corey was sitting on the sofa feeding Stella her bottle when Kathryn and a teenage girl walked in. "Corey, meet Annie," Kathryn said. "She's the best babysitter in the Atlanta metropolitan area." Annie looked to be about fifteen, with long, straight brown hair, and dark-brown glasses.

"Hello, Annie. So, you like to babysit?" Corey asked.

"Yes, ma'am. I have three younger sisters, and one is only nine months old, so I have lots of experience. Hello, Stella," Annie said, sitting down next to Corey on the sofa. "Can I feed her?"

"Sure. I need to get dressed, so that will be great." Corey carefully handed off the frantically eating Stella to Annie without disrupting the bottle. Corey watched for a moment to make sure Annie had everything under control, then motioned for Kathryn to follow her into her bedroom.

"Kathryn, you are the best friend a person could have," Corey said once they were in the bedroom. "I didn't even know how much I needed to get out until this afternoon, when I realized that I could go out tonight."

Kathryn grinned at her. "I do have my moments, don't I? And I have another surprise for you."

"Really?" Corey asked, feeling just a bit of trepidation.

"You know that guy Will, whose condo in midtown I've been redoing?" Kathryn asked.

"Yeah, I sort of remember you telling me about him."

"Well, we've gone out a couple of times, and he's meeting us at Capo's and bringing a friend of his."

"You've got to be kidding me!" Corey exclaimed. "You've set up a blind date! I haven't even lost my baby weight, my hormones are going crazy, and you want me to go on a date the very first time I leave my baby with a new babysitter? I take back everything I just said about you being a good friend. You must hate me to do something like this to me."

"Just trust me. You need this. You need to remember the Corey that existed before pregnancy, before becoming a mother, even before you were a widow."

"I'm not going."

"You have to go. I won't be your friend or your decorator anymore if you don't."

"That's blackmail."

Kathryn laughed. "Maybe so, but you *are* going to go tonight, so stop arguing and let's get you dressed."

Eventually, they found a yellow loose-fitting pre-pregnancy dress that Corey felt comfortable wearing and that contrasted nicely with her dark hair. Kathryn went through the jewelry box and pulled out some large, gold loop earrings. As Corey was putting them in her ears, Kathryn cleared her throat and said in an uncharacteristically serious voice, "I understand that taking off your wedding ring is probably a difficult thing for you to do. But what about taking it off just for tonight? Will's friend might notice it and ask questions that you'd rather not answer. I've seen you tense up when you've had to tell people that you're a widow."

Corey looked down at her ring. She had rarely taken it off. When she and Luke had bought their rings, they'd chosen simple ones that could be worn at all times—whether swimming or running or whatever. After Luke's death, Corey continued to wear the ring because it comforted her. Now that she had Stella, the ring also provided her with protection against rude people who might look at her funny if she had a child and no ring on her finger. However, perhaps Kathryn was right. Maybe it was time she took the ring off, at least for one night.

"Okay." Corey took the ring off her finger. The skin underneath was slightly whiter than the rest of the finger's skin, but probably not so much that anyone would notice. Corey carefully put the ring in her jewelry box.

"Wow," Kathryn said with a sigh of relief, "that was a lot easier than I thought it would be."

Corey smiled slightly. "I'm willing to take it off just for tonight."

"A journey of a thousand miles begins with the first step," Kathryn said wisely.

"Come on, Buddha, let's go check on Annie and Stella."

In the next room, Stella seemed perfectly content with Annie, so Corey couldn't use the baby as an excuse for not going out. She wrote her cell-phone number down for Annie. They grabbed their purses and walked to Capo's. During the walk, Corey felt strange. It had been a long time since she'd gone out at night as an attractively dressed single woman on a date. When they arrived at the restaurant, she glanced at Kathryn nervously, but her friend only had eyes for the extremely tall brown-headed man who was waving at them. Corey should have expected Will to be tall since Kathryn had said he played for the Atlanta Hawks basketball team. Still, Corey was five feet seven and not used to men towering over her. Kathryn looked like a midget next to him. The man standing next to Will was a good foot shorter than his friend, but certainly a respectable height, and Corey had to admit that he was pretty cute.

"Hey, pip-squeak." Will grinned as he looked down at Kathryn.

"Hay is for horses." Kathryn tossed her hair back coquettishly. *Only Kathryn could get away with saying something that corny and making it sound cute,* Corey thought.

"You must be Dave." Kathryn put her hand out to the man standing next to Will. She smiled so brightly that she seemed to light up the dark corner where they were standing. "Dave, Will, this is my dear friend and sometimes client, Corey. You will have to forgive her if she dances on the table or does some other crazy thing. This is her first time out in a long time."

"Kathryn!" Corey felt her face flush red.

"Just kidding, guys." Kathryn laughed. "I'm actually the one who might embarrass you."

"I can vouch for that," Corey agreed.

"Your table is ready. Please follow me," said the hostess, turning around without waiting to see if they were following her. They were seated at a table in the middle of the restaurant, which meant they were surrounded by noisy chatter, which seemed like a very good thing to Corey.

"I've never eaten here before," Will said, "but it seems like a fun place." Corey thought Will looked like a fun guy, and one who was very smitten with Kathryn, as he could hardly take his eyes off her.

"It's a great neighborhood bistro, and I've never been disappointed in the food," Corey said.

"We don't have anything like this out in Norcross," Kathryn began. "I wish I hadn't bought out there; it would be so much more exciting to live in midtown like all of you."

"So where do you guys live?" Corey asked, trying to do her part to keep the conversation going.

"I live in the best-decorated condo in Colony Square," Will answered with a wink toward Kathryn.

"I live in the Midtown Tower. You know, the one next door to the High Museum." Dave sort of reminded Corey of John Kowlowski; he had that smooth salesmanlike air about him.

"Wow, y'all live right across from each other—how convenient!" Kathryn said, eyes wide as if it were the most amazing thing she'd ever heard. Corey had never seen the flirty side of Kathryn before, and she was finding it quite entertaining.

"Yeah, we're always going back and forth across Tenth Street to borrow a cup of sugar. Where do you live?" Dave turned to Corey.

"I live right down the street from here in the Peachtree Arms condos. This is *my* neighborhood bistro."

"She lives in the best-decorated condo there as well," Kathryn offered. "If you want your condo to be the best-decorated condo in the Midtown Tower, here's my card." Kathryn withdrew one of her business cards and handed it to Dave.

"Nice," Dave whistled. "I should hire you to work at my PR firm."

"Your PR firm needs a decorator?" Kathryn asked eagerly.

"No, right now we need salespeople who can sell hospitality suites and packages to Braves games. I bet you could sell ice makers to Eskimos."

"You've got me all wrong," Kathryn began. "I'm only passionate about two things." She paused and winked at Will. "And one of those things is decorating. I'd be a bust trying to sell Braves boxes."

Corey decided to try to get back in the conversation. "Do you guys go to the High Museum a lot?"

"I hate to admit it, but I've never even been there," Dave said.

"Never?" asked Corey incredulously.

"Hey, we're into sports, not the arts," Will explained apologetically.

"What are you into, Corey?" asked Dave.

Corey paused for a moment. She could say *diapers*, *spit-up*, or a thousand other things that would be an instant conversation killer, but it was always safe to fall back on her job. "The law. I work for Landon, Crane, and Forrester," she said.

"It's one of the oldest law firms in Atlanta," Kathryn said, obviously proud of her friend's credentials.

"Do you have lots of decrepitly old clients with lots of old money?" asked Will.

"Nah," said Dave, before Corey could answer. "Old in Atlanta means since about 1972. They do have lots of hot young lawyers, though."

Corey blushed. She had to admit that it felt good to have an attractive man like Dave flirting with her. "Actually, specializing in estate planning like I do, I have more than my fair share of decrepitly old and wealthy clients."

"Ever thought about marrying one of those old widowers for their money? Might not be such a bad deal. You'd have to put in a difficult year or two, and then you'd be an incredibly sexy widow with lots of money." Dave's words fell like rocks, crushing the conversation. Kathryn looked at Corey, whose mind had suddenly gone blank. Dave picked up from the instant stillness at the table that something was wrong. "Hey, I was just joking, guys."

Kathryn came to Corey's rescue. "I guess we might as well tell you. Corey is a recent widow with a six-week-old baby at home."

Will looked guiltily at Corey, and Dave looked distraught. "I'm so sorry," Dave said immediately. "What an ass you must think I am."

"Of course not," Corey said politely. "You didn't know." Corey suddenly wished she could leave and go home. She knew the rest of the night was going to be difficult. She might as well be wearing a sign saying, "I'm a widow; I'm different." However, Corey soon realized that Dave was in public relations for a reason, as he launched into a campaign to save the dinner.

"I never would have guessed you had a six-week-old baby—you look fantastic! Is it a boy or a girl?" Dave asked.

Corey was grateful for his efforts. "I have a girl. Her name is Stella."

"I love that name—Stella," Dave said. "It isn't a namby-pamby kind of name. It has character and strength."

"Makes me think of Marlon Brando screaming, 'Stella!' in one of those old movies. I can't remember which one, but I've seen clips of it," Will said.

"*A Streetcar Named Desire*," Corey replied.

"Yeah, that one," Will said. "I never watched it 'cause I can't stand movies in black and white."

"Me neither," said Kathryn. "They're so dull."

Both Dave and Corey looked at Will and Kathryn as if they were crazy. And just like that, the conversation picked back up, and the dinner catastrophe was averted.

After a leisurely dinner, their group stood a bit awkwardly on the sidewalk outside Capo's.

"You girls want to go somewhere else now?" asked Will.

"There's a great band playing at the Lullwater Tavern tonight," added Dave.

Kathryn looked at Corey longingly.

But Corey had done as much as she could for her first night out. She felt exhausted, and suddenly she wanted nothing more than a glass of wine and a long soak in her tub.

"I'm going to have to call it a night, guys," Corey apologized.

"Oh come on, the night's early," Will said cajolingly.

"Yeah, it is," said Corey, deciding to bring the elephant that had been in the corner all night up to center stage. "But I have a brand-new babysitter, and I would rather not make it too late of a night for her my first time out."

Will turned to Kathryn. "What about you?"

"I brought the babysitter from Norcross, so I've got to take her home."

"All right, I give up, we'll call it a night." Will bent over and gave Kathryn a quick kiss on the lips. "I'll call you soon."

Corey decided to circumvent any awkwardness with Dave by leaning over and giving him a quick kiss on the cheek. "Thanks for dinner. It was great, and I enjoyed meeting you."

"Yeah, me too," Dave said smoothly. "Maybe we can get together again sometime?"

"That'd be great," Corey said, thinking that the odds of his calling her were pretty much slim to none. Still, she wrote her number on the piece of paper he handed her.

"So what'd you think of Dave?" asked Kathryn as they walked back to Corey's house.

"Very nice, very smooth."

"And very cute, don't you think? I bet you didn't think about Tripp's wedding one time tonight, did you?"

Corey was startled to realize that Kathryn was right. How had that been possible?

CHAPTER 18

Diane called the next day to check on Corey and give her all the details of the wedding. It had been in Dothan so that Tripp's father could be there. "It was very small and simple, really very sweet."

Corey thought it ironic that Diane described Tripp's wedding with the same adjective—*sweet*—Tripp had used to describe Lucy. "What does Lucy look like?"

"She's blonde and tiny. Not nearly as beautiful as Martha Anne—but pretty in a simple way. I didn't get a chance to really talk to her, so I can't say what's she's like as a person."

"Does Tripp seem happy?"

"Yeah, he does. He asked about you and Stella."

"That was nice."

"Oh, by the way, I put your name on our wedding gift. You owe me fifty dollars."

"Oh really. What did *we* give him?"

"A leaf blower. I've got to go now."

Corey put the phone down. Life had certainly taken her on a strange ride. How had she reached this point, where she was giving a wedding present to the father of her child?

◆ ◆ ◆

Much to Corey's surprise, Dave did call several days later to invite her to dinner. Luckily, she wasn't able to get to her cell phone in time and got the invitation on her voice mail. She called Kathryn immediately.

"That's great!" Kathryn said excitedly.

"Um . . . I don't know, Kathryn. Millie can't babysit at night, and I don't know where to find a sitter. Annie was great, but driving out to Norcross to pick her up just isn't feasible."

"Aren't there any teenage girls around where you live?" asked Kathryn.

"I'm surrounded by recently married couples; single, young, urban professionals; gay couples; and divorced or retired people. Where would these teenage girls come from?"

"The retired people might be a possibility for the future. You need to start networking for babysitters at your next condo-association meeting; in the meantime, what about Romeo and Gary?"

"I can't ask them for any more favors. Romeo has already volunteered to cover me in the afternoons if Millie has to leave before I get home."

"Well, then, I'll babysit for you. You need to go."

"I don't want to impose on you."

"Why? It's never held you back before." Kathryn laughed. "Let me check my calendar and give you a couple of good dates for next week."

"Uh . . . I don't know, Kathryn. I'm not sure I really want to go out with him anyway. I don't know if he's my type."

"Get a grip, Corey," Kathryn said in exasperation. "We're not talking about marriage here. We're talking about a date—a fun night out with a good-looking adult of the opposite sex. You need to learn to relax and enjoy yourself a bit."

"Okay, okay, you're right. I'll go. Thanks."

◆ ◆ ◆

Kathryn's excitement about Corey's date with Dave reminded Corey of how excited Kathryn had been about Corey's dinner with Tripp. Unlike Kathryn, Corey felt no excitement about this date. As a matter of fact, she felt certain that Dave had only asked her out because he wanted to make up for his blunder at dinner. Corey became even more certain of this when she called him back and he said that their dinner would be at the Braves stadium during a baseball game. Since she knew the team was one of his clients, Corey figured this was probably related to his business and was also likely a free dinner for him. Still, she said nothing that would spoil it for Kathryn.

On date night, Kathryn, who was one of Romeo and Gary's favorite people, had been invited to bring Stella over for dinner at their place, which made Corey feel better about leaving Kathryn to babysit, and also a bit envious of the casual, relaxed dinner they would be having together. She gathered all of Stella's necessities and then walked next door with Kathryn to help with the transfer. She was standing at their front door saying good-bye when Dave arrived to pick her up. *Isn't anybody ever late anymore?*

"Dave, you know Kathryn, she's my babysitter tonight, and these are my neighbors and dear friends, Romeo and Gary."

Dave shook the guys' hands as they clearly sized him up. "Where's Stella?" Dave asked.

Corey motioned for Dave to follow her into the guys' condo where Stella sat snuggled up in her bouncy seat. "She's so little," he remarked.

"Seven weeks old tomorrow," Corey said.

Dave turned from Stella to Corey. "You ready?"

"Everybody okay?" Corey looked from Kathryn to Romeo to Gary.

"Go have fun," Kathryn said.

Corey turned to Dave. "I'm ready."

As the night progressed, Corey found that going to dinner at a Braves game was a wonderful first date. They had a fabulous steak dinner on a plaza overlooking the baseball field. She wasn't a huge baseball fan, but she liked sports in general and found herself enjoying hearing personal stories about some of the players they were watching. Although several people stopped by their table briefly for a chat, Corey never felt as if Dave was working. He seemed genuinely interested in the things she had to say, and not feeling nervous about where the date was going, Corey found it easy to be herself. At some point toward the end of the night, Dave mentioned that he loved to fish.

Corey's eyes lit up. "I think I went fishing before I could walk."

"Really? Freshwater or saltwater?" Dave asked, amazed.

"Saltwater. My family has a beach house in Mexico Beach, Florida. I grew up practically living on the ocean."

"Have you ever been to Fripp Island, South Carolina?" Dave wanted to know.

Corey shook her head no.

"It's a great place for fishing. I just bought a boat, a seventeen-footer, and I have a share in a townhome there."

"How often do you get a chance to go?"

"I own a sixth in the townhome, so I get it every six weeks. It works out well with my work; I couldn't go any more often than that anyway."

"That sounds wonderful."

On their way back to Corey's condo, Dave brought up Fripp Island again. "My weekend to have the townhome is coming up in a couple of weeks. What about you going with me? Then, I could find out if you're just bluffing about your fishing skills."

Corey was shocked by Dave's invitation. She'd felt they were both having a good time at dinner, but an invitation to spend the weekend with him seemed a bit abrupt.

"I would love to," she began, "but I think you've forgotten about Stella. I don't have a babysitter who could stay for the weekend. And even if I didn't have babysitter issues, I go back to work full-time in another week, which is going to be a bit of a rough transition, I'm sure."

"Oh come on, you've got two weeks; you can find a babysitter for Stella in two weeks. Plus, after starting back to work, you're going to need a vacation."

Corey was surprised by his casualness. "I'm afraid you've got a lot to learn about parenthood. It's not like Stella's a dog and I can just board her anywhere. I didn't have a babysitter for Stella tonight—that's why my friends are keeping her."

"Who's going to watch her while you work?"

"I have a nanny during the day, but she can't work nights or weekends."

"Bummer. Well, let me know if you ever think you can get away."

They were back at her condo. Corey opened her car door. "I really enjoyed the dinner and the game." Dave started to get out too. She stopped halfway out of the car. "Don't bother getting out. Thanks again."

Kathryn fussed at Corey after hearing her account of the date. "Well, I guess you've pretty much closed that door with Dave for any future dates."

"I don't care. Right now, my life is complicated enough. I'd rather things not go any further with Dave if he doesn't understand what it means for me to be a single mother."

Kathryn shook her head in amazement. "Corey, you're setting yourself up for a difficult life."

"No," Corey said vehemently, "I'm trying to keep my life from getting any more difficult than it already is."

CHAPTER 19

On Stella's two-month birthday, Corey was to return to work full-time, and she had mixed feelings about it. On the one hand, she was excited about reconnecting with her old life. The thought of sitting in her office, being able to concentrate on only one thing at a time, was extremely appealing to her. On the other hand, however, she hated the thought of leaving Stella all day. The baby was changing by the minute, and Corey hated to miss even one second of her life. Also, Corey was nervous about how things were going to work out with Millie and Romeo. Corey hoped she could transition into doing more work from home. Until then, she was placing a lot of faith in the MARTA bus system to get Millie to work on time in the mornings, and in Romeo's as-yet-unproven ability to handle Stella in the afternoons.

Corey dressed in one of her power suits and was ready to walk out the door when Millie arrived. With no traffic problems, she actually found herself a bit ahead of schedule heading back to work. She felt oddly out of place walking into her office building after so many weeks away. She hadn't felt so awkward since her early days with the firm. Even during that last year of Luke's life, she hadn't taken off more than a couple of weeks at any one time.

Standing at the elevator, waiting to go up to her office as she had so many thousands of times before, Corey remembered the first time she'd stood at those elevator doors, waiting to start her work as a lawyer. She felt as though she'd lived a lifetime since that day. She'd gotten married, made a name for herself at the law firm, discovered that her husband was terminally ill, become a widow, and now she was a single mother. Corey thought, *Why, I've lived more in the years between my first time in front of these elevator doors and today than some people do in a lifetime!*

"Excuse me," said an older woman next to Corey as they walked into the elevator. "I thought you might want to know that you have throw-up down the back of your jacket."

Corey felt her face flush red. "Thanks so much." She said a silent prayer of gratitude that it hadn't been someone at the firm, like Tom Crane, who'd made that discovery. Yes, her life had certainly changed since that day she'd stood in front of those elevator doors for the very first time.

On Stella's first birthday, Corey marveled at how she held court like a princess in her high chair—blonde curls glinting in the sunlight. Her hair color reminded Corey more and more of how Tripp had looked when they were children. Corey hoped no one would stop to question how two dark-haired parents could produce a blonde child.

Stella was delighted with the cupcake Millie had made for her, and also with all the attention she was receiving from the roomful of people. On one side of the high chair stood Romeo and Gary, eating birthday cake but obviously entranced with Stella's every movement. Corey's transition back to work hadn't been seamless, but Romeo—and even occasionally Gary—had filled in admirably whenever Corey had needed them to do so.

In return, Millie had taken it upon herself to thank the guys with some new confection every few days. One day she might make them a key lime pie; on another day it might be a caramel cake. She'd baked them so many goodies that Romeo's stomach was beginning to protrude slightly over his waistband, and Gary had started joking that he'd leave him if it progressed much further.

On the other side of Stella's high chair sat Kathryn and Will. Instead of losing Kathryn to Will, as so often happened when girlfriends got serious boyfriends, Corey had acquired a new friend. Both Kathryn and Will were willing to help Corey with Stella whenever she got herself into a pinch. And no one could make Stella laugh more than Will, who worked hard at coming up with new funny faces to entertain her. Corey never asked Will about Dave, whom she'd heard nothing more from since she'd dashed from his car that night after the Braves game. However, one time while she was out with Stella, Will, and Kathryn at the Piedmont Arts Festival, they'd all run into Dave holding hands with another girl. It really hadn't mattered to Corey, as a romance was way down on her list of desires—somewhere after a bubble bath and eight hours of sleep.

Stella's aunt Diane stood in front of her, snapping pictures with her new digital camera. Corey appreciated that Diane, Jack, and Marcy had come for the big birthday party. But honestly, she would have been stunned if they hadn't been there. After all, they'd driven to Atlanta to celebrate Stella's first Thanksgiving and Christmas. Corey was extremely thankful for their love and support, which had gotten her through so much during the past year.

Stella's adoring Nana sat across from her, now glowing with happiness. Nancy took the Peachtree Wilden bus to Corey's house every time it was headed in their direction. Luckily, Millie and Nancy got along well, and each seemed to enjoy the other's company. Millie had learned more about Nancy in their year together than Corey had learned in the years she'd been married to Luke. Corey had almost stopped feeling any guilt over lying to Nancy. How could she feel guilty when Stella had probably saved Nancy's life? And if Stella hadn't saved Nancy's life,

Corey felt confident that her baby had added significant meaning to it over the past year.

Then, of course, there was Millie, standing quietly in the background, happy to be there but not wanting to be the center of attention. Stella and Millie had such a mutual lovefest going on that Corey occasionally felt a hint of jealousy. Stella said the word *Mimi* for Millie just about the time she said *Mama*. But the happiness on Stella's face when Corey handed her off to Millie in the mornings always made Corey's jealousy disappear. Yes, when Corey counted her blessings, Millie was always at the top of the list.

Corey remembered the sheer panic she'd felt those first few weeks of Stella's life as she realized she was completely responsible for another human being, as well as the doubt she'd felt about whether she could actually pull off this motherhood thing. Eventually, with Millie's help, she began to feel more comfortable in her role as a mother. Yet, Corey equated herself with a recovering alcoholic. She prayed each day for the wisdom and the strength to just make it through that day or night successfully. So far, thankfully, she'd made it through 365 days and nights.

Now Stella's chubby little face creased in smiles more than tears, and she had conquered so many new experiences, from finding her toes to rolling over to eventually crawling. So far, Stella seemed determined to avoid the joys of walking as she continued to scoot across the glossy hardwood floors on her hands and knees. Millie and Diane, as well as Dr. Carrington, assured Corey that Stella would eventually walk whenever she wanted to badly enough.

On the negative side, work continued to be a delicate balancing act. Corey often had to put in an hour or two of work at home, and she relied more on Erica, her assistant, to connect her with her office than she ever had before Stella's birth. Sometimes she could sense frustration in her coworkers or her clients when she had to dash out of a meeting that was running late. Larry had talked to her a couple of times about how she was managing things. Overall, she felt reasonably confident that he was okay with her work schedule. Corey still believed she was doing a good job. Perhaps not quite as good as she had before Stella was born, but good nonetheless. She still believed she would be promoted soon.

Yes, all in all, Corey had a lot to be thankful for. She was even looking forward to her first trip to Mexico Beach with Stella in a few weeks. For Millie, it would be a much-needed vacation. And for Corey, it was time to face her greatest fear—which, surprisingly, wasn't the six-hour trip in a car alone with Stella. Corey knew that she would have to face Tripp in Mexico Beach, and that fear about when she would see him was always nagging at her somewhere in the back of her mind. She hoped that once she faced that fear, she could put it to rest forever.

CHAPTER 20

Stella was insistent. "Go, go." She crawled to the door and reached her chubby arms up toward the doorknob.

"Okay, but first you have to let me put sunscreen on you."

Stella shook her head firmly to indicate "No way."

Corey laughed at her. They'd been at the beach long enough for Stella to learn that she liked playing on the sand and that she didn't like the cold suntan lotion being rubbed on her. "Then we don't go," Corey said. Stella started whining.

"Just come here and then we can go," said Corey. Stella looked at the door, then at her mother, and then back at the door. Finally, with a resigned air, she crawled quickly into Corey's outstretched arms.

After covering the squirming child with lotion, Corey left a note for Diane—who'd gone into Port Saint Joe to do some shopping—and grabbed everything they'd need for the beach. She loaded the umbrella, a chair, Stella's bag of beach toys, two towels, and a cooler filled with drinks and snacks into the beach wagon Diane had purchased for them. Corey put a big, white floppy hat on Stella's head.

"No," Stella said, and immediately pulled the hat off.

"We won't go until the hat is on," Corey said firmly. Finally, after a few more minutes, Stella allowed the hat to be put on, and Corey placed Stella in the wagon and started toward the beach.

Corey reflexively checked the MacKinnon house as they went along. She noted with satisfaction that the blinds were still closed. They'd walked fifty feet or so when Corey realized that Tripp's vehicle was parked underneath, and the back hatch was open. Tripp must have just arrived and was still unloading, but she didn't see him anywhere. For a moment, Corey considered turning back, but she knew that Stella would pitch one of her major fits if she were to try to turn back now. Maybe if they hurried, they could get to the beach before Tripp returned. Once they were on the beach, he might not recognize them. Corey thought they were safe when they'd reached the side of the house without any sign of Tripp. But just at that last second before they reached the beach path, the downstairs storage door opened, and there he was staring straight at them, practically face-to-face.

"Well, hello," Tripp said, walking out to greet them. "I finally get to meet the smartest and the best baby that ever was."

"Sounds like Diane's been talking to you," Corey answered.

"She is one proud aunt." Tripp reached his hand out to Stella, who immediately turned away from him and reached for her mother.

"She's shy with strangers," Corey apologized, picking her up.

"Here, let me help you take your stuff down to the beach. Maybe she'll loosen up in a minute and let me see her."

"That's okay, you've just arrived. I'm sure you want to finish unloading."

"There's nothing that can't wait." Tripp walked over and closed the back of his Yukon, then took the beach wagon from Corey's hand.

"Okay, if you insist."

"I do."

They walked in silence down to the beach. Every once in a while, Stella would lift her head to see if Tripp was still there, and seeing that he was, she would immediately put her head back down against Corey's chest. When they arrived at a good spot, Corey said, "Would you mind dumping the toys out on the sand?"

"Not at all." Tripp took the bag of beach toys and dumped them. Then he started digging a hole for the umbrella and set up the chair.

Corey turned so that Stella could see the toys. Stella released Corey's neck immediately and started saying, "Down, down."

Corey obliged Stella by placing her on the sand and handing her a shovel. "Thanks," Corey said, indicating the umbrella that Tripp had just put into place. "I always have a difficult time getting it in right."

"I remember," Tripp said. "May I join you?"

"Sure," Corey said, "but I only brought one chair."

"Sand works."

"Here, at least use a towel." Corey had known this day was going to come sooner or later, so she supposed she might as well get it over with today. She hoped Tripp couldn't hear her heart beating loudly in her chest. "Oh yeah, I haven't seen you since you got married. Congratulations. I hope I'll get to meet Lucy while I'm here."

"She'll be down tomorrow. She had some nurse party to go to tonight."

Stella was turned away from them so that the brim of the hat hid her face. Contented, she very patiently filled her shovel and dumped the sand into her bucket. "I think I'm going to have to buy a sandbox for home. She absolutely loves playing in the sand."

"How's motherhood going?"

"It's had its difficult moments, I won't lie, but it's been the most amazing adventure. Just when I think I've got it figured out, Stella changes and I go back to square one."

Tripp sat there, silent for a minute. "We haven't told Diane and Jack yet, but Lucy's pregnant. I'm sure she will have tons of questions for you."

Corey's breath caught in her chest. "Wow, congratulations."

"Thanks, I'm really looking forward to being a father."

Stella, who'd been totally absorbed in sand play, suddenly remembered that she had on the dreaded hat. She reached up and pulled it off. Her blonde curls glinted like gold in the late-afternoon sun. "No," she said, looking directly at her mother and daring her to put the hat back on her head.

"She can't stand that hat." Corey laughed at her bravado before noticing that Tripp was looking at Stella with the strangest look on his face. When he kept staring at Stella, and several more minutes had passed, Corey felt nervous. "Tripp?"

"She's my daughter," Tripp said flatly. It wasn't a question but a statement of fact.

Corey felt anxiety hit her so hard and swiftly that she finally knew how it felt to have a full-blown panic attack. "I, well . . ." Corey couldn't think of what she should say next.

"In my parents' bedroom, there's a picture of me sitting on the beach at about that age, and I feel like I'm looking at that picture right now." Tripp turned toward Corey. "I had my suspicions when Diane told me you were pregnant." Suddenly Tripp's face was furious. "Why in the hell didn't you tell me?"

"I'm sorry" was all Corey could manage to get out.

"Don't say 'I'm sorry' like you just spilled a drink on me!"

Finally, she found her voice. "I think I was in shock at first. Luke and I had tried to have a baby for a long time, and I was unable to get pregnant. It never occurred to me that I might get pregnant that night. Then, when I was, I was confused and afraid."

"Afraid of me? *You know me!*"

"Oh come on, Tripp. We had spent six or seven hours together after not having seen each other for years. I really didn't know you all that well."

"But we grew up together. For God's sake, as a friend, didn't I at least deserve a courtesy call from you to tell me, 'By the way, Tripp, I thought you might want to know, I'm having your baby'?"

Corey felt tears streaming down her face. "Yes, I know now that's what I should have done. I was incredibly selfish and . . . wrong not to have told you. I wanted to tell you when you came to Atlanta. And I've almost called you a hundred times since Stella was born. Believe me—I was trying to think about what was best for everyone."

"Yeah, what about Atlanta? I drove all the way up there to see you. I had this hunch that something was wrong. But you convinced me that everything in your life was perfect, happening just as you had planned, and just how you wanted it to happen."

Stella seemed oblivious to the turmoil going on behind her. "I was scared," Corey said again.

"Of what?" Tripp asked harshly. "That things might get messy and ruin your perfectly choreographed life? Or that I might have feelings for you?"

"No," Corey said quietly. "That you wouldn't."

Tripp looked at her strangely. "What?"

"I was in love with you when I went to Auburn. But you never even noticed. It hurt like hell when you became involved with Martha Anne. I thought I'd never get over it. But I did, finally. That night in Atlanta, you never said anything about how you felt about me, only that you wished we could have seen how things developed, and I was afraid of taking a chance again, of getting hurt again."

Tripp looked stunned.

Corey added slowly, "Plus, I was still grieving Luke's loss when I found out I was pregnant. My boss sent me to Florida in the first place because he thought I was about to collapse or have a nervous breakdown or something. I wasn't thinking too clearly when I decided to pretend Stella was Luke's. I mean, I talked it over with my ficus tree—that's how crazy I was at that time."

Corey paused for a moment and gathered her thoughts. "Besides, it's always easier to stay where you are and to keep doing what you're used to doing. Still, after you left Atlanta, I decided the right thing to do was to tell you. I planned to drive down to Dothan on New Year's weekend and tell you everything. I couldn't go any earlier because of work. But then Diane called and told me you had asked Lucy to marry you at Christmas."

Tripp ran his hand through his hair in an agitated movement. "I decided it was time to get on with my life. I wanted children. I told you that in Atlanta."

"Yeah," Corey said sadly, the tears still falling unchecked. "I just didn't know that you were ready to move on so quickly. But even when I was planning my drive down to Dothan to tell you the truth, I couldn't get anything to add up right. What was going to happen once the baby was born? Would we shuttle her back and forth between us? I couldn't imagine you living in Atlanta or me living here. Would that really have been the best thing for Stella?"

Stella crawled over to Corey, sandy and smelly. "Poo, poo," Stella said.

"I've got to go up to the house and change her." Corey wiped the tears from her face with the bottom of her shirt. "Please think about what's best for everyone before you decide what you're going to do next. We've got to think about Stella, Lucy, and now the baby Lucy's going to have."

"Damn it, Corey, I feel cheated. She's beautiful, and I want to be a part of her life."

"We'll figure something out. Just don't tell everyone the truth now."

"Don't you think other people will see what I saw?"

"People see what they want to see," Corey said earnestly. "Luke's mother thinks Stella looks just like her sister, Margie. And Diane thinks Stella looks just like our mother. If you get rid of that baby picture of yours, no one will ever suspect. Please, Tripp, I'm begging you."

"Okay, I won't say anything right now. But I'm making no promises about tomorrow."

CHAPTER 21

Corey tossed and turned all night and was grateful when she heard Stella stirring because it gave her a reason to finally get up. Stella was playing happily with her feet, and Corey felt such a rush of love that she didn't know if she could bear being apart from her if Tripp were to demand joint custody. Stella saw her and immediately pulled herself up to the side of the bed. "Down, down," she said.

After changing her, Corey carried Stella downstairs for breakfast. She was just getting started with the cereal and bananas when Diane walked into the kitchen and went straight for the coffee.

"DiDi," Stella said, reaching her arms out toward her aunt.

"I think she wants her aunt Diane to feed her," Corey said.

"I'm barely awake myself, but how could I refuse that sweet face?"

Corey allowed Diane to take her place in the chair in front of Stella. She watched for a minute or two and then looked out the window at the beautiful morning. "If it's okay with you, I'm going to go take a run. I still have that last little bit of baby weight to get off."

"Yeah," Diane said, laughing. "Good luck, I've been trying to get mine off for the past fourteen years."

Corey ran furiously down the back beach road as far as the El Governor Motel and then decided to return walking along the beach. It was still early, probably only seven or so. She wondered if Tripp had gone fishing or was even up yet. When she started to walk up the beach path, she was relieved to see him sitting at a table, drinking coffee on his front deck. Corey waved at him, and he held up a hand in return. Although he wasn't exactly ushering her up, she took it as a welcoming sign and went up the stairs.

"I've been going crazy wondering what you were thinking," Corey said. "I didn't sleep a wink last night."

"Me neither," said Tripp. "You want some coffee or water?"

"Water would be great," Corey said. When Tripp started to get up, she said, "Just sit, I'll get it."

"There are bottles in the door of the refrigerator."

Corey was stunned by the transformation inside the beach house. The brown shag carpet had been replaced with a tweedy Berber, and the paneled walls had been painted a turquoise blue. Oars were crossed behind the sofa. And a very expensive-looking brass barometer hung on the wall across from the breakfast bar. Corey reached into the brand-new white refrigerator for a bottle of water and longed for the old avocado-colored appliances. The inside now looked like any picture of a beach house you would find in a *Southern Living* or *House Beautiful* magazine. It was not the beach house of her childhood anymore. *The unknown Lucy is responsible for these changes to the house,* Corey thought unhappily, and walked back outside. She sat down next to Tripp, took a long swig of water, and waited for him to say something.

Finally, after a minute or two, Tripp said, "All my life, I've believed that if you really analyze something, look at all of the facts, you'll know the right thing to do. When Martha Anne and I decided to get a divorce, I knew it was the right thing for both of us. When my mother's mental state started deteriorating rapidly, in spite of my father's very strong objections,

I knew the right thing was for her to go to an assisted-living facility where she could get the care she needed. But for the first time in my life, I can't decide what the right thing is, and it's got me all twisted up inside."

"I know. That's why when I found out—" Corey began, but Tripp interrupted her.

"Don't say anything," Tripp warned her. "I'm talking about the right thing to do now, not when you first found out you were pregnant."

"Okay," Corey said in a quiet voice, and she felt strangely calm and unemotional. She *had* been trying to do the right thing. Why couldn't he see her side?

"I feel torn apart," Tripp continued. "I have a beautiful baby daughter, and I want to be her father and see her grow up. Yet, I don't want Stella to be labeled illegitimate. I don't want her to be subjected for the rest of her life to the kind of gossip that small towns thrive on. I also have to think about Lucy. I can't imagine what hearing this kind of news might do to her."

Although Corey had begged Tripp to think about Lucy yesterday on the beach, hearing him so concerned about Lucy's happiness now suddenly really irritated her.

"So what's the bottom line here? Are we making some sort of grand announcement today, or are we continuing the status quo?" Corey's voice sounded hard and sharp even to her ears.

Tripp looked at her coldly. "Neither. I'm not going to tell the truth today. But I want a relationship with my daughter. I want to see her regularly and have a say in the important decisions in her life. And when she's older, and I don't know what age that will be, I want her to know the truth. Do you accept my terms?"

The lawyer in Corey surfaced. "I want our terms to be clear before I agree to anything. What do you mean, 'regularly'?"

"You'll agree to bring her to the beach for at least two weeks every summer. And I'll be allowed to come to Atlanta whenever I can arrange it to see her. In between, you'll e-mail me updates and pictures."

If Corey agreed to these terms, she was agreeing that her life would be forever intertwined with Tripp's. But then, she supposed, her life had become permanently intertwined with his the moment she'd given birth to his daughter.

"I agree," she finally said. "I hope you realize that you're going to have to pretend to be friends with me in front of Diane, Jack, Lucy, and everyone in order for this to work."

Tripp looked at her, and something electric passed between them. "That's what makes this so damned hard, Corey! In spite of how angry I am with you right now, I still care about you. When we were kids, you were one of my best friends. At times I've wondered if there wasn't something more than friendship there. But now friendship is all we can have, and that's what we've got to sell to the group."

And just like that, Corey's calm, unemotional state evaporated. "Diane's going to be wondering what happened to me," she said as the tears began falling freely down her face. She thought for a moment Tripp was going to say something more to her, but he just nodded, and Corey ran down the stairs, wiping the tears from her face with the bottom of her shirt.

Diane was upstairs with Stella when Corey entered the beach house. She checked her face in the bathroom before going upstairs, where Diane was trying to wrestle Stella into a swimsuit.

"Have a good long run?" Diane asked.

"I have to confess I walked half the time; I'm still trying to get back into shape."

"I was thinking you were gone longer than usual. I was also thinking about having a fish fry tonight. What about inviting Tripp and Lucy and Fran and Mark for dinner? Does that sound like fun to you?"

"Sure. I think it's about time I met Lucy."

CHAPTER 22

Corey watched Lucy and Tripp from the window as they walked toward the house. Lucy looked so young, like a child of twelve or thirteen, with shoulder-length bouncy hair and the slender build of a gymnast. When they were close enough for them to possibly see her, Corey backed away from the window. A few minutes later she heard footsteps on the stairs, and then Lucy was standing at the door. Corey opened the door and ushered her into the sunporch.

"I'm so glad to finally get to meet you," Lucy said. "And where's the wonderful Stella?"

"Nice to meet you too," Corey said in return. "Stella is already in bed. She skipped her nap this afternoon, and the beach wears her out."

"Oh no," Lucy said. "I'm so disappointed."

"Don't be," Corey said, managing to bring forth a smile from somewhere. "She'll be up and going early tomorrow morning. Feel free to stop by anytime, especially at six a.m. when she's usually raring to play."

Lucy laughed. "Smells wonderful in here. I thought the guys were doing the cooking outside."

"Do you know my sister? She would never pass up an opportunity to cook for a group of people. I think that's her amazing chess pie you're smelling right now. Let's go see."

They walked into the kitchen, where Diane was in a tizzy because she'd used all the sugar to make the chess pie and didn't have any for the sweet tea.

"I've never heard of a chess pie," Lucy said. "What's in it?"

"This is our grandmother's recipe but pretty standard I think: eggs, a lot of sugar, evaporated milk, white vinegar, and cornmeal."

"Umm . . . it smells a lot better than those ingredients might suggest," Lucy mused.

"I'll run to the store and get you some more sugar," Corey offered.

"I'll ride with you," Lucy said.

"That's okay, you don't have to."

"But it will give us a chance to get to know each other a little better," Lucy said in a genuinely friendly voice. How could Corey refuse?

"Well, then, let's go." Corey walked down the stairs with Lucy trailing behind her. When she reached the bottom, Tripp and Jack were standing off to the side of the stairs, fiddling with the fish cooker. Both men looked up. Corey felt nervous. "We're off to the store for sugar. Do y'all need anything?"

"Actually, I think this propane tank is empty. Do you know how to exchange it for a full one?" asked Jack.

"Let me go," Tripp offered. "Never send a girl to do a man's job."

"No, let us go. I was thinking Corey could tell me all of your childhood secrets on the trip to the store," Lucy said with a provocative look at Tripp.

"That would take a lot longer than just a trip to the grocery store," said Jack, laughing.

"Ha, ha," said Tripp. "Excuse me while I go get the car."

"Here, just take my car," Corey said, throwing him her keys. Tripp reached out and caught the keys with one hand just as Fran and her husband, Mark, drove up in their MINI Cooper.

"I'm afraid to drive something that fancy." Tripp threw the keys back to Corey. "Mark can drive me to the store." Tripp picked up the propane tank and walked to Mark's car, signaling for him to get back in.

As they drove off, Fran, in a flowing, floor-length cotton sundress, walked up to the group holding a bowl of broccoli salad. "I guess Mark forgot he had two bags of ice in the backseat." No sooner had the words come out of her mouth than the MINI Cooper reversed and approached them backward. Mark jumped out and quickly handed the ice bags to Jack. Then he gave a big wave to the group and drove off again.

"I guess the Wizard came through with that brain, after all." Jack laughed and started up the stairs with the ice.

"When I put down this bowl, I'm going to give you a great big hug, Corey. I can't believe that our little Corey is old enough to be a mom," Fran said as they all trailed along behind Jack. "You know, Lucy, Corey was like my baby sister, always tagging along after me and Diane. She was such a little pest. Of course, that was when she wasn't playing with your husband."

"I've heard," Lucy said, looking at Corey with a cautious smile. "Tripp's dad told me that Corey and Tripp were inseparable when they were children. I can't wait to get her alone and find out what he was really like."

Corey didn't say anything as they walked upstairs and into the house. Diane was wiping her forehead and pulling baked beans out of the oven. "I don't know why I decided to make something that had to be cooked in the oven. I swear this kitchen must be one hundred degrees right now."

Fran winked at Corey and Lucy. "Feels fine in here to me, Diane—must be one of those hot flashes. Are you going through the change?"

"Phew on you," Diane said. "If I'm going through the change, then you must be, too, 'cause you are two months older than I am. By the way, I've given you a new name."

"Didn't know I needed one," Fran said, rearranging the refrigerator to make room for the broccoli salad.

"I thought Stella could call you Grannie Frannie," Diane said with a smile.

"Lovely, and what does she call you?"

"I am DiDi."

"How about DoDo instead?"

"You only think you're funny," said Diane.

Corey felt warm inside, listening to these two women argue over what her daughter was going to call them. "Have you heard any noise on the baby monitor?" asked Corey.

"No, and she looked sound asleep when I peeked in on her a few minutes ago," Diane said. "Let's fix ourselves a drink and go sit on the sunporch away from this heat. I've made sangria. Shall I pour a glass for everyone?"

"None for me," said Lucy. "I'll just have a glass of ice water."

"Um . . . no alcohol? I wonder if that means anything," said Fran.

Corey watched as Lucy's face turned beet red, but she didn't say anything.

Taking pity on her, Corey said, "I love this sunporch. But I do sort of miss the old screened porch. I miss listening to the crickets chirping, and those old paddle-wheel fans blowing a cool breeze on us while we played spades."

"Maybe we could get up a game while you're here. How long you staying?" asked Fran.

"She may just stay forever," said Diane. "I'm not sure she can make it back to Atlanta, just her and Stella."

"Bad trip down?" asked Fran.

"Stella's not one of those babies that goes to sleep in the car. It took us eight hours because I had to stop every hour or so and let her out of the car seat for a bit. If there were an airport anywhere close by, I would have parked my car and flown."

"Well, it will get easier," Fran said knowingly.

"And you know this because you have so much experience?" asked Diane. Fran and her husband were free spirits who'd never had children.

"Okay, I'm just trying to make Corey feel better," Fran said sheepishly.

Car headlights invaded the shadows on the sunporch as the guys returned from the store. "Jack!" Diane yelled. "They're back. Let's get some fish frying pronto. I don't want to eat at ten tonight."

It wasn't quite ten when they sat down to eat, but it was close. The three drinking women had downed several glasses of sangria by that time, and Diane and Fran were heavily into catching Corey up on the small-town Marianna gossip. Their information was only of minimal interest to Corey, and she was sure it held none whatsoever for Lucy, who nevertheless managed to smile politely and feign interest. Corey was beginning to develop a slight headache when the guys came up with the fish and hush puppies. When Tripp walked in, Corey felt her pulse quicken. Her eyes locked with his, and for once he was the first to turn away. Then, Corey's eyes fell on Lucy, who happened to be looking at her. Had she seen the look that had passed between Corey and Tripp? Maybe she was just imagining that Lucy seemed to be watching them. Perhaps her guilty conscience was working overtime?

"Oh man, I'm starving," Jack said as he sat down at the table, his plate brimming with food.

After the blessing was said, Lucy turned to Tripp. "Don't you think it's a good time to make our announcement?"

Corey watched as Tripp's face softened, looking down at Lucy. "Uh, yeah, why don't you do it, Luce?"

Lucy's eyes shimmered with excitement. "Tripp and I are going to have a baby."

"Congratulations!" Diane said immediately. "I had a feeling that you might be since you weren't drinking tonight."

In the deluge of good wishes that followed, Corey began to feel a little envious. She remembered how lonely and confused she'd felt when she first discovered she was pregnant. Wouldn't it have been nice to have been surrounded by well-wishers, as Lucy was now, and to have embraced her pregnancy with joy and happiness instead of shock and confusion?

Tripp seemed uncomfortable as they continued to be the center of attention. Corey noticed that he quickly shifted the subject away from the pregnancy to Jack's skill in cooking the fish.

Corey surreptitiously watched Tripp and Lucy together at the dinner table. Lucy seemed to sparkle next to him in a way that she hadn't when it had been just the women. She would place her hand on his arm to emphasize certain points during a story.

Just as they were finishing up dinner, the baby monitor came to life with Stella's cries. Corey jumped up immediately and went up the stairs quickly. Stella was sitting in her bed, crying. "Oh, poor baby." Stella's clothes were wet with sweat, and the room seemed much warmer than it was downstairs. Corey turned on the bedside light and pulled out some dry clothes. After changing her diaper and redressing her in clean pajamas, Corey decided she should get her some water and turn the air-conditioning down. Stella seemed bemused about what was going on when they walked downstairs and she saw all the people at the dinner table.

"DiDi," Stella immediately said, reaching out for Diane.

"Would you hold her while I fix her a bottle of water? It's really hot upstairs. I think we need to turn the air-conditioning down."

"Of course." Diane took Stella from Corey. Stella laid her head down on Diane's shoulder and started sucking her thumb.

When she had a bottle of water in hand, Corey took an unwilling Stella from Diane and carried her back upstairs. Corey rocked her awhile, holding the bottle, before finally placing her back down in the bed. Stella whined a few times but then started sucking thirstily on the bottle.

By the time Corey got back downstairs, Lucy, Fran, and Diane were just finishing up washing the dinner dishes. "Your timing is perfect." Diane laughed.

"I love it when a plan comes together," Corey replied before remembering that Tripp had frequently used that phrase when they were growing up. She stole a look at him and caught him looking at her before he quickly looked away.

"I think it's time that we head out," Tripp said.

"Us too," Mark agreed. "See y'all at the marina at six a.m.?"

"I'll be there," said Tripp.

"Me too," agreed Jack.

CHAPTER 23

Corey didn't see Tripp or Lucy again for several days. On the Fourth of July, they were invited to the MacKinnon house for drinks and appetizers on the deck, and for a better view of the fireworks that would be shot off from the end of the pier. Corey tried to get out of going by saying she was afraid Stella wouldn't like the fireworks. But Diane was having none of it. "Stella will love the fireworks, you'll see."

So Corey found herself sitting on the deck of the MacKinnon beach house, holding a squirming Stella in her lap. Luckily, the deck was quite crowded with people. Fran and Mark were there, as well as several other people whom Corey didn't know. She wondered idly if Lucy's baby had also been conceived at this beach house. But then she stopped her thoughts from going any further in that direction.

Although Tripp was as far away as possible from Corey on the deck, at times she was certain she could feel his eyes upon her and Stella, and she had to restrain herself from looking in his direction to see if her feeling was correct.

When the first brilliant fireworks lit up the sky with loud pops, Stella jerked, flattened herself against Corey's chest, and then started crying loudly. Corey wished she could locate Diane at that moment and say, *See, I told you so.* But instead, she quickly carried Stella inside the beach house to calm her down. After a couple of minutes, Stella started looking at her new surroundings and then wanted to get down and explore. Corey stood her beside the sofa just as the door opened and Tripp came inside.

"Everything okay?" Tripp asked. Stella already seemed to recognize Tripp, because she smiled adoringly up at him. And then without so much as a pause, she let go of the sofa and took a few faltering steps toward him before falling on her diapered bottom halfway to him.

"Oh my gosh!" Corey cried out in surprise. "Stella just took her first steps!" She ran over to Stella, sat down beside her, stood her up, and said, "Come on, Stella, do it again!"

"Really? Her first steps? Hey, Stella, come on, do it again," Tripp said encouragingly as he got down on his knees. And just as though it were no big deal, Stella let go of Corey's leg that she'd been holding on to and started walking again. This time she made it all the way to Tripp. But once there she seemed to have second thoughts about what she was doing; she looked back at Corey and then plopped down right at Tripp's feet.

Corey crawled over to where Stella sat on the floor and hugged her excitedly. And it was just at that moment that Lucy opened the door. Her eyes registered surprise to see the three of them sitting closely together on the floor. "Hey, Lucy," Corey said immediately, "can you believe Stella just took her first steps?"

"I was wondering where you all were. The fireworks are over." Lucy continued to stare at them with intensity.

Tripp awkwardly pulled his tall frame up off the floor. "Sorry for missing the end of the fireworks. Stella just started walking toward me. Can you believe it? Her first steps."

Lucy slowly nodded her head in agreement. "Tripp, some people are starting to leave. Maybe you should come out and tell them good-bye."

"Sure." Tripp offered his hand to Corey to pull her up off the floor. She hesitantly put her hand in Tripp's grip and allowed him to haul her and Stella up.

"And I need to get Stella to bed," Corey said, trying to keep the squirming baby from getting back down on the floor.

"Yeah, I can see how sleepy she is." Tripp smiled.

Corey went outside, found Diane, and told her Stella's big news.

"You little rat," Diane said, shaking her finger at Stella. "After I've spent the last four days trying to get you to take your first steps with me!"

"I'm going to take her home now. She needs to settle down so she'll go to sleep."

"Wait just a few minutes and I'll walk with you," Diane offered.

"Nah, you stay and enjoy. I'll see you back at the house." Corey walked over to Lucy and Tripp, still struggling with Stella. "We had a real good time. Thanks."

"Tripp, why don't you help Corey down the stairs with Stella?" Lucy offered.

Before Corey could respond, Tripp reached out, and Stella lunged toward him. "Come here, you little squirt," Tripp said.

Corey could hardly believe how much the father and daughter looked alike in that moment. She looked quickly to see if Lucy had noticed the same thing. But Lucy had turned to someone else who'd come to say good-bye and was no longer looking their way. Tripp started walking toward the steps, so Corey followed along behind him. Stella, the traitor, seemed perfectly happy without her mother.

Halfway down, Tripp turned back to Corey. "You've done a good job with her, Corey. I can tell you're a great mother."

"Thanks." Corey felt tears pooling in the corners of her eyes. They were at the bottom of the stairs, so Corey reached out for Stella.

"Let me carry her back to the house for you."

"You need to stay here with the rest of your guests," Corey said.

Tripp looked up at the many people still milling around. "Yeah, I guess you're right." He closed his eyes and leaned his face close to Stella's hair for just a minute, as if he were inhaling her smell. Then he held her out to Corey.

Morning came much sooner than Corey would have liked. Perhaps Jack woke Stella when he left before six to go fishing. But for whatever reason, Stella, always an early riser, was up earlier than usual. To keep her from waking everyone else in the house, Corey decided to pack her a "to go" breakfast and take it down to the beach. They didn't need the umbrella so early in the morning, so she just grabbed a chair, some towels, and the toys. Corey imagined they'd have the beach and the sun, which had just risen, all to themselves for a while.

Once on the beach, Corey realized her mistake about breakfast. Stella was too excited to sit still and eat. Finally, Stella managed to eat a few handfuls of Cheerios mixed in with a little sand. They hadn't been on the beach too long, when Corey noticed a tiny dot of a person way down the beach walking toward them. Corey watched the dot for a while until it grew larger, and she realized it was Lucy, meandering slowly, picking up seashells as she went. When she was almost to them, Corey had to wave, and Lucy responded by walking up to where they were sitting.

"Find any good ones?" Corey asked.

"I like this one," Lucy said, holding up a brown-and-white-striped scallop shell, which Stella immediately reached for.

"No, Stella, that's Miss Lucy's shell."

"Oh, it's fine," Lucy said, offering the shell to Stella and then immediately pulling it back. "I mean, if it's okay for her to have it."

"Sure. Did you get left alone today?"

"I'm just a fisherman's widow," Lucy said, and then as if realizing how that must have sounded to a real widow, she added quickly, "I'm sorry. How thoughtless of me."

"Don't worry about it," Corey said. "Don't you like to fish?"

"I like to go out for a pleasure cruise, but that slow crawl they do when trolling for fish makes me seasick every time."

"Tried Dramamine?"

"Yeah, but I just go to sleep. I'd rather stay here and enjoy the day."

"Makes sense. How's the pregnancy going?" Corey asked.

"I haven't had any morning sickness yet, although I keep waiting for it," Lucy answered as she started picking up handfuls of sand and letting it sift through her fingers.

"You're lucky, then. I was sick every morning for about a month. But I'm not complaining. Sitting here looking at Stella, I know it was all worth it."

"I really admire you for having the courage to have a baby alone," Lucy said.

"There was nothing admirable about my decision," Corey said honestly. "It was a purely selfish decision."

"Stella's a cutie. Must have been exciting for you to see her take her first steps last night?"

"Yes, I had been so afraid she would do it while I was at work."

"Do you have someone come in, or do you take Stella to daycare?"

"I have the most remarkable babysitter, who is literally Stella's second mother. Or, maybe, she's her first mother and I'm her second mother. I'm not sure," Corey said with a smile.

"That's what I'm the most nervous about, finding the right child-care. That's why I'm planning on going back to working the weekend shift, so that I can take care of the baby during the week, and Tripp can take care of the baby on the weekends."

"Really? If you're off during the week and he's off during the weekends, when will you see each other?"

"Oh, I just mean for the first couple of years, not forever."

Corey remembered how one week had seemed like two years with a newborn baby. *How would Tripp handle those weekends alone with a baby, unable to go fishing or do anything else?*

Lucy stopped sifting sand and brushed her hands together to get the sand off. "Tripp said that you went off to college at Auburn and have hardly been back here, even for visits. What made you decide to stay away?"

The question—from this person she barely knew—was disconcerting to Corey. Plus, she'd never really thought about why she hadn't made more of an effort to come back. "It wasn't a conscious decision to stay away," Corey said slowly. "It was more like my life just didn't bring me back here. You know . . . I had law school, and then my parents died. I guess it was hard to come back after they died. Then I moved to Atlanta and married someone not from this area who didn't care that much for the beach. Not to mention the insane hours I was working when I was first hired." Corey's words kind of trailed off without a conclusion.

"You've certainly had more than your share of losses," Lucy said empathetically. "Your parents and your husband within such a short period of time. I'm amazed at how you've handled it all."

"Believe me, if there had been an option other than handling it, I would have taken it. You're from Ohio, right? What brought you to Dothan?" Corey asked, trying to change the subject.

"A combination of work and personal reasons. I went through a nasty divorce after discovering that my first husband was having an affair with one of my friends. Then, the hospital where I was working began firing full-time nurses. When I got the pink slip, I decided it was a sign that I needed to move away from Cleveland and make a fresh start somewhere else. Dothan General was the first place that offered me a job."

"You must have gotten married right out of college because you seem so young. How old are you, if you don't mind me asking?"

"Of course not," Lucy replied. "I'm twenty-six, and I got married while I was going to nursing school to my high school sweetheart, the only boy I'd ever dated."

"So . . . is Tripp only the second person you've ever dated?" Corey asked incredulously.

"Yeah . . . ," Lucy said sheepishly. "Things went pretty fast with Tripp, too, I guess."

"And now a baby is on the way."

"As a matter of fact, I probably would have waited a few years to have children, but Tripp made it clear before we got married that he wanted children right away."

Corey, somewhat surprised at her blunt honesty, decided to answer in kind. "I had a similar experience with my husband. But I had just started my law career and I knew I couldn't do both at the time."

"Are you sorry now? Do you wish you'd had Stella earlier?"

Corey was blown away that Lucy was asking questions that no one—not Diane, not Kathryn—had ever asked her. "No, as a matter of fact, now that I have Stella, I know it would have been impossible for me to give Luke the care and time that he needed during those last few months and also care for a newborn baby. I thought going into my pregnancy that I could do it all. But since then, I've learned that having a baby is the most difficult thing I've ever done. You can't imagine how having a baby changes your life."

"Really?" Lucy asked hesitantly, and Corey knew immediately that she'd said the wrong thing to a first-time mom-to-be.

"It may be different for you," Corey said quickly. "Maybe motherhood will come more naturally to you."

"Um . . . I guess we'll see."

Corey was suddenly anxious to end this conversation. "I didn't expect to stay down here this long, and I didn't leave a note telling Diane where we are. I think we'd better head up."

"Oh, okay, well, I guess I'd better say good-bye. We're leaving tomorrow for Ohio to see my folks."

"Is it hard to be so far away from your family?"

"Yeah, I miss them a lot."

"Well, enjoy seeing all of them this week. And good luck with the pregnancy!"

"Thanks!"

CHAPTER 24

Late in the afternoon, Jack headed back to Marianna because he had to work the next day, and Marcy went with him to go to a friend's birthday party. For once, Diane said she was tired of cooking and wanted to go to Port Saint Joe for some Mexican food.

"I don't know . . . ," Corey said. "I'm not sure how Stella will do in a restaurant."

"Come on, Corey, you've got to start living a normal life with Stella."

Rather sheepishly, Corey agreed, "Okay, let's go."

Pecos, the Mexican restaurant, had a mariachi band that night, and Stella was enraptured with the music and the hats and the instruments the musicians played. She laughed at the men when they came by their table, then stared at them intently the remainder of the time. Diane ordered a jumbo margarita straight up because Corey was driving.

"See, she's just fine," Diane said, reaching for a chip. "You really need to lighten up and take her out more often."

"You're right, I know. It's just that she was so bad for so long that it's hard to get over it."

"It'd be easier if you had someone to share the responsibility with," Diane began. "I think—"

Corey interrupted her. "No joke. But I really don't need you to tell me I told you so right now."

"Excuse me, I wasn't about to say anything except that I wish you lived closer to me so that I could help you."

The mariachi band came back at that moment, making it impossible for Corey to answer her. Finally, when they moved away a little bit, Diane continued, "Why are you living in Atlanta anyway?"

"My job is there, for one thing," Corey said. "Plus, there's so much to do: plays, museums, sports."

"Really, what do you do other than work?"

"Since Stella was born, I really haven't had time to do much of anything, you know."

"Before Stella, what did you do?"

"Well, Luke was ill."

"And before that?"

"I don't remember."

"My point exactly. I think you love your job. But other than that, you've got no reason to be living there."

"I have friends and Nancy."

"You see Nancy once a week, and you have Kathryn and Romeo and Gary. Who else?"

"Okay, you've made your point. I need to make some more friends."

"You see, Corey, I feel like you're living Luke's life. Not *your* life."

"You don't know what you're talking about," Corey said angrily. "I think the tequila is doing your talking."

"You know, there are other jobs. If Marianna is too small for you, you could move to Tallahassee or Dothan. I'd love for you to move somewhere where I would be close enough to help you with Stella."

"Well, it's not all about you," Corey retorted.

"Yeah, I know. It's always been all about you."

"What do you mean?"

"Do you ever think that maybe I get tired of always going to Atlanta to see you? Do you ever think that maybe I'd like to do Thanksgiving at my house one year? Do you ever think that I miss Mom and Dad too? I miss our family, and I'd really like to have my sister and my niece— what's left of my family—around me more often!"

Corey was stunned when she saw the tears brimming in Diane's eyes. Something in the universe shifted, and Corey realized that it hadn't always been easy for Diane to take care of her, even though she'd never complained. Perhaps it was because she was now a mother, but Corey suddenly realized that she'd been selfish in her behavior toward Diane, always taking and hardly ever giving anything back.

"I'm sorry, Di. You're the best sister that's ever been, and I'm the worst."

"No, I think you were right the first time," Diane said with a tearful hiccup.

Corey looked confused.

"I can't drink tequila."

Later that night after Stella was sound asleep, Corey lay in bed staring at the ceiling. She couldn't get her conversation with Diane out of her mind. Corey remembered how Diane had sent Jack to Ole Miss to tell her about their parents' accident and bring Corey home to Marianna so that she hadn't been forced to make that long drive home alone. It had never occurred to Corey before, but when Diane sent Jack to her at Ole Miss, Diane had been left alone to take care of Marcy, as well as their mother, who was in the hospital, and to make funeral arrangements for their dad. She also remembered how disappointed Diane had been when she and Luke decided to get married in Atlanta. Still,

Diane had managed to arrange an amazing wedding for Corey over the phone, and she'd always traveled to Atlanta to look at wedding dresses, or whatever else Corey needed. She'd never appreciated all the sacrifices Diane had made for her.

The next morning, for once, Stella slept in a bit later than usual. Corey had tossed and turned all night so was happy to have a little extra sleep. When she finally got up and took Stella downstairs, Diane was already sitting out on the sunporch, drinking coffee. Corey paused at the entrance.

"I'm sorry, Diane." Corey began.

"For what?"

"For not appreciating all that you've done for me over the years. I've been incredibly selfish and self-centered. But I promise you I'm going to do better."

"Just promise me you'll think about moving back."

Corey put Stella down on the floor. Stella immediately ran over to Diane, who picked her up and gave her a big hug.

"Diane, I've got to think about what's best for Stella. In Atlanta, she'll be exposed to a variety of different types of people and cultures. I just want her to have a different childhood than I had—one filled with limitless possibilities."

Diane looked shocked. "That sounds like something Luke would say. I didn't know you felt your childhood had been so lacking. I mean, despite growing up in such a primitive environment, you were able to make it through college and law school. You were able to become a hotshot lawyer at a big-time law firm in a big city. What more did you want?"

"Oh come on, Diane," Corey said, frustrated. "You know that for every person like me, there are a dozen more who never make it out of Jackson County."

Diane's face turned red, and she turned to Corey angrily. "Like me? Like Jack?"

"Well, no, of course I wasn't talking about you and Jack. You both went away to college, you have professions, and you chose to live in Marianna. I just want Stella to know that there's a different kind of life outside of northwest Florida."

"Corey, don't you think it's time you started living *your* life? Not the life Mom and Dad wanted for you, not the life Luke wanted for you, and not the life you want for Stella. What do *you* want? You would think that, after losing Mom and Dad and Luke, you would realize that life is way too short to be going through the motions without really living, like you've been doing for years."

"You don't know how hard it was for me to even go through the motions of living after losing Luke on top of Mom and Dad. I mean, you still have Jack and Marcy."

"I can't imagine how hard that was. But you've got Stella now. Corey, you and I grew up with family around—people who knew us. And we grew up in Marianna, and it seemed to work out okay for us. I really want to be a part of Stella's life, and I miss my little sister. Just think about the possibility of moving somewhere closer to us. Tallahassee or Dothan would be good possibilities. I hear they do practice law in a few places outside of Atlanta, you know."

Corey smiled at Diane's weak attempt at humor. "Okay, I promise to give the possibility some thought."

CHAPTER 25

The trip back to Atlanta was as torturous as the trip down had been. Stella was like a trapped animal in her car seat. She squirmed and fussed and carried on until Corey wished she'd kept some of the drops Dr. Carrington had given her to calm Stella as a baby. They stopped at every McDonald's playground between Dothan and Atlanta so that Stella could get out of her car seat and run around awhile. About an hour outside of Atlanta, Stella gave it up and finally went to sleep.

Corey savored the sudden peace in the car, as she hadn't been able to think straight with Stella's constant fretting. She kept going over and over her conversation with Diane, and she kept wondering how she was going to fit Tripp into Stella's future life. She ought to be making a plan for how things were going to work with Tripp. But she really felt clueless about what that plan should be.

Then a line from one of John Lennon's songs popped into her head: *"Life is what happens to you while you're busy making other plans."* That had certainly been true for her. When she'd gone to law school, she had fully intended on moving back to Marianna and opening her own law practice—secure in the familiarity of family and friends. Her parents' deaths had changed that plan. By marrying Luke, Corey had chosen a different path, but one that had seemed just as secure and comfortable as the previous one. Yet, Corey had watched that security dissolve in the few moments it took a doctor to utter the word *cancer*. Corey wasn't sure how she'd ended up where she was today, but one thing was certain—she sure hadn't planned it this way.

Once back in Atlanta, Corey was happy to get back into her routine, and Stella was excited to be back with Millie. Corey told herself that Millie was the same thing as family to Stella, and, of course, Stella also had Kathryn, Romeo, and Gary, as well as her nana in her life. Stella did have her family around her.

Corey was also glad to be back because Nancy had been sick during their absence. She'd come down with the flu the day after they left. She hadn't been sick enough to call Corey to return, but Nancy still hadn't recovered fully, and Corey wondered why it was taking so long. Nancy was pale and weak and spent much more time in bed sleeping than she ever had, to Corey's knowledge. She was going to have to somehow get Stella over to visit with Nancy now that she couldn't come to them. But realistically, between her job and Stella, Corey wasn't sure she could do much more than she was already doing.

One night about a month after she'd returned from the beach, her cell phone rang at eleven, jolting her out of an incredibly sound sleep that she'd been in for only thirty minutes or so. Her first thought was, *Oh no, something's happened to Nancy.* She picked up the phone hurriedly and said a terse "Hello."

Only half-awake, she heard a vaguely familiar man's voice say, "Oh, I woke you up. I'm sorry."

"Tripp?" Corey asked. "What's wrong?"

"I know it's late, but I want to come to Atlanta tomorrow and see Stella."

Corey sat up in bed, trying to clear the confusion from her head. "Tomorrow?"

"I just found out there's a banking convention in Atlanta. I told Lucy that I'd been on a waiting list for a cancellation, and I just found out there's an opening."

"You mean you're lying to Lucy about going to a banking convention?"

"There *is* a banking convention in Atlanta for the next three days."

"But you aren't going?"

"Well, no."

"So . . . that's lying."

"Yeah, it's kind of like saying you're pregnant by artificial insemination when you got pregnant the old-fashioned way."

"I guess I deserved that."

"Look, I didn't call to get into a fight with you. Can I please come tomorrow?"

"I guess so . . . but next time, please give me a bit more warning."

Corey left work early the next afternoon to make it home before Tripp was to arrive. Still, when she turned into the building's parking lot, she wasn't surprised to see that he was already sitting in his white Yukon out in front of her building. Was the jumpiness she felt due to seeing Tripp, or the fact that she'd worked through lunch without eating anything? When she pulled up next to him, she could see through his lowered window that he looked a little sweaty. It was probably ninety-five degrees, and she wondered how long he'd been sitting in his car in the heat.

"Fear of Atlanta traffic again?" she asked, getting out of her car. Tripp smiled weakly at her as he got out of his SUV. He wore a pair of faded jeans that she wouldn't have noticed had they been at the beach, but that seemed oddly out of place in front of her condo. "You could have gone inside. I told Millie we were having company this afternoon."

"It is rather toasty out here today." Tripp wiped his hand across his face. "Millie is Stella's nanny?"

"Yeah." Corey walked up the sidewalk. "Come on in before you pass out."

As Corey walked through the front door, Stella came running up and threw herself at her mother's legs, almost knocking her over. "Hey, darling," Corey picked her up and swung her around in a circle in their little afternoon ritual.

Millie came out from the kitchen just then. "You're home early today. Oh, and your company is already here."

"Yes, Millie, this is Tripp MacKinnon. Tripp is a childhood friend of mine. And, Tripp, this is Millie Simpkins, my saving grace."

"Nice to meet you, Ms. Simpkins," Tripp said, holding out his hand politely and flashing her one of his most charming smiles.

Corey swore that Millie started blushing.

"Just call me Millie, please," she said in her soft southern drawl. "Ms. Corey, everything is ready in the kitchen. Do you mind if I go on even if it is thirty minutes early?"

Corey realized that Millie already had her large carrying purse in her hand and was ready to walk out the door. "Of course not, Millie," Corey said. "I'll see you tomorrow morning."

Once the door closed after Millie, Tripp turned to Stella. "Do you remember me?" he asked, holding out his arms to her.

Stella put her head down against her mother's shoulder and then immediately peeked back at him. "She's just playing hard to get." Corey laughed.

"Come here, you rascal," Tripp said, continuing to hold out his arms. Stella looked him up and down for a moment or two more before she finally leaned over into his outstretched arms. Tripp pulled her in close and twirled around in a circle, much like Corey had done when she'd first come through the door.

"Not fair," Corey said. "She'll never leave your arms as long as you're doing that." The funny feeling in her stomach seemed to be spreading into her throat as she watched Stella laughing so freely in her father's arms.

"Well, then, why don't you go get changed out of that fancy suit, since we don't need you here."

"Okay," Corey said slowly. "I'll be right back."

Corey went into her bedroom and grabbed a pair of jeans and a white top. She then decided to brush her teeth and put a bit more powder on her face. *Why not?* she thought defiantly. But she stopped short at putting on some lipstick, which might imply too much effort on her part. *Why is Tripp here?* Her day had been so crazy that she hadn't had time to worry about his visit until her ride home today. *What does his unexpected arrival mean?* Corey had a really bad feeling as she walked into the great room. She was surprised to see Stella riding Tripp's back in a circle around the sofa. "Stella, do you want some animal crackers?"

Immediately, Stella started trying to dismount. Tripp reached around and caught her before she fell, and then sat her carefully on the floor. Stella jumped up and ran happily toward Corey.

"No fair. How can I compete with cookies?" he asked.

"Come on into the kitchen. I have a couple of beers if you'd like one."

Tripp followed Corey and Stella into the kitchen. "Smells wonderful in here."

Corey got a sippy cup down from the cabinet, poured some juice, and put Stella in her booster seat at the table with her juice and cookies. Stella happily sucked on one of the cookies before taking a big gulp of juice. "Millie is a fabulous cook. She cooks dinner during the day and leaves it for us to eat at night. I hope you like pot roast—it's one of her specialties."

"I love pot roast." Tripp stared at Stella sitting in her booster chair. "How can she look so much bigger in just a few weeks?" Tripp asked.

"Sometimes I think she gets bigger during the day while I'm at work. Is Bud Light okay?"

Tripp nodded. Corey turned toward him, holding a Bud Light and a Coke in her hands. "You not drinking?" Tripp asked.

"Not usually during the week, and never until after I get Stella bathed and to bed. Let's sit here until she finishes her snack." Corey sat down on the bench across from Stella, and she took a long sip of her Coke. She decided to go ahead and ask the question that had been bothering her since eleven the night before. "So, why are you here?"

Tripp looked more uncomfortable than Corey had ever seen him. After several sips of beer, he said, "Lucy lost the baby."

Corey was stunned. She wasn't sure what she'd expected him to say, but that hadn't been it. "I'm sorry. What happened?"

"We went in for her first doctor's visit last week, and the doctor couldn't find a heartbeat."

"How did Lucy take it?"

"She was upset that day, but actually she's taken the news better than me since then. I think she feels that she's young and has plenty of time to get pregnant."

"She is and she does."

"Yeah, but now she's decided that this is some sort of sign that she's not ready to have children. She says she wants to wait a few years, maybe even until she's thirty."

Corey remembered their conversation on the beach and immediately felt guilty. "That's not that long, just three or four years." Stella had finished her snack and was ready to get down from the table. Corey got up and wet a paper towel to wipe her mouth. Once she was clean, Corey stood her up on the floor.

"Whir, whir," Stella demanded of Tripp, holding up her arms.

"See what you started?" Corey asked. "Come on, let's go into her room. Maybe we can distract her with some special toys that I keep hidden away for emergencies."

"Let's show your room to . . ." Corey stumbled over the right word to use. She'd started to say Tripp but then thought he might take offense at being addressed so informally. Finally, she said, "Come on, let's go play in your room." Corey started down the hall, with Stella and Tripp following behind her.

"Is this your room?" Tripp asked Stella as Corey reached behind a box on a shelf in the closet. She pulled out a toddler-style piano, and Stella clapped her hands together in excitement.

"I try to keep this put up because it makes so much noise, but she does love it," Corey said.

"I see what you mean," Tripp said, as Stella immediately sat down in front of it and started pressing every key at once.

"She'll be okay in here for a little while. Let's go back to the great room, where we can hear each other speak."

They walked back into the other room, and she sat down across from Tripp. Corey couldn't think of what she should say, so she just sat there fidgeting with the fringe on one of the sofa pillows.

Tripp cleared his throat. "I know I should have given you more warning that I was coming. But I've been missing Stella, and this thing with Lucy losing the baby has sent me for a loop. When I saw the advertisement for this banking conference, I just decided on an impulse that I had to come."

"It's okay this time." Corey continued flipping the pillow's fringe. "However, I'd appreciate a bit more warning next time."

"I'll give you at least two weeks' notice, I promise." Tripp smiled warmly at her, and Corey felt her heart skip a beat in response.

Suddenly there was a shrill cry from the bedroom, and both Corey and Tripp immediately jumped up and ran back to Stella's room. Stella was sitting on the floor where they'd left her, but tears were coursing down her face. She held her hand out toward them. "Boo-boo."

Corey took her hand and saw that the corner of one of her fingers was red. "She must have pinched her finger somehow."

"It doesn't look too serious."

"I guess I shouldn't have left her alone in here. I've hardly ever done that."

"Relax, Corey, she's fine. You can't be with her every minute."

Corey realized he was right and that she was overreacting. "You want Mommy to kiss your boo-boo?" Corey asked Stella, taking her hand.

"No, him." Stella said, sniffling and holding her hand out to Tripp.

Tripp leaned over and kissed it. "Come on, princess, let's whir some more." Soon Tripp had her laughing again while Corey took the piano and put it back in its hiding place. She couldn't help thinking how much easier everything would be with two parents.

"Stella usually eats dinner about now. I skipped lunch, so I'm starving. Could you possibly eat this early?" Corey asked.

"I can always eat," Tripp said, giving her another one of his adorable smiles that made her heart flutter.

When the three of them sat around the table, Corey couldn't help but think that this was what a real family looked like at dinner. When it was just Corey and Stella, she always felt like they were pretending to be a family. Corey suddenly imagined Tripp helping to give Stella her bath and putting her to bed, and the pictures that flashed through her mind were so appealing that she had to force herself to remember that she wasn't his wife and this wasn't his home. He had a wife and a home in Dothan. This fairy-tale picture of domesticity she was conjuring up in her mind was dangerous in many ways.

To avoid any more imaginings, Corey told Tripp to watch some television while she bathed Stella. When she finally brought Stella out clean and dressed to tell Tripp good night, she was surprised to see that he was just finishing up the dishes, and the kitchen was immaculate.

"Thanks for cleaning up," Corey said. "Stella, say good night." Instead, Stella squirmed in Corey's arms to get down. She ran over to Tripp and hugged his legs. He picked her up and kissed her head while holding her close.

"Could I carry her back to bed?"

"She'll probably settle down faster if you don't. I'll be back in five minutes or so. The remote for the television is on the table by the sofa."

Coming back from Stella's room, Corey was surprised to see that Tripp hadn't turned on the television but was looking through Stella's baby book that had been sitting on the coffee table. He looked up at her with a look in his eyes that she couldn't read. Was it anger?

"Will you tell me about all of these pictures?" he asked.

Corey sat down next to him on the sofa. As he flipped through the pictures, she narrated. "That was the day she discovered her feet. That was her six-month birthday. That's Millie's daughter, Deborah, holding her." And on and on they went, until they finished the entire book. When he finally closed the book, Corey realized how close they were sitting, and she moved back a little.

"I wish I could have been there for every one of those things," Tripp said slowly. Corey didn't know what to say, so she didn't say anything. For some reason, she was suddenly finding it hard to breathe. "Since Lucy lost the baby, I've been doing a lot of thinking about you and Stella," he continued.

"Don't go there, Tripp," Corey warned, and she started to get up from the sofa. Tripp reached out and grabbed her hand. His touch sent a shock wave through Corey that made her freeze. When he leaned in toward her, she knew she needed to get away from him, but for some reason her body didn't move. Looking straight into his eyes, she knew he was going to kiss her, but she didn't even try to pull away. Their mouths met, and she couldn't help but respond to his kiss. She felt his hands on the back of her head pulling her in closer, and she still didn't try to stop him. Yet somehow when his hands started down her back, she found the strength to wrench herself away, and she stood in front of him, gasping for breath.

"Stop, Tripp. We've been down this path before, remember?"

"It just feels so right."

"But it's not right. And you have a wife now."

Tripp ran his hands through his hair in an agitated manner. "I know, I know. But I'm beginning to wonder if I didn't marry Lucy just so I could have a family. Corey, I think about you and Stella all the time." He looked up at her in a pained way. "I want you so badly right now, and you want me, too, or you're a pretty good actress."

"Tripp, it would be so easy for me to just go with what I'm feeling right now. But I allowed myself to go with my emotions once before with you, and it changed my life forever. I won't do it again. So don't come to Atlanta thinking anything else. You can see Stella. You are her father, but keep your hands to yourself."

Tripp's face changed from conflicted to stormy. "You were sitting there all cuddly next to me, sending out all kinds of signals, and you know you were."

"I think you'd better leave," Corey said, walking toward the door.

Tripp closed his eyes and took a deep breath. When he stood up, the anger seemed to have left him. "I'm sorry, Corey. You're right. I just feel so confused all the time. I'm constantly comparing Lucy to you and wondering if maybe I didn't rush into marriage too fast with her."

"I'm sorry, too, Tripp," Corey said in a conciliatory voice. "But the facts are that you do have a wife, and she doesn't deserve for her husband to be lying to her and doing things like this. You need to go home and figure out what it is that you do want. I like Lucy—she seems like a nice person. Don't you think she deserves better from you than this?"

"Is there a chance for you, me, and Stella to be a family?" Tripp asked, standing at the door.

"Tripp, why didn't you ask if there was a chance for you and me? I don't want you fooling yourself into thinking that you care for me just because I happen to have your daughter."

"I don't. You have to admit that when we're together, there are sparks."

"Yes," Corey said unemotionally and calmly, "you're right. There's always been something between us. I just don't know what it is. I compare it to what I had with Luke, and it doesn't seem like love. Luke and I had a relationship based on trust as well as passion. I've never been able to trust you, Tripp. You've let me down more times than you can possibly know. And I've reached the point in my life where I won't settle for anything less than what I had with Luke. Not even for Stella's sake. Go home to your wife, Tripp. Grow up. And if one day you find yourself single, then maybe, just maybe, you and I might start to think about building a relationship. But please know that I'm not promising you anything."

"What about Stella? Can I see her tomorrow before I head back?"

"Yeah, you can come over for as long as you want while I'm at work. Just be gone before five thirty." Tripp squared his shoulders and waved wordlessly as he walked out the door.

CHAPTER 26

Corey called Kathryn to talk over what had happened, but she didn't answer. She left Kathryn a message and went to take a shower. When she got out of the shower and saw that she had a message, Corey quickly retrieved it, hopeful that she might get some sleep if she was able to review everything with her friend.

"Ms. Bennett, this is Peachtree Wilden. Please call Laney Hill immediately at extension 501."

With a racing heart, Corey quickly punched in the number to Peachtree Wilden. "This is Corey Bennett," she said when connected to the appropriate person.

"Ms. Bennett, we think Nancy had a stroke tonight. She didn't come down for dinner, which isn't that unusual, but when we realized that she hadn't called for her meal to be delivered to her room, we decided we better check on her. They found her unresponsive on the floor. She's being transported to Northside Hospital by ambulance."

"I'll be there as quickly as I can," Corey said, immediately thinking about who she could get to keep Stella while she went to the hospital. Kathryn still hadn't returned her call. Romeo and Gary had taken a few days off and gone to New York. She could call Ralph and Judy—they could probably fill in for a few hours—but she wasn't sure how long she might be, and they both had to work the next morning. She could take Stella with her but was afraid of what she might face at the hospital. Corey had a sudden thought. *What about Tripp?* Without stopping to think much, she found his number in her cell phone and hit the "Call" button.

Tripp answered after the first ring. "Corey?"

"Something has happened to Luke's mother, and she's on her way to the hospital. Do you think you could come over and stay with Stella so that I can go to her?"

"I'll be there as quickly as I can, probably in about fifteen minutes."

"Thanks so much, Tripp. This means a lot to me."

Corey changed back into her jeans and sweater and applied a quick touch of makeup to her face. She was just finishing up when she heard a faint knock on the door. When she opened it, she could tell from the concerned look on Tripp's face that their earlier argument was forgotten. Corey was so thankful to see him standing there that she wanted to throw her arms around him and give him a big hug. But she restrained herself and just launched into what he needed to know. "Stella probably won't wake up, but if she does, just give her some water. Here's her sippy cup, and maybe rock her a bit before putting her back to bed. I don't know how long I'll be, but I'll call you as soon as I get some idea. If you get sleepy, the guest-room bed is made up with clean sheets, so feel free to go to bed."

Tripp said, "We'll be fine—go see about your mother-in-law."

As she drove to the hospital, Corey couldn't help but think about what a blessing it was that Tripp happened to be in town and available to stay with Stella. Corey had never considered what she would do in an emergency situation like this. She really needed to establish more of a support system.

When Corey walked into the hospital, the antiseptic smell of industrial cleaning agents—so familiar from her frequent visits to the hospital when Luke was there—made her suddenly feel queasy. She went to the information desk, where a gray-haired woman in a starched pink jumper was reading a book. "May I help you?" the woman asked.

"Have you admitted Nancy Bennett?" Corey asked.

The woman punched keys on a computer for a few moments and then looked back up at her. "She's still in the emergency room with Dr. Aziz. Do you know how to get there?"

Corey nodded her head. She'd made this trip more than a couple of times. "Thanks, I know the way," she said as she headed toward the double doors that would take her to emergency.

Dr. Aziz was not at all what Corey expected. Ironically, when the emergency-room nurse took Corey to where Nancy was, Corey thought the dark-headed young woman with the shockingly red streaks in her hair and the row of earrings must be an orderly of some sort. When she turned around and introduced herself as the doctor, Corey was momentarily stunned.

"Are you her relative?" Dr. Aziz asked, pointing to Nancy, who lay on a bed attached to myriad machines. One of the machines was making a whooshing sound that Corey found oddly calming.

"I'm her daughter-in-law. I got here as quickly as I could. How is she?"

"Not good," Dr. Aziz said bluntly. "She's having trouble breathing, and the scans show that she's suffered a significant brain hemorrhage. Unfortunately, I suspect that she had the stroke several hours before she was found."

"Will she recover?"

Dr. Aziz looked at her for a moment or two. "I'm not going to sugarcoat this. Unless we see vast improvements in the next twenty-four hours, her odds are pretty grim."

Corey felt as though she'd been punched in the stomach. "What can I do?"

"Stay with her; talk to her. Hopefully, you'll get some sort of reaction that will show us that she's cognizant about what's going on around her. We're going to have to move her out of emergency and up to a room in intensive care." She sighed deeply. "Do you know if she has a medical directive or a living will?"

"No, I don't. Her son, I mean, my husband," Corey stuttered, "died fairly recently. I never talked about this kind of stuff with her."

A fleeting look of compassion crossed Dr. Aziz's face. "Well, maybe tomorrow you might try calling someone who handles her affairs and see what you can find out."

"It's that serious?" Corey asked, sounding remarkably calm in spite of her racing heart.

"I'm afraid so." Dr. Aziz turned to look at one of the machines that was suddenly—and apparently unexpectedly—beeping. She pushed a button and the noise stopped. "I'm going to go, but I'll be back in a moment to oversee her transfer."

"I need to make a quick phone call," Corey said, following Dr. Aziz into the fluorescent-lit hallway. As Dr. Aziz went behind the nurse's station, Corey dialed Tripp's cell-phone number.

He answered on the first ring. "Everything okay?"

"It's pretty serious. I probably need to stay the night here. Can you stay with Stella? Millie will be there in the morning, and sometimes Stella doesn't even wake up before Millie gets there."

"Sure, Corey. Don't worry. I'll call you if I have any questions."

"I really appreciate this."

"You don't have to thank me, Corey. She's my daughter. I wish I could spend every night with her. Good night."

◆　◆　◆

Later, after Nancy was transferred out of emergency, Corey sat beside her on the hard leather chair, listening to the whoosh, whoosh of the machines, and the periodic ping of the elevator doors opening and closing in the hall. Corey talked to Nancy, as the doctor had suggested. She told her about all the latest things Stella had been doing, and Corey peered at her carefully to see if there was any reaction. Finally, after a couple of hours with no sign of a response, Corey put her head down on the bed beside Nancy's arm and cried. She cried for Nancy, for Luke, for her parents, but mostly she cried for herself because she felt so overwhelmingly alone.

Dr. Aziz unexpectedly walked in, took one look at Corey sobbing on the edge of Nancy's bed, came over, and put her hand on her shoulder. "I'm sorry," she said. "I'm sure she had a full life and wouldn't want to linger in this kind of state."

"I . . . know . . . that," Corey sniffled. "I think I'm crying more for myself than for her."

"It may sound like a bunch of crap, but it's true—getting all of that emotion out of you can really make you feel better. Sometimes there's nothing like a good cry."

Corey smiled at her weakly, thinking how bizarre it was being comforted by someone who looked more like a punk rocker than a physician. Then, suddenly it hit her that tomorrow was also a workday. Her mind started sorting through all the things she needed to do. She needed to call Larry and let him know about her situation. She had one appointment that couldn't be postponed and would have to be shifted to another associate. Everything else could be postponed for a day or so. She felt guilty thinking about such mundane things when Nancy lay before her in such a critical state, possibly even dying.

"Well, this is it for me tonight," Dr. Aziz said. "Tomorrow, Mrs. Bennett's physician, Dr. Randall, will take over. If I don't see you again, I wish you well."

"Thanks. I appreciate everything you've done."

"You're welcome." And with a slight wave, she was out the door.

Corey napped for a few minutes at a time, off and on for the remainder of the night. When Dr. Randall came in around seven the next morning, she was just about to go out into the hall and call Tripp. Corey had met Dr. Randall only once before when she'd taken Nancy to a doctor's appointment. Unlike Dr. Aziz, Dr. Randall was the stereotypical doctor who would have been right at home on any weeknight television show involving doctors. He wore a crisp white coat, introduced himself in a brusque manner, and immediately went to work, checking the hospital's charts and Nancy's pulse and other vital signs. When he turned to her, he didn't beat around the bush. "The results of her EEG aren't promising. They don't show any sign of brain activity. At her age, and with her already deteriorating health, I don't see the possibility of a good outcome here."

"So, what are you saying?"

"I'm saying that she is unlikely to recover from this vegetative state. I think you and her other family should start talking about what Nancy would want."

"She doesn't have any other family, and I'm just her daughter-in-law. I don't feel qualified to make these types of decisions for her."

Dr. Randall looked somewhat sympathetically at Corey for the first time since he'd entered the room. "Well, you don't have to make any decisions today. How about I send someone in from counseling to talk to you?"

Corey nodded yes. A counselor might be a good thing. She'd never felt so alone in her life. At least when decisions had to be made for Luke, she'd had Nancy to help her.

"I've got to finish my rounds now. I'll have the nurses contact me immediately if there is any change."

Corey nodded her head again, and the doctor was gone. She looked down one more time at the immobile body in the bed, which already seemed less and less like Nancy. She went out to the hall to make some calls. She called Millie first. She didn't want her to be surprised when she arrived to find Tripp there, but Millie must have already left, because no one answered her phone. Next, she called Tripp, and he provided her with a factual exchange of information in answer to her questions.

No, Millie wasn't there. Yes, Stella had slept through the night. No, Stella wasn't up yet. Yes, he would be careful not to scare Millie when she arrived. Finally, he was able to get a question in of his own. "Do you want me to stay another night? I'm not expected back in Dothan until tomorrow."

Corey thought hard about her alternatives. Millie might be able to get someone to stay with her daughter so that she could stay with Stella overnight. But that was a long shot. Kathryn, who had yet to call her back, might be able to stay. Having another night to sort through the situation would be a good thing. "That would help me a lot," Corey finally said at last.

"Okay, then once Millie gets here, I'll go check out of my motel and bring my stuff here. Can I come to the hospital and bring you some lunch?"

Corey felt her eyes tearing up. "Sure, that would be great. I'm at Northside Hospital, room 317."

After gaining some composure, she dialed Larry's cell phone. When he answered, she could tell he was driving from the noise in the background. "Larry, my mother-in-law was admitted to Northside last night after suffering a stroke. She's in the intensive care unit, and it's not looking real good."

"I'm so sorry," Larry said apologetically.

"I need to be with her as much as possible today to take care of some things."

"Of course," Larry said. "Do what you have to do. And keep me posted if anything changes."

She returned to the room, where Nancy remained exactly as she'd left her. Corey supposed she'd better go home and change and then go over to Peachtree Wilden to look for Nancy's living will. If she was lucky, the facility would have a copy of the document on file there. I'll be back as soon as I can," Corey said to Nancy before squeezing her hand. "I love you, Nancy."

CHAPTER 27

What a strange feeling it was to walk into her home and see Tripp playing with Stella. The baby was still in her pajamas and was happily rolling a ball back and forth on the floor to Tripp. The two didn't even notice she was standing there, so engrossed were they in their game. The picture of domestic tranquillity overwhelmed her.

Tripp finally looked up in surprise and saw her standing in the foyer. "So . . . do you think she has any ball-handling ability?" Corey asked. Stella also looked up then and delightedly ran to her mother.

"Did anything happen?" Tripp asked, concerned.

"No, no change. I just decided to come home and freshen up a bit." Corey put Stella down, and the baby ran back to the ball. "I've got to drive out to Nancy's retirement home and look for a copy of her living will."

"Oh," Tripp said, his forehead wrinkled with the seriousness of the situation. "Millie's making Stella's breakfast, and I was just about to leave to go check out of my motel. I could wait and ride with you, though."

Corey felt touched by his consideration. "I don't think so. I'd rather you bring me some lunch later. I know from experience that the food at Northside Hospital leaves a lot to be desired."

"Where should I go to pick up food?"

"Millie can just fix me some leftovers from last night," Corey said, rubbing her head. "Last night seems like a long, long time ago right now. I'm going to go shower and get changed."

She headed for the bedroom. Once there, she called Erica and went through each appointment that was on her schedule for the day. She decided to have Erica call Peachtree Wilden to see if they had the living will on file while Corey took a quick shower.

Listening to her messages after the shower, Corey was relieved to hear that Peachtree Wilden did have the living will on file and would e-mail it to her if she'd call and provide her e-mail address. Now that she no longer had to make the long drive, she brushed her teeth, put on some basic black pants and a white blouse, and carefully applied her makeup. *One could handle just about anything,* she thought, *in basic black pants and good makeup.*

Suddenly she heard Stella crying outside her door. She opened it and realized that Tripp must have left, and her daughter now wanted her attention. "So, what am I now? Third best?" She picked Stella up and went to look for Millie, who was in the laundry room putting clothes in the washing machine.

"I've got to go now," Corey said. "Tripp will be back later. He's going to bring me some leftovers from last night, if you don't mind packaging them up. Also, he's going to stay here tonight with Stella, but he has to leave tomorrow. I don't know how long I'll need to stay at the hospital with Nancy. Do you think there's any way you could stay overnight with Stella for a night or two? Or if it would be easier for you, you could bring Deborah here, and I'll be glad to pay for a taxi to take Deborah to school and back."

Millie didn't say anything for a few minutes. "Let me think on that, Ms. Corey, and I'll let you know. Deborah has a real hard time adjusting to changes."

Corey ran her fingers distractedly through her hair. "Thanks, Millie. If I can get in touch with Kathryn, she might be able to help. And I'll call my sister and see what her situation is like." Then she gave Stella a kiss on the head and handed her off to Millie. "Bye, love. Be good for Millie."

"She always is," Millie said.

Parking at the hospital, Corey felt a sense of déjà vu. How many times while Luke was here had she parked in this very same parking deck and walked alone down this cold metal staircase in the early-morning hours? The only difference was that now, in addition to worrying about her loved one in the hospital, and her job, she also had Stella to worry about. She suddenly felt panicky. *How am I going to handle everything that I have to handle?* Corey concentrated on taking one step at a time and breathing deeply, so that gradually, by the time she reached Nancy's hospital room, she felt back in control of her body. She opened the door cautiously. Nothing had changed except that the room was filled with light because someone had come in and opened the blinds. Nancy still lay exactly as Corey had left her, chest moving rhythmically up and down.

"Hello, dear," Corey said in her most cheerful voice. Then she walked over and gave Nancy's hand a gentle squeeze. "I'm back."

When a nurse came in later, Corey told her she had a copy of Nancy's living will and medical directive. The nurse wrote "DNR"—do not resuscitate—across the top of her chart and inserted the documents in Nancy's records. With nothing else to do, Corey opened her laptop computer, plugged in her Internet card, and began to do a little work.

Much later, the door opened quietly, and Tripp stood in the doorway holding a picnic basket.

"Come on in and meet Nancy," Corey said. Tripp walked in and hesitantly approached the bed. "Nancy, this is Tripp. Tripp, this is Nancy."

"Uh . . . hi, Nancy." Tripp nodded uncomfortably in Nancy's direction. He turned back to Corey. "Is there someplace you'd like to go and eat?"

"There's a little family room right around the corner."

Tripp opened the door, and Corey led him to the empty family room. She sat down at a little table and started unpacking the basket. "I hope you're eating with me. There's a lot of food here."

"I am, and you are so right—Millie is a jewel."

"I know. If only she were available to stay nights, she would be perfect." Corey looked Tripp in the eyes. "Thanks for everything. I'm not sure what I would have done last night if you hadn't been able to stay with Stella. I might have had to bring her to the hospital with me, and I'm not even sure they allow that."

"How do you manage?"

Corey looked at him curiously while she opened containers of food and spread out the paper plates. "I'm not sure what you mean."

"I mean, you've got an awful lot of responsibility resting on your shoulders."

"Having a routine helps a lot. It's only when something like this comes out of the blue that it's really difficult." Corey began spooning pot roast and green beans onto their plates.

"What are you going to do when I leave tomorrow?" Tripp asked.

"I'll figure it out." Corey sounded much more confident than she felt. "If I can connect with my friend Kathryn, she might be able to help. Also, Millie may be able to stay with Stella. I'm not sure."

"Have you called Diane?"

"No, I haven't. I'll call her when I have a better idea of what's going on. Knowing Diane, she'll want to drop everything and come up here, and I'm really trying to stop taking advantage of her so much."

Tripp picked up a fork and played with it for a moment. "I'm not sure Diane would see it as being taken advantage of."

"I know. That's why it's so hard not to take advantage of her."

Tripp looked down at the paper plate full of food Corey had placed in front of him. "Listen, speaking of taking advantage of someone . . . uh, and last night. I want to apologize for my behavior. I shouldn't have kissed you. And I certainly shouldn't have said some of the things I said to you. I've got a lot of thinking to do. First and foremost, like you said last night, I've got to figure out my relationship with Lucy. I hope you don't think too badly of me."

"I don't think badly of you. I know the situation you and I are in is confusing. I can even understand the emotions that you're feeling because I'm feeling a lot of the same stuff too. I mean, every time I look at you and Stella together, my heart does strange things. But right now, I think we just need to focus on Stella. I know you love Stella. I can see it in your eyes when you look at her, and hear it in your voice when you talk to her. I just don't want you to confuse what you feel for Stella with how you feel about me. And I don't want what I feel for you to be confused with wanting a dad for Stella. I think you're right. You need to go home to Lucy and figure out that relationship first. Let's just agree to be honest with each other, okay?"

"Deal. Let's eat up," Tripp said. "I've got to get back to Millie so she can show me what to do with Stella tonight. I've never given a toddler a bath or fed her dinner before."

"You'll be fine. If fifteen-year-old babysitters can do it, you can too. At least that's what I told myself a lot of the time right after Stella was born."

Tripp smiled at her gratefully, and they finished their lunch in silence. After Tripp left, Corey spent the rest of the afternoon sitting with Nancy, talking to her when she could think of something to say, trying to work, and thinking about Tripp taking care of Stella. She wasn't worried that Tripp couldn't do it. She just wished she had a hidden camera so that she could actually see him trying to figure things out. In spite of her situation, she smiled just thinking about it.

Late that afternoon, Dr. Randall returned. A quick hello and he was about business as usual. When he finished his evaluation, he turned to Corey. "As you can probably tell, there's been no change in her."

Corey nodded her head. "Is she in any pain?"

"No. As a matter of fact, she doesn't need to be in intensive care anymore. We'll move her to a regular room tomorrow and then start thinking about a long-term facility if you want to go that route."

"What other route is there?"

"We could disconnect the life-support system and see if she can survive on her own."

Corey looked down at Nancy, praying that she couldn't, in fact, hear what the doctor had just so callously said in front of her. "Don't you think it's a bit premature to be talking about such things now?"

"Just being realistic," Dr. Randall said. "Also, there is no reason for you to be here around the clock. She doesn't know that you're here, and the nurses will call you if there's any change."

"May I say that, in my opinion, your bedside manner could use a little polishing."

"Well!" Dr. Randall said with a huff. "I guess I'll be on my way, then."

When the door closed, Corey felt angry tears forming in her eyes. How dare that supercilious jerk just write Nancy off as though she were so much trash that needed to be gotten rid of. She sat down next to Nancy and touched her hand. It felt cold and lifeless. She picked it up and enclosed it in her hands in an effort to transfer some of her body's warmth into the hand. Corey sat there and thought about the uncomfortable decisions they were trying to get her to make. How could she be responsible for another human being's life, or rather, death?

"I'm sorry you had to hear that. He is *not* my favorite doctor." Corey sighed, still holding on to Nancy's hand. "I just wanted to tell you that I love you. I remember the first time I met you. You were so welcoming and warm that all of the awkwardness I'd been feeling just melted away. And you were a great mother who raised a great son. Also, I couldn't have made it through Luke's illness without you. You were always there when I needed you."

Corey felt tears falling unchecked from her eyes. "If you could just do one more thing for me, please don't make me make this final decision for you. Either open your eyes and come back to me, or go be with Luke. I'm sure you can't wait to be with him again anyway, and I'm sure Luke is anxious for you to be with him too."

Corey sat up and wiped her eyes. She felt empty and spent. She decided that perhaps the doctor had been right about one thing: she might as well go home. She found a piece of paper in her briefcase and wrote out her home and cell-phone numbers. She stopped by the nurse's desk and gave the information to the nurse on duty. "Please pass this along to the nurse who relieves you. And please call me if there's any change."

On the way home, she called Tripp to tell him she was on her way. But he didn't answer his cell phone. When she opened the door, she could hear happy noises coming from Stella's bathroom. "Hello!" Corey called out loudly, not wanting to startle them by coming in unexpectedly. She peeked into the bathroom and saw Stella splashing water at Tripp. "Stella," Corey said disapprovingly.

Tripp jerked back in surprise. "Oh no, we're busted, Stella. I was planning on having the evidence cleaned up before the authorities got here."

"Tripp, that's not a good habit to be forming."

"I know, I know, it's just that she was having so much fun. Hey, what are you doing home?"

"Nothing seemed to be changing with Nancy, so I decided I might as well come home and get some sleep."

"Despite evidence to the contrary, I've got everything under control here. You go take a bath and relax."

Corey looked at Stella smiling happily and decided she would take him up on his offer. "Okay, thanks. I'm going to call Diane first."

Corey went into her bedroom and called Diane, who answered on one of the first rings. Corey decided not to beat around the bush. "Nancy has had a stroke, and it's not looking too good."

"Oh no. What are they saying?" Diane was instantly concerned.

Corey rubbed the side of her head where it was throbbing. "Basically that Nancy could remain in this totally unresponsive vegetative state for a while and then die. Or they can unplug the machines and speed the process along."

"I'm so sorry. Do you want me to come tomorrow?"

"Why don't you wait and let me call you tomorrow."

"And Stella? What are you doing with her?"

"Well, there's nothing I can do at the hospital. I don't think Nancy even knows I'm there, so there's really no need for me to stay overnight. Everything's okay for now. I'll call you as soon as anything changes."

"I'm here if you need me."

"I know you are. I love you, Di."

"Love you too."

"Hey, listen, Kathryn's calling on the other line, so let me go."

Corey realized that it had been two days since she'd left the message for Kathryn to call her. Although she hadn't known about Nancy when she left the message, it seemed odd that it had taken Kathryn so long to get back to her.

"Guess what?" Kathryn said excitedly when Corey switched over.

"What?" Corey knew from the sound of Kathryn's voice that it was something big.

"Will and I flew to Las Vegas on Tuesday and got married. It has been such a whirlwind that I'm only now getting around to calling people and letting them know."

"Congratulations!" Corey tried to put some enthusiasm into her tired voice. "Why didn't you let me know before you left?"

"I didn't know myself. I thought the surprise trip to Las Vegas he sprung on me Tuesday was my birthday present. But on the plane, Will proposed. He said that since we'd both been married before, he thought a nice, quiet wedding—just the two of us—would be perfect. So he threw me a surprise wedding for my birthday. My birthday was why you were calling, right?"

What a terrible friend I am, thought Corey. After everything that Kathryn had done for her, Corey had forgotten that Tuesday was Kathryn's birthday. In this situation, Corey decided a tiny white lie was appropriate. "Yeah, although later that same night, Nancy had a stroke. She's at Northside Hospital now, and things aren't looking very good."

"Oh no! What can I do to help you?" Kathryn sounded alarmed.

"You can be happy and enjoy being a new wife. I'm fine right now. Call me when you get back to Atlanta."

"Keep me updated about Nancy."

"I will."

Corey realized after hanging up that her slightly throbbing headache had spread to her entire head. She decided two Advil and a good, long soak in her tub were just what she needed. She started to go and check on Stella and Tripp but decided against it. Everything sounded calm. She filled the tub with aromatic soaking beads and then took two Advil while she waited for the tub to fill with hot water. Moments later, Corey eased herself into the steaming tub. She leaned back on her bath pillow, placed a hot rag on her face, and closed her eyes, trying to sort through all the events that had occurred over the past couple of days.

Monday had been just a regular day until Tripp had called that night. Since then, it had been one hellacious week. And she had a sneaking suspicion that it was going to get worse before it got better. She felt the Advil and the hot water having their desired effects. Maybe she could just close her eyes for a few minutes and take a short rest while relaxing in her tub.

A persistent knock came from the other side of the bathroom door. "Are you okay?" Tripp asked.

Corey woke with a start.

"I'm fine," Corey answered groggily through the closed door. "I just fell asleep in the tub. Is Stella okay?"

"Yeah, but I'm not sure she's going to go to sleep for me. I've been trying for a while, and she only seems to want to play."

Corey reached for a towel as she stepped out of the now-lukewarm water. "I'll be right out." She toweled off quickly and slipped into her blue bathrobe, not wanting to take the time necessary to find some clean clothes to wear. It was heavy, old, and fuzzy, but she didn't care. She ran a comb through her hair to straighten the wet ends, then opened the door.

A drowsy-looking Stella in Tripp's arms reached out for her as soon as the door opened. "Mama," Stella said impatiently.

"Let's go find your blanket," Corey said as they walked back to Stella's room, leaving Tripp standing there alone.

"I'm going to go outside and make a call," Corey heard him say from a distance.

Stella went to sleep rather quickly, much to Corey's surprise. She walked cautiously back into the great room. Tripp was kicked back on the sofa with his eyes closed. Corey chose the chair across from him. "How's Lucy?"

Tripp opened his eyes. "She's fine. Stella asleep?"

"Yeah. What time are you leaving tomorrow?" The conversation seemed like that of two polite strangers.

"I think I'll try to leave as soon as Millie gets here. Is Diane coming?"

"No, I told her to wait."

"You going to be okay alone?"

"I'll be fine," Corey said, again sounding much more confident than she felt. However, it struck her that she really was going to be alone now. Kathryn was in Las Vegas and wasn't available to help her. Gary and Romeo wouldn't be back from their trip until Saturday. And Nancy was dying. Corey felt tears in her eyes as the loneliness washed over her.

"Don't cry," Tripp begged. "If you start crying, I'm going to have to come over there and comfort you. And if I do that, while you're sitting there all clean and sexy in your big blue bathrobe, I may forget about all of those promises I made to myself and to you earlier today."

Corey had to smile, as she knew there was no chance her fuzzy bathrobe could in any way be considered sexy. "Thanks, Tripp, for everything you've done for me and for Stella."

"I've loved every minute of it. But I'm going to bed now." Tripp stood up and stretched. "You know, a man can only maintain his control around a bathrobe like that for so long." And leaving her with a halfhearted smile, he walked rather quickly to the guest room.

CHAPTER 28

The next day, Corey woke early and called the hospital to see if there had been any change in Nancy's condition. With no reported change, she started her morning routine. She went to get Stella out of her bed but was surprised to see Tripp already dressed and up with Stella. It was no wonder Corey hadn't heard Stella calling for her to get her out of her baby bed; she'd already been sprung. She watched the two silently for a few moments, marveling at how attached Stella seemed to be to Tripp already.

When Millie came in, Corey watched her face brighten like a young girl's in response to some flirtatious comment Tripp made. Tripp was like a thread of gold in the dull fabric of their lives, adding a bit of sparkle that wasn't necessary but certainly appreciated by all involved. *It is good that he's leaving today for many, many reasons.*

Later, she was sitting at her desk sorting through e-mails when Larry stuck his head in. "Got a minute?"

"Sure."

"How's your mother-in-law?"

"No change."

Larry looked down uncomfortably at the arm of the chair he was sitting in and then back up at Corey again. "I know this is terrible timing. But it can't be put off."

Corey felt her heart start a rapid staccato beat; she wasn't sure she could take any more bad news today. "Yes?"

"We are announcing today that John is being promoted to partner."

Corey couldn't believe that Larry had said the words she'd just heard. "John has less seniority than I do. I trained John."

"You've had too much on your plate for a long while now. We know some of it has been beyond your control. But some of it you've brought on yourself. You haven't been producing as many billable hours as John for over a year now, and to be quite frank with you, we don't see you being able to do any more than you are currently doing for a long while."

"This is bullshit and you know it." Corey jumped to her feet. "I'm one of your best lawyers, and by passing me over for partner, you're saying that my work isn't good enough."

"The work that you do is very good. And if it were only up to me, you would have been a partner long ago. It's just that the other partners don't feel that the quantity is where it needs to be. Corey, I told you, remember? You can't do it all."

"You mean I can't be a mother and a partner?" Corey asked indignantly.

"No, not right now. Maybe when Stella is older."

"I'd be a partner already if I were a man."

"That has nothing to do with it," Larry objected. "Please sit down and let's talk about this calmly."

Corey sat down but glared at Larry. "I've had to work harder than any of the male associates just to be in the running for partner. But just so we're clear about the facts, for seven of the eight years I've worked here, you've had no complaint about my work. I was one of the top producers in the firm. Now, I'll admit that for the past year or so my numbers have been down somewhat. Still, I can't believe that you're going to promote someone who has less seniority and, quite frankly, isn't as good as I am, to partner instead of me."

"Of course we'll reconsider your promotion if you post consistent numbers in the future."

Corey sat there looking at Larry without saying anything for a long time. She wanted to choose her words carefully, as she'd looked upon this man almost as a father figure for a long time. When the silence had become uncomfortably long, Corey finally said, "You won't have to reconsider anything in the future. I'm going to submit my resignation today before I go back to the hospital to try to decide whether or not I should have the doctors unplug my mother-in-law from the machines that are keeping her alive."

Larry looked at Corey in shocked surprise. "You are obviously in no state of mind to make this type of decision today. Let's just table this discussion until after things are settled with your mother-in-law."

Corey felt remarkably calm. "No, I don't think so. You know, one thing you said to me today has really struck home. I can't do it all. And if I have to give something up, it's this job. Everything else in my life is much more important to me and is nonnegotiable."

"This isn't what we want," Larry said.

"Well, we don't always get what we want, right? I wanted to be a mother and a partner in this law firm. But I guess that's not going to work out either. If you'll excuse me now, I need to get busy on that resignation letter. I'll have it on your desk within the hour."

Corey printed copies of her resignation letter for each partner in the law firm, put them in envelopes, and asked a stunned Erica to distribute them for her. As she rode the elevator down from her office, she recognized that it had been an incredible struggle for her to try to do the work she'd always done and also try to be a good mother. She knew now that she couldn't have kept it up indefinitely. She felt as if she had been granted an unexpected reprieve from a prison sentence she hadn't even known she was serving. Now she would look for a job that would allow her to enjoy being a mother as well as a lawyer.

She called Millie on her way to the hospital and was relieved when Millie told her that she and Deborah could stay the night if needed.

"Thanks, Millie. I'll let you know as soon as I check on Nancy."

As Corey walked through the hospital, she ran into the emergency-room physician, Dr. Aziz, who said, "I hear there's been no change in your mother-in-law."

"No," Corey answered. "I'm just going up to see her now."

"Mind if I tag along and take a look?"

"I wish you would."

When they walked into Nancy's room, Corey thought that Nancy looked worse than she had the day before. Dr. Aziz picked up her arm and felt for her pulse while looking at the monitor. "Her heartbeat is very weak. I don't think she'll make it through another twenty-four hours."

Corey burst into tears. Strangely, she felt a twinge of happiness, the first she'd felt in days. "I just want her to go on her own," she said softly.

"I know," the doctor said comfortingly.

After the doctor left, Corey sat with Nancy for another hour, holding her hand and talking with her about how she'd just quit her job. Suddenly the heart-monitor machine set off a beep, and a nurse came running into the room.

"She's leaving me, isn't she?" asked Corey.

The nurse nodded.

"I'll just stay with her, if that's all right."

It was over soon. As the nurse unplugged the machines and moved them away, Corey thought that Nancy looked like herself again, only incredibly peaceful. Corey was thankful that she'd been there, and she felt an amazing sense of relief. She left the room and called Erica to tell her that she wouldn't be coming back to the office that day because her mother-in-law had died. Although she'd resigned, she was going to work long enough to transition her clients to other associates.

She called Nancy's church, talked to the rector, and scheduled the funeral for Monday. She called Diane, who said she'd be there the next day. She called Kathryn and left her a message. And then, just because he'd been so instrumental in helping her get through the past few days, she called Tripp. When he answered, Corey could tell by his tone that he was unable to talk freely.

Corey said quickly, "I just wanted you to know that Nancy died and that I appreciate your help more than you can possibly know."

"Thank you for that information. I'll get back to you as soon as I can."

"You don't have to," Corey said quickly. "That's all I wanted—just to let you know. Bye, Tripp."

At home, she broke the news to Millie, who became more upset than Corey would have expected. After calming her down, Corey realized that she needed to address one more delicate issue with Millie.

"I, uh, want to ask you to do me a favor, Millie."

"Of course, Ms. Corey, whatever you need, I'll be glad to do it for you."

"Uh . . . would you mind not mentioning to my sister that Tripp has been here for the last few days?"

Millie looked somewhat insulted by her question. "Well, of course, I won't be talking about Mr. Tripp being here. It's not my business to be talking about you."

"I'm not implying that you would be gossiping about me. I'm just saying that if somehow his name comes up, I would prefer for you not to mention that he'd been here this week. Okay?"

"Okay," Millie said, and with a huff she went to answer the door. She came back carrying a huge bouquet of fresh-cut flowers that the firm had sent. The flowers, coming after the firm's recent betrayal, meant nothing to Corey. She felt like telling Millie to throw them in the trash. But instead, she just commented on how pretty they were and put them out of her mind.

CHAPTER 29

The day of Nancy's funeral was sunny and extremely hot. Corey, sitting between Diane and Jack at the graveside, could feel a bead of sweat rolling down the inside of her leg toward one of her black peep-toe pumps. She wanted to lean over and stop its progression, but instead, good manners made her sit perfectly still. She felt odd sitting in the same place where she'd been just a few years ago for Luke's funeral. Corey knew that she had smiled and responded and acted perfectly normal that day because people had remarked to her later about her composure. But she'd been operating on autopilot, mouthing words and engaging in actions without any true knowledge of what she was doing. Thinking back now, she realized she might have been on autopilot for at least that first year, maybe longer.

Now she could barely remember the day they'd buried Luke. She'd been functioning on very little sleep and on zigzagging emotions, so that by the time Luke died, she was mentally and physically spent. What she did remember was the overwhelming fear she'd felt and the question that had echoed over and over again in her head: *How am I going to carry on without Luke?* Luke had centered her after her parents' deaths, providing her with direction. Because he believed she was capable of doing certain things, Corey had found the confidence to do them. He had thought she could get the job at Landon, Crane, and Forrester, so Corey had gone for the interview and gotten the job. Luke had believed she would be the first woman partner, so Corey had made that her goal as well.

Corey wondered how her life would have progressed if she'd never met Luke. She had almost not stopped in Atlanta to visit her sorority sister. Where would she be today if she'd just kept right on driving? It was strange looking back to see how her life had been shaped by such a seemingly meaningless decision at the time.

She looked around at all the people from the law firm who were in attendance: Larry and Sherri, Erica, John, and even Larry's assistant, Barbara, stood at the edge of the tent, trying to stay out of the direct sunlight. Corey appreciated their thoughtfulness in coming, but she realized that it made no difference in her decision about her job. The relief she'd felt walking out of the law office, without worrying about what she was leaving behind or what else she needed to do, made her confident that she'd made the right decision.

The rector was wrapping up the service, so Corey brought her attention back to his words. Then, they formed a receiving line for people to pay their condolences. When Larry and Sherri, looking uncomfortable, approached her, she reached out and gave them both a big hug. Larry leaned in close to her and said in a voice that only Corey could possibly hear, "Corey, we hope you will reconsider your resignation. Come in tomorrow and let's talk."

"Larry, I've made my decision, and I'm really happy about it. But thanks for coming today. Let's have lunch sometime."

Larry looked relieved. "Okay, call me."

Three days after the funeral, Corey sat in another attorney's office waiting for Nancy's will to be read. The lawyer, Donald Blakely, of the law firm Blakely and Blakely, appeared to be about Nancy's age and seemed to be having some trouble organizing the papers on his desk. After a good five minutes or so, he finally began, "Ms. Bennett, unless you want me to read the will in its entirety, and knowing that you are trained in the law, I'll just give you the specifics."

"That would be fine, Mr. Blakely."

"Very well. Your mother-in-law has put her entire estate in a trust for her granddaughter, Stella. You are designated as the trustee, and the money can be used however you see fit in order to care for your daughter. She has made a few special gifts, one for the perpetual care of the cemetery lot where she and Luke are buried, and another to the family of her longtime housekeeper. But that's about it. Currently, the estate is valued at just a little under a million dollars, which should be plenty to provide for your daughter's care and education."

Corey sat speechless. She had no idea that her mother-in-law had accumulated that much wealth. She'd known that the Buckhead house had been worth a lot of money, but she'd also known that living at Peachtree Wilden was extremely expensive. Corey supposed that after Luke died, she should have gone over Nancy's estate with her. After all, she'd done that sort of thing for other people every day in her job.

"Ms. Bennett, do you have any questions? Everything's here if you want to review it."

"I'm sure everything is in order. But if I have any questions after I look at the documents, I'll give you a call."

Corey walked out of the Blakely law office into the sunshine, feeling another type of relief. With this money from Nancy, and the nest egg Corey already had established, she wasn't going to have to worry about how she would make the next mortgage payment. Now finding another job wasn't nearly as important as it had been just a few hours before. She felt humbled and grateful to Nancy for her incredible gift to them.

A few minutes later, Corey's mood had darkened considerably. She sat in a traffic jam on Peachtree Street and hadn't moved for ten minutes. A gang of rough-looking youth hanging out on the corner by a bus stop noticed her and began making crude gestures at her. Corey's heartbeat quickened, and she felt vulnerable and scared. One of the guys approached her car and tapped on her window. "Hey, lady, wat ya got in there? You got any moneeeey? I need some money." Just as another boy was about to knock on her passenger window, the traffic started moving forward, and Corey let out a deep sigh of relief.

Her hands were still shaking when she pulled up to her condo. Corey thought, *I don't want to deal with situations like that anymore.* And then her next thought was, *I don't have to deal with situations like that anymore. I can move anywhere I want to move.* It was an exhilarating and liberating feeling. She went inside. Millie was giving Stella some juice, and neither of them seemed to notice how rattled she was. "Millie, do you plan on moving back to Cairo one day?"

Millie looked up at her in surprise at this totally unexpected question. "It's funny you should ask that, Ms. Corey. I had a meeting at Deborah's school last week. She's learned just about all they can teach her. They think she's ready to take the next step, to get a job, maybe something working with plants 'cause she loves watering them and taking care of them. You know, she's done right well at that school, and they have taught her how to take care of herself and to be more independent. But if she's done with school, it would be easier for us if we moved back home." She shook her head. "I sure hate the thought of leaving Stella. I was going to talk to you about this as soon as things settled down a bit. I just hated to put one more worry on your shoulders."

Corey felt like she was receiving a message from the universe that was loud and clear. She was not meant to live in Atlanta anymore. "Millie, I've been having some of the same thoughts myself about moving home. I'm beginning to see that it would be a lot easier for Stella and for me if we were to move back home too."

"Well, I'll be . . . I know Ms. Diane is sure gonna be happy about that!"

Corey smiled. "I'm sure you're right about that."

CHAPTER 30

It was a typical Indian-summer day in November. Corey enjoyed the warmth of the sun on her face while she waited in the parking lot of the First Baptist Church of Port Saint Joe. One of the best things about Corey's new job at the legal-aid office was that it was across the street from the church-sponsored Mother's Day Out program Stella was attending. If Corey had to work late, all she had to do was pick up Stella from next door and let her play for a while in her new kid-friendly office. After only two weeks of work, Corey felt as if she'd already made more of a difference in people's lives than she had in all her time working at Landon, Crane, and Forrester.

Corey knew the Mother's Day Out routine by now. Stella's class would come out of the building slowly, each child dutifully holding on to a loop attached to a long rope held by the teacher. The class looked like a giant caterpillar with the teacher as its head, meandering toward the place where the parents stood waiting. Sometimes Corey's precocious toddler came hopping or skipping from the building. Sometimes Stella stumbled out looking exhausted from a hard morning of play. But regardless of how she looked coming out of the building, when Stella spotted Corey, her eyes lit up, and only the teacher's most severe warnings kept her from letting go of her loop on the safety rope and running across the parking lot to Corey's side. Each day, Corey experienced a moment of pure unadulterated joy when she saw that look on Stella's happy face. And at that precise moment each day, Corey had no doubt that she'd made the right decision in moving her child from Atlanta to here.

Their move from Atlanta hadn't been without a few bumps. As Corey had promised, she continued to work at the law firm until all her clients had been transitioned to another lawyer. However, she'd been amazed by how happy she felt going in to work each day knowing that the number of days she had to spend there were limited. It had been challenging getting the condo on the market. However, it had sold within days of being listed. Romeo and Gary had at first been furious with her about her moving. But when the condo sold to a young gay couple, they suddenly didn't seem nearly as sad to see Stella and her leave.

Corey had arranged for movers to help Millie and Deborah with their move back to Cairo. And she surprised Millie one day with a car, which Corey said was a gift from Nancy. It wasn't true, but Corey knew Nancy would have given it if the idea had crossed her mind. Corey almost gave the ficus tree to Deborah, since she loved plants so much, but then decided that she and the ficus had too much history together for her to let it go. In fact, she felt almost superstitious about the ficus tree; somehow its renewed health and vitality seemed connected to the renewed health and vitality of her own life.

Leaving Kathryn was definitely the hardest part about moving from Atlanta. Yet, Corey knew that since her friend had just started a new married life with Will, things probably wouldn't have been the same between the two women anyway. She made Kathryn promise her that they wouldn't allow their friendship to die after the move.

Corey's original plan had been to move in with Jack and Diane in Marianna. It was to be only a temporary stay until she could find a place of her own. At first it had been great fun being surrounded by family. But after a few weeks of constant attention, Stella had started acting like a spoiled brat, and Corey began to feel like a visitor overstaying her welcome in their home. In addition, none of the jobs that Corey considered in the small town seemed quite right. She began to wonder if she'd made a mistake moving to Marianna at all until she saw the advertisement in the Sunday issue of the *Jackson Country Floridian* for a part-time attorney at the legal-aid office in Port Saint Joe. Why she even considered going on the interview, she didn't know. But when she got there and met the people, she realized it was a special place. And when she saw the children at the church school next door being picked up after school, she knew it was the perfect place for her and Stella. Unfortunately, Diane hadn't agreed.

"You don't know anyone in Port Saint Joe. Why would you even think about taking a job and living there?" Diane chastised her.

"I wasn't thinking about living in Port Saint Joe. I want to live at our beach house. The fifteen-minute drive to Port Saint Joe will be nothing compared to my commute every day in Atlanta. I'll get a feel for how I like living at the beach without too much of a commitment."

"Well, in that case, I guess it sort of makes sense. You can try it out, and I'll keep looking for something for you here. That way, when you realize your mistake, we'll have a plan."

"Why does it have to be a mistake? The people next door in the yellow house live in Mexico Beach year-round. And Fran and Mark have retired there. I may decide I never want to live anywhere else."

"We'll see," Diane said, which meant she totally disagreed with Corey.

Corey realized that Stella's class had reached its assigned spot on the sidewalk. Once there, the children were allowed to release the rope, and parents were allowed to fetch their children and take them home.

Corey walked over to claim Stella, who seemed more animated than usual today.

"Beach, beach, beach," Stella sang in a rhythmic voice.

"Yes, we're going to the beach." Corey took Stella's hand as she sang and danced her way delightedly to the car.

Corey fed Stella lunch, put the dreaded sunscreen on her, and then grabbed a few sand toys and a couple of beach towels. The process went much faster now that she'd learned to travel lighter. Once at the beach, Corey watched Stella play tag with the waves. She had a vague memory of playing the same game herself as a child while her mother sat watching her. Finally, Stella lay her slightly sandy body down on a beach towel and fell into an exhausted sleep.

Next to them, seagulls floated up and down on the breeze effortlessly, and Corey felt an unusual connection to them. Like the seagulls, she'd found a breeze. Everything she did these days seemed easy to do, from taking care of Stella to working at the legal-aid office. Corey's life felt effortless. In Atlanta, even before Luke died, even before Stella, Corey had never felt this carefree. In Atlanta, she'd been more like a duck. She might have looked serene floating on the pond that was her life, but underneath the water, she'd been paddling like hell just to stay afloat.

On an intellectual level, Corey knew this tranquil feeling wouldn't last forever. Life would throw her some curveballs, and Tripp was likely to be the first one coming at her real soon. Corey hadn't seen him since the night he'd left Atlanta, and she'd talked to him only twice: the night she called to tell him Nancy had died, and then a week or so later, when Tripp called to tell her that he owed it to Lucy to try to make their marriage work.

"I'm going to stay in Dothan for a while," Tripp had said, "and Lucy and I are going to go to marriage counseling. Until I figure out this part of my life, it's probably better if I don't see Stella, even though it will kill me not to."

Since then, Corey had heard nothing from Tripp. As rapidly as he'd returned to her life, he was suddenly gone again. She'd moved to Marianna and then to Mexico Beach, and now had been living at the beach for two weeks, and she'd still heard nothing from Tripp. Every time she looked at the MacKinnon house, she wondered how things were going between Tripp and Lucy. A shadow suddenly covered Corey, and it was almost as if she'd conjured Tripp with her thoughts, because when she looked up into the bright sunshine, he was standing there in shorts and a faded fishing shirt.

"She looks pretty comfortable." Tripp motioned toward Stella, who was sprawled out on her side with her thumb in her mouth.

"She ran in and out of the waves for about an hour and then just collapsed. I guess it's as good a place as any for an afternoon nap." Corey put her hand to her forehead and squinted up at Tripp.

"Do you want me to go up and get an umbrella to cover her?" he asked.

"No . . . thanks. I think she's fine. I covered her in sunscreen before we came down, and I'm not going to let her sleep too long anyway, or she won't go to bed tonight. I wish you'd sit down. The sun is blinding me when I try to look at you."

Tripp sat down on the sand beside Corey. "I suppose she'll be taking more of these beach naps, since I hear from Jack that you've moved to Mexico Beach."

"For now," Corey replied.

"Was I one of the reasons you decided to move here?" Tripp asked quietly.

Slowly, Corey turned to face Tripp. "Honestly . . . no."

"That wasn't the answer I was hoping for," Tripp said raggedly.

"Well, you weren't a negative to moving here." Corey gave him a slight smile.

"I guess that's something."

"Where's Lucy?" Corey studied Tripp's face carefully.

"She's probably halfway to Ohio by now," Tripp said grimly.

"Marriage counseling didn't work?" Corey asked softly.

"Our counselor was a big proponent of honesty in relationships, but I think Lucy may be thinking that the whole honesty thing is a bit overrated." Tripp looked straight ahead as he spoke, still as a statue.

"So she knows about Stella?" Corey swallowed.

He nodded. "The news didn't go over very well, but by that time, I had pretty much decided that our relationship wasn't going to end well anyway."

"I'm sorry." Corey avoided looking at Tripp when she said it.

Tripp turned to her and placed a hand on hers. "Corey, it was hard for me to work on my marriage when all I could think about was you and Stella, but I tried. I swear I tried."

Corey gently pulled her hand away. "Were you thinking about Stella and the fact that I'm Stella's mom? Or were you thinking about the three of us together as a family? Or were you thinking about how you wanted to be with me?"

"How about all of the above?" Tripp's voice sounded strained.

"What do you want, Tripp?"

"I want you and Stella. I want a family. It's hard for me to believe that I'm approaching forty and that my life is as screwed up as it is right now."

Corey paused and let the silence stretch out for a moment. "Yeah, I know what you mean. I often wonder how I ended up a widowed, single mother. I certainly never planned for my life to turn out this way."

"There wasn't much you could do about your husband getting cancer."

"Perhaps not, but I sure could have avoided becoming a single mother."

The stain of embarrassment colored Tripp's cheeks, and after a long pause, he said, "What do you want, Corey?"

"I've been trying to figure that out myself. I've spent most of my life not really thinking about what I want, or what makes me happy. I went to law school because of my dad. I moved to Atlanta because of Luke. I didn't even realize how unhappy I was in Atlanta until I moved from there. I think choosing to have Stella was the first decision that was one hundred percent mine."

"Well, it was a good one." Tripp looked over at their daughter, who lay sucking her thumb contentedly.

"I agree. Look, this is all I know for certain. I don't miss Atlanta. I don't miss my old job. I do miss Luke sometimes, but not nearly as much as I used to. I want to be the best mother to Stella that I can possibly be. I want to be close enough to Diane and Jack to see them often. I want to feel passionate about my work. And I want to live at the beach. That's the full extent of all I know." Corey smiled at him crookedly. "And tomorrow, I may not know half that much."

"I was hoping I rated at least an honorable mention."

Corey smiled at him carefully without saying anything.

"But what about me and Stella?" Tripp asked. "What are your plans as far as my relationship with Stella goes? I've missed her so much these past few months. It's hard to believe that I could miss her so badly after knowing her for such a short time. And looking at her now, it's hard to believe how much she's grown. Now that I'm free, I want to spend as much time as I can with her to make up for the time that I've missed."

Corey took a deep breath. "That's not for me to decide. It's really your decision. You are her father. You do have legal rights, and I can certainly understand if you want to formalize those legal rights and make your relationship with Stella public. However, I hope you know that you can see Stella as much as you want, and that I would never keep her away from you. Stella loves you, and that isn't going to change. I guess

I'd prefer that we just kind of go on like we are for now. I just want to let life happen for a while without any sort of plan."

"That doesn't sound like the Corey I know."

"I know, but I've changed. My goal now is to focus more on living. Besides, none of the plans I ever made prepared me for where I am today."

"I guess I'm okay with things remaining like they are for right now as far as Stella is concerned."

Corey ran the sand through her fingers. "Okay, we'll take it one day at a time and see how it goes."

Tripp looked up at the sun sinking lower on the horizon. "I'm going to do a little fishing. I'm not going out far, just trolling along the shoreline. You and Stella want to come?"

"It gets so choppy in the afternoon. I'd kind of like Stella's first trip on a boat to be smooth. Invite us for a morning trip sometime."

"You got it. Can I see Stella tomorrow?"

"Of course. Hey, Tripp, why don't we apply my new philosophy to our relationship as well? Let's forget about everything in our past. Let's start fresh, get to know each other as adults, and just take it day by day. We don't have to rush into anything."

Tripp nodded and said, "So . . . as an adult asking another adult, would you and our lovely daughter like to accompany me to dinner tomorrow night at the Sunset Grill?"

Corey started to refuse because Diane was coming down to the beach tomorrow. But then she changed her mind. *Why not?* They might as well start their new relationship sooner rather than later. "Sure, sounds great. But if we're taking Stella, we need to go early."

"Five thirty?"

"It's a date."

Tripp stood up and gave a slight wave. "See you tomorrow."

Corey watched Tripp go up the path, then turned back to her sleeping child and watched the brilliant afternoon sun sink lower and lower toward the horizon. Movement down the beach caught her eye. As the people came closer, she realized they were the same elderly couple she'd seen on the beach several years ago. She remembered how she'd cried, watching them, longing for the years of happiness that they'd spent with each other. And they still appeared to be just as much in love as before. They were holding hands and talking animatedly to each other as they walked. Corey felt a sudden urge to talk to them. Love like theirs deserved to be acknowledged.

She looked down at Stella, who was still sound asleep. She waited until the couple was directly in front of her, and then she jumped up and walked toward them, waving. The couple stopped and waited for Corey's approach.

"I've seen y'all walking on the beach before, and I just had to tell you how special it is to see two people in love like you are."

The couple looked at each other, confused as to her meaning.

"I mean, you're so obviously still in love after all these years. Do you know how lucky you are to have spent your life with your soul mate?"

The couple looked at each other, and something was communicated wordlessly. The man looked back at Corey and said, "We hate to disillusion you, but we didn't find each other until about five years ago. Both of us had previous marriages that didn't turn out so well. But you are right about one thing—we couldn't be happier now. And we are very lucky to get to spend what's left of our lives with our soul mates."

Corey felt her face flush. "I just thought . . . well, I'm sorry to have bothered y'all. Anyway, you do inspire me with your happiness now."

"Thanks. We're glad," said the woman, with an adoring look at the man, which held more meaning than anything she could have said. "Well, we better turn around; we walked farther than we had intended, without realizing it."

Corey nodded her head. "That's easy to do, I know. Hope to see you around again."

The man nodded in agreement. They turned and started ambling back the way they'd come.

Corey went back to her beach towel and sat down. Once her embarrassment started to fade, she couldn't help but start laughing at the awkward situation she'd just created. Stella must have heard Corey laughing because she opened her eyes and looked at her questioningly.

"Hello, dear. No, Mommy's not going crazy. It's just that I've realized something. A long time ago, I saw those people on the beach, and I cried and felt sad because I wanted to be living their lives—well, at least the fairy tale of their lives that I'd created in my mind. Not that those people aren't happy now, but their lives haven't been the 'happily ever after' I imagined. You know what, Stella? I think we'd all be better off if we focused more on living in the now."

Stella rolled over and sat up, rubbing her eyes and making little grunting waking-up noises. Corey reached over and brushed some of the sweaty hair out of her eyes. A feeling of love swelled in her heart as she looked at Stella's sleep-swollen face. "Look, Stella." Corey pointed to where the sun's setting had suddenly turned the sky into a blaze of orange. "Isn't it amazing?"

Stella didn't seem impressed. "Juice!" she demanded.

"Okay, Stella, let's go get you some juice." Corey threw the toys into the middle of one of the beach towels, picked up her daughter, and grabbed the towel full of toys with the other hand. "And then, how about you and I start to work on a real happily ever after?"

ABOUT THE AUTHOR

Born in the small town of Marianna, Florida, J.A. Stone left home for college at Auburn University. After completing her degree, she moved to Atlanta, where she took a job as a technical writer for an insurance trade association. Although she'd always loved dreaming up stories as a child, it wasn't until she turned fifty that Stone began writing *Life Unexpected*, her debut novel and her first book published by Lake Union. J.A. currently resides in Augusta, Georgia.